THE HIDDEN GEMSTONE

An MBA Saga...

SUSMIT SARKAR

Published by InkQuills Publishing House
www.inkquills.in

First Edition 2024

ISBN: 978-81-967124-7-1

Author's Biography

Susmit Sarkar works as a Business Technology Associate at a multinational firm in Mumbai. He has done his MBA in Business Analytics from IIT (ISM) Dhanbad (2021-23). Before that he had worked as a System Engineer at an IT firm in Mumbai for 5 years (2016-21). He has done his B. Tech in Electrical Engineering from NSEC, Kolkata in 2016, 12th boards from DAV Model, Durgapur and 10th boards from ST. Xavier's, Durgapur. He started off his literary journey in 2016 wherein he got published in 8 anthologies. He contributed short stories for the following books - "Minds@Work 4" by First Step Publishing House, "The Master Stroke" by Write India Publisher, "Blessings" by Xpress Publication, "I'm Done with Love" by Inked Company, "Mocktales" by M.A.D Publishers, "Meri Kahani" by LAB Academia, "Shades of Life II" by Shades Publication, "I Had a Last Wish" by Inklovers Publication.

He is a musician as well. Trained as a rhythm guitarist in 2017 at Guitar Grund Institute, he loves to compose and write a variety of songs in Hindi, English and Bengali. His first song titled *College Days* got launched in 2018 and he keeps on uploading his original compositions regularly on *YouTube/Susmit Sarkar*. His hometown lies in Durgapur, a city you can easily pinpoint on the map of West Bengal, India.

Social Media Links –

LinkedIn - www.linkedin.com/in/susmit-sarkar-mba/

YouTube - www.youtube.com/susmitsarkar

Facebook – www.facebook.com/susmit.sarkar.94

Instagram –www.instagram.com/sarkar.susmit/

X – www.x.com/s_susmit11

Acknowledgement

It has been 8 years now, since I had written my first short story. Never thought that I will resume the journey again that too with a full-fledged novel. And this would not have been possible without the following people.

First and foremost, my parents, Mr. Nityananda Sarkar and Mrs. Sumitra Sarkar who have supported me unconditionally. They didn't even let me do any house chores during the vacations, so that I can focus and complete the entire book at one go.

Next comes my alma mater IIT (ISM) Dhanbad. Had it not introduced the MBA Business Analytics program, this book wouldn't have ever been written.

Then comes my professors and colleagues at the firm.

All my friends and batchmates without whose help and support this book would have never been possible. They are Sambuddha, Pramit, Sushant, Priyatham, Bhavay, Antara, Apurv, Harigaran, Sudhakar, Bhavesh, Chirag, Kushagra, Hemant, Asish, Sushanta, Nihal, Somanshu, Parvez, Tanmoy, Piyush, Megha, Sonu, Silpamoy, Shubham, Yeshita, Tania, Shilpa, Nasreen, Nazneen, Faiz, Yashvardhan, Shruti, Prateek, Siddhi, Shashank, Tarun, Reshav, Mayank, Pratibha, Pragati, Pragnya, Shubhadeep, Arnav, Tamal, Geetanjali and Surbhi.

My close friends and well wishers – Jay, Anoop, Dhananjay, Punit, Rajneesh, Ummed, Magesh, Dolly, Mandar, Sumanth, Afshaan, Ankur, Ranit, Sayantika, Bidyut, Ranajit, Rudrangshu, Ankita, Soumya, Priyankar, Dhirajraj, Pooja, Anurag, Rakhi, Harshita, Reshmi, Laxmi, Tejashri, Amar, Amit, Dheeraj, Ganesh, Rahul, Akshay, Swarnali, Santosh, Snehanjan, Arijit, Rajith Bhaiya, Pushkar Bhaiya, Pobitro Da and Arnab Da.

My cousins, Sanket, Sarbesh, Ankan, Supriti and Rintu.

And last but not the least, God without whom this journey would have never begun.

Contents

Part 1

Part 1

Chapter 1 --- The CAT is out of the Bag

It has been 4 years now since Rhiyan had joined a multinational IT firm as a system engineer. Looking at the desktop screen, he started thinking, *What next!* Monitoring alerts on a desktop with 4 big LCD screens sketching one graph after the other that too at 2 am in the night is not something he had aspired for his future after B.Tech. But nonetheless he was getting paid decently without any layoff worries. "Hey Rhiyan, how are the alerts looking?", asked Ajay as he started getting ready for his part of the shift. "Yeah, all good", Rhiyan replied. Ajay brought out a few books from his bag as he sat down for his shift. "What are those for?", asked Rhiyan's curiosity. "Oh, I am preparing for CAT. You know how the typical Indian career graph goes, right? First B. Tech, then 2 years work experience, preparation for CAT, doing an MBA and finally settling down in a metropolitan city with a consultant role and a huge amount of debt on your back", replied Ajay's not so enthusiastic words. "Wow, seems like you are on your way to hell", commented Rhiyan's sarcasm with a smile on his face. "Why don't you join me? You never know when the road to hell might end up giving you a perfect ride", winked Ajay. "Nope, I am happy with my musical world as of now", smiled Rhiyan.

Rhiyan, a musician by heart got trained as a guitarist under the strict yet friendly guidance of his mentor Ivan for almost a year. That one year of training had taught him more than he could have ever imagined. Ivan helped him improve his pitch, rhythm and vocals as well. A year later he even managed to launch his first song, *College Days* on his YouTube channel. But as the beginner's luck would have it, the song didn't garner much views. But still, he didn't give up. He still made it a point to perform at least one show at some mall or the other every weekend, thanks to the band he had managed to form a music band with his colleagues. Even the next week he had a show, this time for a promotional event on behalf of a D2C brand.

The clock struck 8 am. Night shift over and Rhiyan back at home for some good sleep. The maid had already made the breakfast and lunch. So, no worries about that. The moment Rhiyan's head hit the pillow; the world moved upside down. It was a different world altogether. A world where he performs his own self composed songs and the world listens. That's what he enjoys the most, a world full of music and peace. He was swaying to the rhythm when suddenly some spiders started crawling up his fingers, slow and steady, moving up bit by bit, waiting for the right moment and BANG! He woke up aghast. "Thank God! It was just a dream", as he started checking his fingers for any bite marks. Seems like, it has been rightly said that a person suffers more in his dreams than in reality. He checked his phone for the time. It was 9 pm and the date blinked as 24th March 2020. He could not believe he slept like a log of wood the entire day. But apart from the date, there were around 10 missed calls from Ajay. *I know, you are going to arrive 1 hour late again today. No need to call so many times for that Ajay*, thought Rhiyan's words as he splashed some water across his tiresome face. The phone rang again and this time in non-silent mode. *"And there you go, as expected its from Ajay"*, Rhiyan smiled, completely unaware that Ajay's next few words would change his life completely.

"I know you will be late once again today Ajay", started Rhiyan as he picked up the call. "No, you idiot. I am not going to come at all", he shouted back. Rhiyan was taken aback. "What! Are you out of your mind? I can't do the entire shift alone", Rhiyan exclaimed back. "Rhiyan, splash some more water on your face and turn up the news. Our Prime Minister has announced a nation-wide lockdown for the next 30 days to contain the Covid 19 spread". Now Rhiyan was more awake than required.

"What! Come again", Rhiyan was still finding those words difficult to digest. Putting the phone on speaker, he searched all latest news on Google Chrome and YouTube. After browsing through for around 10 minutes, things started sinking in. "From today, we will do Work from Home. Instructions from Dhiraj Sir", said Ajay. But more than the work, Rhiyan's mind was engrossed in something else. *What would happen to my upcoming shows?* That's what he had been training for... To become a musical heartthrob across the nation. He read the news more carefully now. Reading between the lines again, he heaved a sigh of relief. *Thank God, it's just for a month*, he thought again. Coming back to his present reality, Rhiyan cut the call and checked for flight tickets back to his hometown. To his surprise the prices were sky high. But still he booked one for the next week, completely unaware that all flight tickets were going to get either cancelled or rescheduled months after months... *because the lockdown would never have an end date.*

As expected, work from home became a way of life with no possibilities of diving into the world of live music anytime soon. For most IT Professionals the working time extended from 9 hours to almost 12 hours, all thanks to work from home nuisance. But Rhiyan had somehow managed to create a timetable for his team to cap the working hours to 8 hours and yet cover all 3 shifts in a day.

Days passed, weeks passed, months passed but the lockdown stayed exactly where it was. STILL VALID! Rhiyan, while working from home was pondering upon how his entire music band got dismantled because of the pandemic and his dreams of becoming a musician laid shattered. Drowned in his thoughts, he was just going to reboot his laptop when suddenly a paper plane flew in and landed on his keyboard. "Not all dreams get fulfilled in months son, some take *time* to land", remarked his father who was reading a newspaper and was trying out some origami to fly in a smile towards his son. "Yes Dad", that's all Rhiyan replied as he started unfolding the plane and came across an advertisement of CAT preparation by Studos, an online EdTech platform. He immediately got reminded of Ajay, who by now had managed to crack a decent B-School. "Maybe you want to give a shot at it", suggested Rhiyan's father. And that, brought a smile on Rhiyan's face.

Back in 2005, inspite of Rhiyan topping the class 4 batch and receiving a scholarship, his father took a decision to switch his school for the best in town because he knew that more than topping it's the competition with the best that would make his son resilient. Rhiyan knew this. And moreover, he was fed up with his current job. So just like the rest of the engineers in India, he started off with his CAT 2020 preparation.

Date – 8ᵗʰ February, 2021

By now CAT results were out. Rhiyan had not received any IIM calls. And the affordability score of the private colleges was dwindling like hell. So, in a last attempt, on the last day he somehow convinced his heart to fill the forms of some top IITs along with IIT Dhanuj. "Seriously, an MBA from an IIT. Does that even exist?", Ajay remarked over the call. "Yes, I know, I might have to give another attempt next year but let's see once how this IIT thing turns out", even Rhiyan didn't seem convinced a few days ago, especially given the placement scenario of the past few batches. But inspite of everything Rhiyan was interested in two things. One, the course fees of an MBA at IIT Dhanuj was one of the lowest in the entire country and two, a specialized course named MBA in Business Analytics, a course that had not been introduced even in some of the top IIMs yet.

Date – 20ᵗʰ March, 2021

Professors on the interview panel asked their first question, "What is Regression?". Forget answering that question, Rhiyan had never even heard of that term before. But one thing that Rhiyan knew was, being honest about himself was the real key. "Sorry Ma'am, I have never heard that term and I don't know what regression means", spoke out his truth. "No problem, can you tell us what is digital marketing?", asked Ma'am. Now this Rhiyan knew and so safely swept it out of the boundary. Like this, it went on and off for the next 15 minutes and finally the zoom call ended. Rhiyan didn't expect any call for MBA Business Analytics after the interview. But to his surprise, he got a position in the waiting list when the results were out. Now the only way he could get Business Analytics was if some applicants in the first list opted out. Rhiyan having a 4 years' experience in the IT field knew the potential of the course. But unfortunately, many in the first list didn't. The only thing they wanted to see were the past placement figures. And MBA Business Analytics being a new course didn't have any. And this logic was exactly what Rhiyan was counting upon to secure a position.

Date – 7ᵗʰ June, 2021

Ting! An email arrived. Rhiyan opened it and it read as "Congratulations. You have been selected for the MBA Business Analytics course at IIT Dhanuj." Rhiyan's joy knew no bounds. His hypothesis had worked. Many freshers who didn't find the past placement figures had opted out passing on the chance to the subsequent candidates. Rhiyan's parents were happy because their dreams of seeing their son enter an IIT had finally got fulfilled. Till now inspite of some anxiety, there were some hints of predictability. But now things were not. He felt completely clueless of how that one email would change the entire course of his life.

Chapter 2 --- The Risk Taker

This time he jumped but… without any expectations!

Sushant was happy with his work at a multinational industrial firm. Dealing with clients face to face, bringing in deals, swiping off the company's credit card and enjoying a lavish corporate life had become a part of his day-to-day life. And yet the disappointment of not being able to crack a government job was bothering him, all thanks to the Indian society's obsession with govt. jobs. "Seems like you don't want to give up, huh", commented a father who wanted his son to move on. It has been almost 8 years now and inspite of having a lucrative style life, his pen moved trying to solve a few quant questions. "What can I do? This pen is not ready to give up yet", smiled back a tired yet confident Sushant, who had come home for a short vacation. Sushant had been preparing for Govt. Exams for quite a long time. He had already cleared the SSC CGL exam Tire 1 and 2 and was getting ready for Tire 3. Thinking of taking a break, his eyes fell on the day's local newspaper. He was going through the usual headlines when something caught his eye. *Inspite of launching a new course like MBA Business Analytics this year, 20 seats laid vacant at IIT Dhanuj.* He felt a bit bad, because having worked at Honeywell, he knew how important data was for the future. But unfortunately, instead of looking at the course curriculum, students preferred the past average packages while deciding on a B-School. And MBA Business Analytics being a new course didn't have any. He felt a bit worse since the college stood right beside his own house.

"When are you returning back?", Sushant's manager asked over a call. "Next week, Sir", he replied. "I hope you have got the briefing about the next assignment, Sushant." "Yes Sir, I have", and after a few more detailing the call ended. Sushant had always wanted to reach the managerial position but somehow or the other the lack of an MBA degree always became an obstacle. He looked at the headline again and this time with a bit more curiosity.

*Date – 29*th *November 2020*

Sushant reached the CAT exam center just a week after he had written the SSC CGL Tier 3 exam. He had filled the form but with the preparation of a Govt. Job exam. His heart wanted to take a chance inspite of all uncertainties but since he had not given enough CAT specific mock, he didn't have any idea as to what was coming his way. Verbal, the first section opened up. As his eyes went through the first question, his heart started beating fast and a bit later, even faster. *Damn! What is this!* It was as if he was reading Greek the only difference being that the alphabets were in English. Somehow, he managed to read between the lines, understand and attempted a few of them. He was confident that he would make it up in the reasoning and quant section. And just as the reasoning section opened up, only one thought came to his mind. *Damn! Rs 2000 just wasted. Could have used it for at least 10 Chicken Biriyanis over the month.* He wanted to leave the exam hall but couldn't, thanks to the rules of the exam. The clock was ticking and time was passing by. He took a look at his fellow mates. Some were busy scribbling through the paper and some were badly tensed. Unable to leave, Sushant went over again and identified two questions that he felt could be solved. The approach that he took was not something usually people take. Instead of solving the question, he picked up options and tried back tracking to see if he could reach the data given in the question. He tried it for two sets and *voila!* It worked for two sets. The rest he left. It was just the quant section that he solved with some level of confidence.

1ˢᵗ January, 2021, 11 pm

A messaged popped up on Sushant's phone. *Cat results have been declared. Check it on the link below.* The way the exam went, he knew how superb he had performed. *No, I don't want to get my mood off on the first day of the year.* With that he switched off his phone and went back to sleep. *He was still regretting the 10 Chicken Biriyanis he could have had with the money.*

On the morning of 2ⁿᵈ, he thought again and finally opened the result's link. As he zoomed the screen, the LRDI percentile popped up. It was 96.3 percentile. The phone slipped down from his nervous hand and fell off, fortunately on the bed. He picked it up and checked the other sections. Quant showed as 86 and English a bit lower. He called his brother to recheck and confirm once. "Well, seems legit to me", said his brother. With that Sushant knew which college and course he wanted to apply for.

Date – 20ᵗʰ March, 2021

The interview day arrived, two professors on the panel. Just like Rhiyan, Sushant flunked 4 out of the 5 questions asked. With no idea on correlation and statistics, Sushant stood quite clueless. The only silver lining was that one answer which he had somehow managed to give correctly. And that one answer finally got him selected.

But as they say it, when the day goes well, it goes too well. The same evening 2 more mails dropped in his inbox. *Job Offers!* Not one but two and that too with a great role and package, one of them being an onsite opportunity in Brazil. He had given the final interviews for these two around a month ago. With no further response Sushant had given up on them, but now here they were. He had to choose among 2 certain opportunities and 1 uncertain one. His family was almost sure that he would take up the Brazil offer but what they didn't know was how desperately he wanted to switch from the engineering role to a top-class managerial position. Sushant knew what he wanted but just to clear the cloud of doubt, he called up and spoke to 3 of his close mentors from the corporate world. By next morning, he confirmed his will to his family. And not to mention, his family was very disappointed with his final decision. *We hope the risk you are taking will be worth it,* blessed his parents.

Chapter 3 --- The IITian life begins!

As you know it… or maybe as you don't

The admission process was over but the pandemic was not. Work from home was still the norm and online classes were about to become the usual for Rhiyan and his friends. Oh yes! Rhiyan had already made some new friends inspite of not meeting them face to face. All thanks to the initiator, Sushant. Usually after 8 years of experience, people go for an Executive 1-year MBA. *You know what they say about opportunity loss. Don't you?* But this guy wanted to do something completely out of the box. Just a few days before the classes, he called up Rhiyan, a complete stranger and took him directly into a conference call with another stranger from Chennai named Harigaran. And all this because of a renowned case study competition called *Shooting Wires* that gets held once in a year for fresh MBA students. If you crack any of the Top 5 positions, you get a PPI along with prize money. For those new to the field, PPI stands for Pre-placement interview and PPO stands for Pre-placement offer. They gave it their best shot but unfortunately couldn't crack it.

Anyways 16th August 2021 arrived and the first semester officially began. All the Business Analytics students had logged in at 8 am to learn a course that gets taught very rarely in an MBA course at least… *Machine Learning.* Personally, Rhiyan had no idea about it. He was as clueless as anyone else in the Google Meet. All cameras were off, only names popped up in the participants tab. Rhiyan went through all names like crazy and realized that there was just one girl in the entire batch. Not that he was seeking something romantic anytime soon but half of his hopes had already vanished by now. *17 boys and just 1 girl, that's very unfair,* thought his thoughts. "So, any idea about Machine Learning?", asked Ma'am's first question. No one spoke up. "Considering the silence, I'll take it as a No. Today we are going to learn about Supervised vs Unsupervised learning", and with that she started off. Rhiyan literally enjoyed the first class. Machine learning was a completely different world for him. Training a model with the help of labelled and unlabeled dataset, testing and checking for accuracy using Python programming language was not something he had ever done even while working at his IT firm. Initially Rhiyan thought he could pull it off easily but what he didn't know was that the more he dives in, the more complex it would get. *Life was coming to punch him out soon.* After the class ended, he thought of chatting a bit with others but even before his eyes could blink, an email notification dropped with another Google Meet link… *Financial Accounting and Reporting.* Finance was something Rhiyan had always been dreadful of, mostly because he assumed it to be a tough quantitative paper. *Finally, the toughest subject has arrived,* assumed Rhiyan, completely unaware that by the end of the course he will fall in love with the subject he dreaded the most.

A screen popped up with a huge cycle on it. Starting from assets to liabilities to operating cycle, everything was circling each other like crazy. Rhiyan's head was already spinning by now and so were the others. "Is that Rhiyan?", asked Professor Jayesh. Rhiyan's heartbeats had already touched the sky heights. *How did he know my name?* he started thinking only to realize later that he had left his mic on by mistake. As a result, his name blinked at the top. "Yes Sir", he replied meekly. "It seems like your mother wants you to finish off your breakfast", remarked Sir's words. Had it been an offline class, the entire class would have burst into laughter. Rhiyan was so engrossed in finding the class link, he had forgot about the food his mother had served him half an hour ago. "Yes Sir. Sorry Sir", Rhiyan fumbled. "That's okay. Just make sure to keep the mic off during the lecture and unmute only if you have a question", instructed Sir's stern words. And after that it was a whole new story about cash, credit sales, inventory, sales revenue etc. *I must say professors of IIT treat time like oil, not in the mood of wasting even a drop of it,* came a ping on the Business Analytics WhatsApp group with some laughing emojis following the statement. It was only after a few weeks that they realized it to be a universal truth. All the IITian professors valued time immensely. And with time that got imbibed even in the students' character.

Every Sunday the MBA Business Analytics students used to have a casual google meet. And there Rhiyan met with Priyatham, Sudhakar, Chirag, Bhavay, Asish, Apurv, Nihal, Hemant, Kushagra, Kabir, Bhavesh, Somanshu and last but not the least *that one mystery girl in the batch… Antara.* He already knew Sushant and Harigaran, thanks to the *Shooting Wires* case study competition.

Data Mining

"I forgot, how did you guys end up here?", asked Professor Trivedi as the Data Mining class began. "By clearing CAT and the interviews, Sir", replied Antara. "And how did you know about this course and its entrance exam?", intrigued Sir a bit further. "From the college website, Sir", added Antara. "Absolutely correct", smiled Sir and then continued, "Do you see the pattern? You gathered info from various sources, put them in one place, analyzed the pros and cons and finally took the decision to join the MBA Business Analytics course. And that's exactly what forms the basis of Data Mining", explained the professor, "Common, now tell me about some good data sources?" "Sir, Wikipedia", spoke up Harigaran. "News articles", added Chirag. "Hmm… good. Yes, they are good sources but here I am talking about SQL database, excel files, cloud etc. and to collect Wikipedia data, well, you will have to master the art of Web Scrapping, an art that we will use for sentiment analysis via Twitter today", elaborated his words. As the clock ticked in, everyone starting falling in love with his lucid explanation. In fact, a few concepts resonated with those in machine learning and this led to a more coherent understanding among the students.

But the actual fun began when the practical started. "Ready to share the screen Sushant?", asked Sir's words suddenly. In an attempt to blurt out *Yes Sir,* Sushant spilled the water he was about to drink. "Don't get shocked. It's just my way of checking your online attention", laughed Sir as he guided him in opening the Twitter developer website and applying the authentication key. "So, on what topic do you guys want to run your analysis today?", asked Sir. Somebody said fintech, others e-commerce. "What about something trending? Something like Covishield Vaccine?", suggested his words. Wasting no time Sushant typed in all the hashtags possible. #Covishield #CovishieldVaccine #Covishield_availablity etc. Trivedi Sir guided him with the codes as well, while explaining each one line by line to the class. Finally, when the graph's code ran, a bar chart appeared showing the levels of various emotions, happy, sad, anger, disappointment etc. "Hmm… seems like the nation is really positive and happy with the life saver", smiled Sir's words, with everyone still trying to understand the magical codes. An hour passed by just like that. "Hope you enjoyed the show. Meet you again soon", with that Sir ended the class.

The following Sunday evening…

"Hey Antara, how are you?", called up Rhiyan. "Hi, I am doing fine. But may I know who is this?", came her sharp reply. *What! There are just 18 members in the entire WhatsApp group and she didn't even save the numbers.* Rhiyan was already heart broken. "Umm… This is Rhiyan, from MBA Business Analytics", replied his voice. "Oh yes, Rhiyan. So sorry, I didn't save your number", Antara. "That's okay. So, enjoying the classes?", said Rhiyan, trying to divert the awkwardness. "Not so much. Machine Learning combined with Finance is spinning me out like hell. What about you?", asked Antara. "Same as yours. But Data Mining by Trivedi Sir and Managerial Economics by Irfan Sir turned out to be life savers. They are the ones keeping me steady", he replied. "Oh yes, completely agreed on that", replied her short reply. "You know this machine learning is getting complicated day by day. With so many mathematical derivations revolving around, sometimes I don't even get the concepts right. I am getting a bit doubtful if I have chosen the right branch of MBA or not?", Rhiyan was indeed suffering a minor depression because of the complexity of the subject. "I completely agree with you but that does not mean you will change the branch, right?", empathized her words. "See, in life nothing will be easy. We have to make it easy. Try out some videos on similar topics on YouTube. I am trying the same", advised Antara. "Hmm… you don't give up easily, do you", smiled Rhiyan. "Not at all. And if you ask me, you shouldn't too", smiled her words back.

After the call ended, Rhiyan started his search on YouTube. He knew that nothing can beat the detailed elaborate teachings of an IITian professor but maybe he needed a different flavor this time. With some efforts, he came across a channel that discussed some sort of machine learning concepts but in a different way. After listening to some of its videos, Rhiyan started understanding the basic concepts. He was hooked to that channel for the next 7 days. Bit by bit he became more confident with the subject and by the 8th day he had a beautiful smile across his face, not because he had understood all concepts with perfection but because now, he knew how to deal with complex subjects, be it Machine Learning or Financial Accounting and Reporting.

Rhiyan tried calling Antara but she didn't pick up. So instead, he wrote a big Thank You note to Antara and hit the send button. *But oops!* Mistakenly he had sent it in the main group instead of just to Antara. But before he could hit 'delete for everyone', it had been seen by most of the members. Suddenly his phone rang up. It was Sushant's with Harigaran already in conference. First there was an awkward silence and then Sushant spoke up, "And here I thought we were your best friends, huh!" "Only in case studies I guess, not in machine learning", added Harigaran's disappointed voice. "Guys, nothing like that. You are getting it all wrong", tried Rhiyan's justifying words. "Yeah, we know. Only Antara gets it right. Isn't it?", sighed Sushant. There was another moment of silence. And suddenly both the pranksters burst into laughter. "Sorry Rhiyan, we just couldn't let go off the fun", both were still laughing. "Seriously guys?", Rhiyan heaved a sigh of relief. Now all three were laughing. "But I must say guys, Antara is indeed a spirit lifter. Without her emotional support, I would have slipped into some major depression you know", added Rhiyan. "Sure. But next time we want your call first", winked Hari as the call came to an end.

Date – 20ᵗʰ September 2021

As per the rituals, it was time for the club and committee inductions. "Look, I don't want to waste my time in these things. But if anyone of you guys wanna stand up, I will definitely support", Sushant made his stand quite clear in the beginning itself. "What about you, Rhiyan?", asked Harigaran, over the conference call. "Well, I like Consulting Club. Would like to join that one and that one only." *According to Rhiyan's presumptions that was the only club where he could have fun and learning, both.*

As the induction process began, multiple tasks were given and only those who cleared all levels had the chance of getting selected. Acing the task and interview round, Piyush, Apurv, Pragnya, Bhavay and Sudhakar got selected as the coordinators of Placement Committee. MBA Core guys dominated the Media and Branding Committee. Alumni Relations Committee also got filled up soon. Now the only one left was the Consulting Club. Rhiyan, Sushant, Hari, Priyatham, Bhavay, Sudhakar and a lot of others made it past the first round. Sushant didn't want to join but to help Antara with the case study he did the first task. Once students' selection was done, it was time to select the coordinators. Initially no one raised their hands. The seniors were a bit surprised. "In our time, people were damn interested. What happened to this batch?", the seniors looked a bit confused. To ease out the situation, they explained the responsibilities in a bit more detail. Rhiyan wanted to but was lacking some confidence and that's when pings after pings started crowding his WhatsApp. Sushant kept on pinging until Rhiyan finally raised his hand and after that came up a few more. All these things were happening online. As a result, everything seemed anonymous. After a small live speech by each candidate, it was time to vote. To keep the voting anonymous, Telegram was chosen. Some were confident but others in dilemma kept on fidgeting with the toggle buttons, choosing one at the last moment. The voting bars finally came to a rest and words spoke up. "Congratulations Rhiyan and Siddhi. Seems like you have a lot of responsibilities on your shoulders now", congratulated the seniors followed by their batchmates. And from that day the duo never stopped. Starting from case studies, guesstimates, quizzes to guest lectures, they left no stone unturned to carry forward the legacy.

Chapter 4 --- Online Exams (Boon or Bane?)

Date – 22ⁿᵈ November, 2021

"Any idea how is it going to be?", asked Harigaran over the call. "No, my friend. But one exam that I am pretty confident of is Business Statistics, all thanks to you Hari", smiled Rhiyan back. Initially Rhiyan used to struggle a lot with statistical concepts and whenever in doubt, he rang up Hari. And Hari helped him out every single time. Same went for Priyatham. Him being a machine learning and deep learning expert, everybody knew whom to approach in case of trouble. Peer to Peer learning has been the norm of Indian B-Schools for ages and instances like these proved it true. Many a times adverse conditions bring people together and the MBA Business Analytics students were going through a similar phase this time.

5 Questions, each 20 minutes and 5 minutes to scan and upload the answer scripts. Initially everyone thought of exchanging answers via WhatsApp Web but what they didn't know was that, on the other side stood the most experienced professors of all time. The first exam arrived. Financial Accounting and Reporting. As the first question opened up, everybody went into a fix. *Forget WhatsApp web, even with the entire internet available at your disposal, you can't solve the question unless and until you have understood the concept in the class.*

What is this? Messaged Chirag. *A sheer conspiracy against us,* messaged Hari back adding a laughing emoji to it. Messages kept on coming but not the solution.

By the time the fifth question had arrived everyone's dream of having a gala time had been washed off perfectly. *This is one thing about IITs. Be it any subject, questions are developed from scratch with no links to previous year. And all this just to test the conceptual understanding of the students. And if you have bunked the class, you have flunked the exams, especially in Finance.*

The next day came with another ordeal, Machine Learning. "See I'll tell you one answer and you tell me one", Bhavesh told Kabir over a call just a few moments before the exam. Both have had a very dwindling attention span in that particular class over the entire semester, many a times even skipping one or two for a cup of coffee. "Which chapter have you prepared?", asked Kabir. "The one you didn't, Linear and Logistic Regression", replied Bhavesh's confidence. "Idiot!", screamed Kabir from the other side, "I asked you to prepare the unsupervised part, the 2nd half of the portion." "Which part have you prepared?", asked Bhavesh's meek voice. "Same as yours. Now we are both stuck with just the first half", replied Kabir.

The 1st question opened up. It was something related to confusion matrix. *You know, nowadays its very rare to find chapters so aptly named, because it was indeed a very confusing matrix.* Rhiyan's head was spinning by now as to what to put in those 4 boxes that screamed as True Positive, False Positive, False Negative and True Negative. He was already confused with positive and negative, when an additional dish of True and False came up to add to the already confused mind. And on top of that, he had to find out the required accuracy, precision and misclassification rate. For a second, he opened his notebook and immediately closed it, realizing that it was nothing but a futile effort. *Concepts Rhiyan, concepts,* cursed his own thoughts. And it was not just him, almost everyone was sailing in the same confusion boat. Scribbling something on the paper, he moved on to the next only to realize that his heart was about to sink a bit deeper. Q2 was all about Neural Network. *With terms like perceptron and auto encoder, the only thing that came to his mind was Priyatham, help us!* He was the only one who knew how to tackle it, but he was busy solving too. Rhiyan went through the question again and identified two sub parts that he thought he could solve. Combining one layer with the other, he solved for the NOR and XOR outputs. Taking one stride after the other, he moved forward and so did the others. An hour later, the clock hit the end. Everyone heaved a sigh of relief. The ordeal was finally over!

But nor for Sushant. For others, things were tough, but for Sushant things were even tougher. His uncle had been admitted to the ICU just a day before and the epitome of responsibilities had fallen upon his shoulders. He had to arrange 3 bottles of blood amid the exam crisis. And to add to that no one was there to help him out, all thanks to the Covid Crisis. Almost on all days, he was having to stay back late in the hospital and appear for exams in the morning. Somehow with the help of IIT Dhanuj's Gymkhana President, he was able to get one bottle of blood. He had already given a bottle of his own blood. By God's grace he was able to find a third bottle with the help of an NGO a day later. On one side were students who were giving exams comfortably from their homes and on other side was Sushant struggling to keep a life alive. His only savior was the amount of attention he had paid during the online classes.

Date – 5ᵗʰ December, 2021

Results were about to come out in a few hours. Sushant's uncle was stable as of now. "Who do you think is going to top it?", asked Rhiyan over the call. "I think it will be a tie between Hari and Priyatham", replied Sushant's meek voice, as he was worried about his. "Don't worry. You have fought to save a life. I am sure God will not disappoint you", consoled Rhiyan. "In this moment uncertainty, let me ask you something. I know it may sound strange but still", continued Rhiyan in an effort to cheer up Sushant, "What is that one thing that you will ask for, if granted a wish by God right now?" *Rhiyan expected answers like best grades, best placement and best career. But what he heard shook him to his core.* "I would ask for only one thing, a fair life", answered Sushant. "What? I didn't understand", Rhiyan sounded a bit perplexed. "See Rhiyan, money will come and go, life will have ups and downs but if it stays fair to you, you will never regret that fact that you tried your best and still didn't get any result", elaborated Sushant. Rhiyan was completely speechless. He literally couldn't speak a word. And suddenly *Ting!* A message pooped up saying, *Results have been declared.* Both of them still on the call, opened up the portal and viewed the results. "Is it bad?", asked Rhiyan. "Seems like my wish just got fulfilled. Its 8.75 out of 10", replied Sushant. "You will not believe. I have got just the same", smiled back Rhiyan. As expected Harigaran and Priyatham had topped with 9+ pointers.

Chapter 5 --- A New Club is born

But is it just one?

Things were going smooth with the consulting club under the leadership of Rhiyan and Siddhi, but somehow Sushant felt a bit of disconnect with the club activities. His heart was into analytics projects but that was never the focus of consulting club. It was around 25th December when Rhiyan and Siddhi organized a live online Case Study competition with Professor Singh as its judge. "These solutions look fine but you know what is missing?", asked Ma'am. "Data. That's exactly what I feel is missing. When you are presenting hypothetical solutions like these, it is always a good practice to back it up with some data, you know", explained her words. Although it seemed like a normal comment to others, Sushant's eyes lit up because he felt that Professor Singh was the exact person he was looking for, not for any project but for something he wanted to create.

Ma'am, I liked your explanation about data inclusion during the case study session. And I was thinking that it would be great if we can establish an Analytics Club that can help the students learn Python, excel basics and give them a head start to build some astounding projects. I wouldn't have asked. But with the rise of Generative AI and Machine Learning models, how could our department remain behind. The need for Tech MBAs is imminent, Ma'am. With this, Sushant hit the sent button from his mailbox.

After around two days, Ma'am confirmed and with HOD's permission the club was set up. "Hmm, and here I thought that you were the least interested in clubs and committees", Harigaran was surprised when the mail came in his inbox. "I was. But now I am in and you will join hands with me", Sushant smiled back. "Who me? No way", replied a shocked Hari. But later Sushant managed to pursue him to join. Sam, Prabhash, Sreeman, Kaustav, Prakash and all other MBA BA seniors joined hands in full support and helped Sushant structure out everything right from the start to finish. Initially people had the notion that no one could beat the Consulting Club activities but now a new and strong contender had stepped into the arena, Analytics Club. Because it was not just a club, it was the brain child of Sushant. The way Analytics students structured it, it felt as if they had set up a full-fledged organization. With Advanced Excel, VBA sessions by Sam to automated car simulation projects by Prakash, Analytics Club became an icon within a very short span. And this led to chain effect with other clubs and committees ramping up their activities aggressively.

Sushant was happy. Not because he had taken the initiative but because he was able to create a place where the students themselves could have a peer-to-peer learning in the field of analytics.

The Igniters

"Come on Bhavay, it's time to spend some money and party", Tarun sounded excited. Bhavay (BA), Reshav (HR) and Tarun (Finance) have recently won their first quiz on D2C with a prize money of Rs 2500. "Yeah sure, but after we win the next", replied Bhavay as he tried to hold on to those strings of the wallet a little longer. "No way, we are going to enjoy tonight itself", reinforced Reshav. After a bit more persuasion, Bhavay agreed and send their shares via UPI. They ordered pizzas and cokes respectively to celebrate their first win. *Par kab tak dusron ke ghar ki parties enjoy karenge? Kabhi khud ke ghar pe bhi honi chahiye na?",* Tarun hinted towards the concept of having their own club. For the past few days, D2C, a platform for hosting case study competitions and quizzes had been running a special campaign to select a student from each IIT and IIM colleges who could represent their brand on their respective campus. "I agree. Let's apply for the D2C Chief Igniter selections in the next slot", added Reshav. "And, what if we fail?", Bhavay seemed a bit skeptical. "Really? Is that an IITian speaking?", Reshav raised an eyebrow. "Hmm… okay let's give it a shot then", agreed Bhavay.

On the next week, all three appeared for the D2C Chief Igniter selections. Interviews were tough. Questions came in from the corners they haven't even visited. Yet the trio tried defending as many as possible. When the results got out, only one made it through.

"Hello, am I speaking to Bhavay?", spoke up a female voice over the call, a few days later. "Yes, may I know who is this?", asked Bhavay. "This the marketing head of D2C platform and I have called to discuss about your department's D2C Igniter page", elaborated her words. "Oh yes, please continue", Bhavay said. "First of all, congratulations on cracking the interview. You have been selected as the D2C Chief Igniter for your department. As a part of this privilege, you will have a dedicated page for your management department wherein you can post articles regarding your internship diaries or anything to help your college standout. You can host case study completions, quizzes free of cost along with other perks", added her words.

As the call ended, Bhavay felt overjoyed. Within the next few days, he formed the Igniters Club with Tarun, Reshav, Tania, Sam, Sourav, Harigaran, Sanjiv, Silpamoy and started off with their work. Now the management department of IIT Dhanuj could post and host competitions pan India and that too completely free of cost, ultimately helping them improve their MBA Branding score.

Chapter 6 --- Second Semester Begins

Date – 5ᵗʰ January 2022

The online classes were finally over and Rhiyan had stepped into IIT Dhanuj, *The Hidden Gemstone.* The gate structure resembled that of the Japanese gates called *Torii,* which symbolizes a transition from the mundane to sacred. As the auto progressed, Rhiyan's eyes fell on the most iconic attraction of the campus, the Heritage building. At first look, it looked nothing short of the parliament building with a huge Ashoka Stambh attached at the top of it. And it looked more so because of the beautifully trimmed garden circling the front. Some unique colourful flowers surrounded the garden with a few plants grouped together and trimmed to bring out a few alphabets into prominence. Pushing up his head, Rhiyan tried to see what it read. It read as IIT DHANUJ.

Finally, the auto arrived at the first-year hostel named Jasper. And that's where he met Priyatham and Sushant for the first time in person. Sushant who had already taken up a room *(after a sweet fight with the warden of course)* helped Rhiyan and Priyatham with the hostel entry formalities. Rhiyan had spoken to Priyatham quite a number of times over the phone but this time they stood face to face as each other's roommates. "These rooms are too small for two people", remarked both of them together as they opened the door of room D-251. The room size was nothing more than 10 ft by 6 ft. Only a king size bed could fit in comfortably, not sure of the people on it. "Thank God, the fees of 2-year MBA course at IIT Dhanuj is just 4 lakhs, otherwise I would have had a huge disappointment with respect to hostel food and stay, I guess", remarked Rhiyan. "Do you always justify your experience in terms of numbers like that?", asked Priyatham's sarcasm with a smile. "Not always", laughed back Rhiyan.

The rooms were quite dusty. The admin had sent floor cleaning people, two for each floor. It was only after six hours that all rooms got cleaned and students got settled in. Rhiyan just had a trolley and a laptop bag. He settled in quickly and started watching Priyatham's unpacking. He started unpacking one jar after the other on the table. These jars were of hand-made pickles stuffed in with a variety of flavors inside. Rhiyan was like, What the hell? Personally, Rhiyan was not a big fan of pickles at all and here the entire room was smelling with it. "I hope you have brought some air-tight jars along", remarked Rhiyan's uncomfortable words. "Definitely not. I love the aroma. Get used to it brother", winked back Priyatham with a sarcastic smile on his face.

On the other side Sushant and Shubham from MBA Core had already taken up the room D-306. Sushant was quite settled down when Shubham started unpacking his items. The first thing that came out was an Apple MacBook and along with that an iPhone. *Kaafi raees banda hai yeh toh!* (Looks like a pretty rich guy), thought Sushant. As he further unpacked, came out a huge World Map. *"Duniya ki sayer abhi karna hai kya? Course khatam hone tak toh ruk jao"*, smiled Sushant's sarcasm. *"Arey nahi bhaiya, yeh toh inspiration ke liye hai. Taki aisi naukri lage ki duniya ghum sakein"*, smiled back Shubham's words. But that was not just it. Starting from a table lamp, a table cloth to window curtains and a flower vase, he had come prepared to set up the 10 by 6 ft room like a mini hotel room. After a decorative effort of another 15 minutes, Sushant was like *"Bhai, mujhe iss hotel room ka rent toh nahi dena padega na?"* And with that both burst into laughter.

"I think it's time to step out of this boring hostel, what do you say Priyatham?", asked Rhiyan as the Sunday evening dawned upon the sky. "What for?", Priyatham. "To explore the campus of course and to meet a few girls, maybe", winked backed

Rhiyan. "Nope, I am a bit busy with my deep learning project. You carry on", came back his stern reply. "Are you always this boring, huh?", asked Rhiyan when suddenly the door opened with bang. "Hey guys, want to explore the campus?", asked Sushant who had just barged into a peaceful conversation. "And meet a few girls? Well, Rhiyan is already up for it. Take him", replied Priyatham's sarcasm, as his fingers stayed busy typing in some codes and his eyes focused on the output.

"Okay come on, Rhiyan. Let me give you a tour. I have been here since childhood. Nobody knows the secret spots better than me", replied Sushant's confidence. With that they took off. "Students are not allowed to use bike within the campus. Only bicycles allowed", continued Sushant's words as they reached the Jasper Hostel gate, "Now, as of now we are at one end of the quadrilateral. If you go straight down the front road, you will reach the Management Department. On the right, you will find the B. Tech, M. Tech and MBA senior boys' hostels Amber, Topaz, Sapphire. On the left, stands the Central Library and a bit further down the road stands the girls' hostel Ruby and Rosaline. So which way do you want to go first?", asked Sushant. "The left sounds a bit interesting. Shall we?", Rhiyan gave a nod towards the left. With that they headed off straight left down the ally. The moment they reached the Central Library, they found some commotion going on. Sushant was about to ignore it when he stopped and looked back once again. "What happened?", asked Rhiyan. "Isn't that Shristi, from MBA Core?", asked his voice. For those who don't know, Shristi was the Finance girl, a title she had earned after the first semester, not because she scored the highest in finance but because she was the professors' favorite target when it came to tricky questions. And this happened because of a joke she cracked in the middle of an online class with her voice that was unfortunately quite loud.

"I am the one who has found this book. So, I get to keep it", screamed her voice. "No, it was me who told you about this book. So, I get to keep it", countered Kabir's voice back, an MBA BA guy. On a closer look, Sushant noticed what the book was actually about. It was a palm thick Corporate Finance book with a weight of around 2 kg for sure. "Guys, relax", Sushant stepped in. Oh, forgot to mention even Sushant had earned a title for himself in the first semester, *The Diplomat*. He did have some witty tricks up his sleeve when it came to disputes, you know. "Before you fight over this 2 kg of burden, has anyone of you has gone through the syllabus of Corporate Finance?", asked his question. "No", replied both. "Very good. In that case let me assure that as much as knowledge this book may contain, at the end of the day it won't serve you more than a laptop stand." Rhiyan burst out with laughter. "Do you know why?", continued Sushant. Shristi and Kabir looked at each other, completely clueless. "Because, that book's content surpasses our actual syllabus by almost a mile", he remarked pointing at the complete title of the book. It read as Corporate Finance for Entrepreneurs by P.K Nandi. They have chosen the wrong book to fight over. And with that everyone burst into laughter. Shristi and Kabir couldn't stop but smiling at each other.

"What are you all doing here?", asked Rhiyan, as he could see most of his batchmates present there. "Seems like you missed the WhatsApp message", commented Harigaran (aka Hari) as he appeared from nowhere, "We were all supposed to meet here at 7 pm. Did you miss it too Sushant?" "Of course not. Who do you think brought Rhiyan here?", winked back his diplomatic reply. Rhiyan looked back at Sushant. He was like REALLY? All this was a trick? With that everybody met each other. The girls were quite friendly in nature and so were the boys. Rhiyan met Antara and thanked her personally for lifting him up from the drenches of depression during the first semester.

Discounting, Compounding and Sinking Fund

(Flavours of Corporate Finance)

"Who can tell what would be the value of these 100-rupee notes after 10 years?", began the Professor Jayesh as his hand fluttered 5 notes in the air. "Sir, I think we have to adjust it with inflation rate", answered Kabir. "Really? Are you sure?", shot a googly from Sir. "And what if you earn this 5 notes every year for the next 10 years, what would be the future value then?" Kabir became a bit nervous. Seeing his worrisome expressions, Sir laughed off. "Don't worry, I was just pulling your leg." Cooling off the environment with a smile, he explained how to calculate the present value of regular cash flows at a certain interval of time. "This compounding formula will give us the future value, while the discounting one will give us the present value", elaborated his words.

"Kabir, I want to ask my second question now. Can you suggest someone whom can I ask?", asked Sir's smiling words. Kabir literally stood up and took a 360-degree bird view to identify the next target. His eyes finally rested on Bhavesh, sitting just beside him. Bhavesh and Kabir's eyes locked on each other. *If you take my name, I am going to rip your heart out,* Bhavesh's eyes tried to warn Kabir. "Sir, I think my friend Bhavesh can take a shot", blurted Kabir's words out. *Damn!* Sank Bhavesh's heart. "Very well then Bhavesh, can you please tell if you have a habit of saving money for the future or not?", Jayesh Sir was in a good mood. "Oh yes Sir, I do", answered Bhavesh. "What for?", Sir tried to intrude a bit further. *To buy an iPhone,* Bhavesh wanted to say. "Umm… for bad times or emergencies, Sir", Bhavesh blurted out instead. "Exactly! And the same goes for a concept call the Sinking Fund. A fund that allows businesses to payout a bond's liability at maturity. It is like a piggybank where in you put some cash at timely intervals to payout a lumpsum amount at the end", explained Sir's enthusiastic words as everyone started falling in love with the subject. After the class got over, Bhavesh did settle his debt with Kabir. But how, no one knew.

Stochastic Processes and its ordeals!

Gradually, other subjects like Marketing, Human Resource, Operations and Advanced DBMS made an entry. But again, just like Machine Learning, another subject that was poised to spin out everyone in the coming days was none other than Stochastic Processes.

Usually, the normal classes were held at the department, but the Stochastic one got shifted to the Old Lecture Hall. And for the BA students, it was a completely different world. "What is this place?", asked Somanshu, as they stepped in for the first time. "An architectural mammoth that has been vandalized to a wreck, I guess", replied Rhiyan. "The college had been established in 1926, almost 97 years ago and this is one of the first lecture hall established during that era which now stands as an iconic heritage", elaborated Sushant's words. Being a localite, he had some idea. "But why does it look like a deserted field?", asked Bhavay, "Look around, seems like we are the only ones who have been assigned a class out here." It was like a gladiator war arena, classrooms arranged in an asymmetrical circular fashion with a stage as the center.

"Welcome guys. Welcome to the historical era of Stochastic Processes", shouted a husky voice from behind. As they turned, they saw an Indiana Jones like figure enter the arena. "I know what you are thinking. My first reaction was exactly the same when I came here for the first time", continued his words, "By the way I am your Stochastic Processes professor and fortunately or unfortunately your only guide out in here." As he walked, others followed. "Sir, couldn't they have adjusted the 18 of us back at the department?", asked Kabir's curiosity. *"Kabhi toh AC ki duniya se bahar nikal ke socho. Aur waise bhi itihas ke beech class karne ka maza hi kuch aur hota hai"*, tried some of the Professor's encouraging words. "Come on, open it", Sir nodded towards him. Kabir gave his best. At first shot, the door didn't even budge. "Maybe a more delicate touch would do the trick", smiled Sir as he unlocked a side latch and gave a gentle push. As the door opened, it unveiled a huge hall with seats scattered across and some huge rusty rod like structure coming down the ceiling, a fan attached to each. "I am going back to register a complaint at the department", Kabir turned to walk out. "No, you are not", Sir turned him another 180-degree helping him inside the lecture hall. "Make yourselves comfortable guys", said his words with his fingers busy switching on the lights.

"Stochastic Processes is a convoluted web of probability and statistics and if you wish to undo that web, kindly do not miss the regular classes", and with that began a series of Markov chain and queueing theory. After around 1 hour the class ended. "Wasn't so bad after all. What do you say Kabir?", asked Sir as he started wrapping up his notebooks. "Sir, to speak the truth, I just hope I get the passing marks in this subject", blurted out his inner truth. Sir could do nothing but smile. "As already said, it's a convoluted web. Undoing it will take some time, my friend", winked Sir as he waved everyone a goodbye.

Two Life Saviours Identified!

Amidst all this convoluted crisis, Marketing came as a saviour.

"The 4Ps of marketing aka Product, Price, Place and Promotion will serve as the four pillars this semester with this as your holy grail", began Professor Singh with a book of Marketing Management by Philip Kotler swaying across her hand. "So, what is a product?", asked her first question. "Ma'am, starting from the chalk in your hand to the desks we are sitting across, everything is a product", answered Tania. "Also, mobile applications and computer software make up the category of Digital Products", added Yeshita from the other side. "Correct. I would love if others could contribute something on Price, Place and Promotion too with respect to these categories." Akaash, Piyush, Sonu and others spoke up enthusiastically to answer as much as possible. *Thank God, at least in one class I can be at ease. The marketing guys can handle the arrows out in here,* relaxed Kabir.

Kabir had some similar expectations in HR, but unfortunately didn't happen that way. For the BA guys, HR was a modular subject. As a result, a new professor had been assigned specifically for the 18 of them. "Do you know her name?", asked Kabir. "Nope", replied Bhavesh. *I hope this subject turns out to be a life saviour, not a destroyer,* thought Kabir. And with that entered our Professor Basu, a young lady with a book and attendance sheet in her hand. "Hello everyone, I will be teaching you Human Resource starting today. From talent acquisition to performance management to compensation, I will take care of everything", started off her confident words. *Two life saviours identified;* Kabir heaved a sigh of relief.

Chapter 7 --- An Unexpected Encounter

Inspite of being in the IT industry, Rhiyan never really had to use SQL for his work. Although he had tried on a few basic commands on his own, but that's it. Never had the thought of going beyond that limit had crossed his mind. But here, forget the basics, he was about to take a direct plunge in the advanced version. And the best part, it took place at the Old Lecture Hall, the same place where Rhiyan and his friends had encountered the ordeals of Stochastic Processes.

"Good morning, kindly have a seat. And it will be better if you focus on the lecture rather than the historical surroundings around you", began Professor Rathi. Going by the usual format, Sushant and Somanshu took seats in the second row, Sudhakar, Bhavesh and Priyatham almost the last, Antara somewhere in the middle and Rhiyan pretty much confused. *If I sit too close, the first question would hit me. If I sit far, Sir's writing won't be visible.* Rhiyan was still dabbling in confusion, when Sir's rough voice spoke up, "Hey you? Where are you looking around? And who have you left those seats empty for?", his duster pointing towards an almost empty row in the middle with just one girl turning the pages of her notebook. "Yes Sir, I was thinking in the same direction", Rhiyan immediately took a seat beside the girl.

"I had mailed you the lecture plan yesterday for Advanced Database Management System *aka* ADBMS. Anyone had a look", asked Sir's words, his hands busy clearing the blackboard. Sensing the silence, he himself gave a smile and replied, "Seems like no one. Anyways, today we are going to start with relational algebra." On the board he sketched six symbols which looked nothing but Greek. On a closer look, Rhiyan could identify two of them. One looked like a sigma, the other like a rho. "Union, Cartesian Product and the IIT

Dhanuj's gate!", exclaimed the girl beside Rhiyan. "What! Our IIT gate?", Rhiyan exclaimed and took a closer look. And yes, it did look like the Japanese gate at the college entrance. Rhiyan was still in a state of disbelief. Suddenly the list of misconceptions broke when Sir spoke out, "At first look, these might look like Greek but in relational algebra, they represent select, union, cartesian product, rename and this which looks like some gate is *project*", his fingers pointing at entrance gate. Both Rhiyan and the girl chuckled off in silence. "Hi, I am Rhiyan", started off the intro as Sir turned towards the blackboard. "Hi, I am Surbhi", replied back the girl. "So, which branch are you from?", Rhiyan got a bit curious. "I thought by now you would have known", answered her googly with a smile. "What!", Rhiyan looked confused. "Let me give you a hint. We might have had a common course in the first semester", gave her clue. "Where you were asking a lot of question, yet somehow struggling to understand the intricacies", extended her clue. *No way! Impossible. She was there? How did I miss her presence?* Doubts were hammering him down when he spoke up. "You were there in Machine Learning course with us. *Damn!* I am so sorry; I was so busy struggling that I never scrolled down the participants' list beyond my Business Analytics friends", apologized Rhiyan. "Not your fault. Those times were a spinning wheel even for me. By the way, I am from M. Tech Data Analytics branch", clarified Surbhi. "Well, in that case you can help me sail through these Greek alphabets, what do you say?", smiled Rhiyan. "Don't worry. We will all sail it together", smiled her words back.

But it was not just Rhiyan, Surbhi was very close to Antara as well. Both were the best of the best friends, never letting go of each other at any point of time, which Rhiyan was not aware of at the moment. "Hmm… seems like you guys have bonded well, huh", commented Antara as the class ended. "All thanks to ADBMS", chuckled off the trio as they walked back towards the hostel.

Later as the course progressed, things started getting into a turmoil when concepts of decomposition and normalization came into picture. "What are all these? 1NF, 3NF, BCNF?", Rhiyan didn't have any idea. "Welcome to the world of Advanced DBMS. Anyways, don't worry, the practical part will be much easier", consoled Surbhi. And so, it was. Rhiyan enjoyed the practical classes as much as he disliked the theory ones. Surbhi being quite good in both, helped out Rhiyan occasionally. But the real relief came when the course drifted towards Data Mining concepts. The second half was almost similar to what Professor Trivedi had taught the BA guys in the first semester. And this is where Rhiyan took an edge and helped out Surbhi in case she had any doubts.

Senator Election

It is said that politics is in everyone's blood, just in different forms. But what the MBA and MBA BA students were worried about was whether they can show their true colours or not. "There are 3 seats for group E, Masters. To win it we need 100 votes. And our combined MBA strength is no more than 70", sighed Arnab, a marketing student.

A senator at an IIT acts as a student representative who can voice out issues with respect to hostel, sports facility, availability of sufficient food stalls etc. in front of higher authorities. And food quality at the hostel was going really out of control those days. *Now I hope you get the point, don't you!*

"In that case we have to apply 2 strategies. One to make sure all MBA students vote one common person and two, convince a few MSc students to vote for us", spoke out Sushant aka the Diplomat. Starting from initial meetings to candidate speeches, almost everything happened in his room. Convincing Kushagra to back out was not easy but Sushant somehow made him understand how the MSc guys were trying to split the votes between the MBA Core and MBA BA guys, so that no MBA candidate can achieve the majority. Later after a lot of debate, Anas was chosen as the one to stand from the MBA side. The only part left was convincing 50 MSc students to betray their clan and vote for Anas.

"Coming up with a manipulating idea is great but I don't think it would work just verbally", suggested Tamal, "Getting on the ground and showing proof of concern might work better". Everyone kind of agreed to the suggestion. And from the next day itself, Anas, Shivendra, Faiz, Tamal, Shubhadeep, Arnab and even Kushagra got down to work.

Many a times, if you don't have budget to build a fully functioning product, even a small prototype works as it serves as a Proof of Concept. And that's exactly what they did. Be it in the hostel mess or casual chats over a game, they spoke to as many MSc students as possible, tried to learn about the issues they were currently facing and with Anas, tried solving them in front of their eyes. Impeccable timing was exactly what grabbed the eyeballs at the right time. Be it shifting the breakfast by half an hour or be it the regular cleaning of the washrooms, they tried to resolve each issue one by one. And the final results of the election turned in Anas's favour. The MBA guys managed to win that one seat at the Senate.

Mid Sem Crisis

"Damn!", sighed Sushant. "What happened?", asked Rhiyan. The mid-sem exams just got over and the first paper that came out was of Corporate Finance. The exam was out of 26 and most have managed at least something above 10. But when Sushant opened his paper, only one digit popped up, 3! 3 out of 26, Sushant was shocked and heartbroken at the same time. "What happened?", Rhiyan asked again but this time with a different tone. "Over-confidence! That's exactly what happened, I guess." Sushant submitted the sheet and went out to reflect upon how he could make it up in the end sem.

Finance has always been a tricky subject for everyone. The marks across the board didn't reveal any better. Understanding the critical concepts was not everyone's cup of tea. But as far as Rhiyan knew, the *Risk Taker* was far from giving up just yet.

Chapter 8 --- The Trio Joins Hands

"Hey guys, has anyone seen my razor?", Sudhakar was squandering around left, right and center to find the one thing he needed at the moment. "Nope", replied Bhavay and Hari who had just come to his room for a small discussion on a Stochastic Processes problem. "As complex as it already is, on top of that we have to submit a term paper now", cursed Bhavay. "True", agreed Hari. "By the way, is anyone hungry. I am looking for some parathas on Zomato. Let me know if you guys want to add something", asked Bhavay, his fingers busy scrolling down the menu. "*Damn!* Except aloo paratha, nothing is available. I wish I was in Chandni Chowk now. Starting from double egg to paneer paratha, you can find anything there", added his words, disappointed. Sudhakar's mind was still focused on finding the razor when suddenly the door banged open and Bhavesh, Sudhakar's roommate made an entry. "Hey guys, did you check your mail? The case study problem statement has arrived", spoke his words as his hands placed a razor on the table. Everyone's eyes fell on the razor first and then on Bhavesh. Sudhakar's eyes locked with Bhavesh's. There was a complete silence for 15 seconds and then suddenly out of nowhere *swoosh!* A pillow hit Bhavesh. He almost fell down but Bhavay caught him. Bhavesh somehow got up and was still recovering from his momentary unconsciousness when Sudhakar's deep voice spoke out, "Next time, ask first." Both Hari and Bhavay burst out into laughter and explained Bhavesh what just happened. Bhavesh took a complete minute to assemble the words together and reach its meaning to realize his minor error.

Sudhakar changed the blade and went to the shave off some unnecessary beard from his face. Seeing the lack of variety in parathas, Bhavay chooses to manage it out with some choco biscuits and snacks that he had brought along. Harigaran opened the mail to read the problem statement. "Oh!", sighed Hari. "What happened?", asked Bhavay still munching on. "See for yourself. Your paratha just got delivered, I guess!", laughed off Hari. Perplexed with Hari's words, Bhavay took a look himself. The problem statement read as – *Find the most optimum route and buffer time for the last mile delivery using a machine learning model. #Parathawala.* Bhavay looked at Hari, whose laughter was still reeling out loud and clear. "Funny", smirked Bhavay. "Here you were thinking of ordering some parathas to eat and instead you got a problem statement in your hands", flew Hari's comments.

The next day all three sat together to make out some head or tail of the enormous dataset that had been provided along with the problem statement. "Traffic density, latitudes, longitudes, restaurant popularity score, peak times etc. What are all these?", Bhavay looked more confused than he had been in the finance classes. "I think before jumping to data analysis, we need to understand the problem statement first", commented Hari. "Hmm… Or maybe we need to understand the real food first. Anyone up for a Paneer Tikka roll", flew in Bhavesh's comment from one corner. "Yeah, but I was thinking of having a Bhavesh tikka roll instead. Should I order?", flexed Sudhakar's arms along with his voice. "Oh no! I have heard it's not at all tasty, you know", replied Bhavesh as he slipped out of the room with a book in his hand. Sudhakar noticed and smiled a bit. "I didn't know Bhavesh is into reading", said Harigaran. "He wasn't until I bought him that thriller for his birthday", smiled Sudhakar's words.

"Okay, back to the problem statement", continued Bhavay, "Initially we thought that this last mile delivery is the distance between the restaurant and the society given in address. But in reality, it speaks of the distance between the society gate and the exact flat of the customer." "So, you mean to say, if we take

IIT Dhanuj's main gate as the starting point and Topaz Hostel gate as the ending point, we need the build a model that can help us find how much time it would take between these two, right?", asked Sudhakar for clarification. "Yes, and in case of a society", Bhavay was about to begin when a voice spoke up, "Time to reach from the society's gate to the exact flat of the customer", Harigaran completed the statement, "Understood, you have already said this before." "Oh, didn't realize that. Anyways, so now we have to do something with this dataset provided along", Bhavay. "Let's start by cleaning the dataset. Its looks very dirty", suggested Sudhakar. With that they uploaded the dataset in Python Jupyter Notebook and began with the first step. Missing data imputation meaning filling out missing data using some mean and mode approximation. "But what to do with these latitude and longitude data?", asked Hari when the door opened and entered the deep learning expert of the batch, Priyatham. "Your timing is just impeccable, my friend", Bhavay had a huge smile on his face, "Kindly help us a bit with these coordinates." "Umm…actually I came to ask you guys out for lunch at the mess", Priyatham looked pretty much confused, which got resolved once he took a look at the dataset. "I see. Well, you guys need to pull off some feature engineering tactics here", shot Priyatham. "I know a library that can help you calculate all distances based on these co-ordinates. Once you get that, you can use it to create a geo map. And then probably use these traffic density, peak time and restaurant popularity data to build a XG Boost model as your solution." The trio looked at each other for a minute before they could even comprehend the words just spoken. "No wonder, Bhavesh left with a thriller novel in his hand", sighed Hari. "Guys, I know this sounds complicated but if you are able to pull this off, you can use it as a spike on your resume", tried Priyatham's motivating words. "Understood. We will try building the XG Boost in the evening. For now, let us boost our energy with some delicious mess food", laughed out Bhavay. "By the way, with a few more variables integrated, you guys can find the optimum route as well", added Priyatham. "Enough my friend. Your words are just increasing my hunger", replied Sudhakar, as they moved towards the mess.

In the evening the trio did give it a try and by the end of the 7th day were able to build a model that could predict the last mile buffer time. But none of it came without extensive research across various research articles on the internet. They were happy that at least they managed to crack half the problem.

Chapter 9 --- Summer Internship Selections

*Select * from IIT_Dhanuj where candidates = 'Desperate'*

Bit by bit as offline classes progressed the internship placement season came around. The first in line was RTIGO. It had registered and arrived with 6 business analyst profiles across different industries. "Hey Sushant, did you hear RTIGO had come with 6 profiles for the internship?", Rhiyan was excited. "Have you heard that Tinder has come along with it?", remarked Sushant's not so excited voice as his eyes hovered on the job descriptions. Harigaran and Rhiyan looked at each other. "What do you mean?", Hari asked. "He means that the firm just gave half of our batch a left swipe with its Job Description capping the experience from 1 to 2 years max", shot a heavy voice from outside the door. As the door banged open, we heaved a sigh of relief. It was Sudhakar, another business analyst student with a herculean body. When he is alone, he is a saint but if someone annoys him… *Let's not get there.* "Finally, here you are", Rhiyan was very happy on seeing him. "It's okay. We will wait for the next company", remarked Hari. "No, we are not", shot Priyatham and with that *Ting! Ting! Ting!* Everyone's WhatsApp boomed up! Priyatham had sent a list of open positions via Internshala. "According to my analysis, IIT Dhanuj had faired quite poorly in summer placements in the past few years. So, we are going to do it the old school way. *Off-campus!*' Agreeing to his proposition, all four started searching for suitable profiles and good companies on Internshala. And the best part, they did it for all branches.

Sushant wasted no time in scheduling the Zoom Meet for all MBA students. Sam, one of the BA seniors who had cracked an off campus full time program manager role at a multinational product firm, had also joined the call. On special request from the juniors, other seniors like Prabhash, Kaustav from BA, Shreyashi from Finance, Pramitesh from Marketing, Anurag from Operations and Ankita from HR have also joined in. "Guys, the past record of summer internships doesn't look great. I think you need to unite and start applying off campus", began Sam as everyone joined the meet. "I don't think anyone from our batch has experience in that", commented Shristi. "But you do have the expertise you require", commented Prabhash back. And with that he started explaining how to prepare a kick ass one page resume, highlighting and quantifying past experience and projects in terms of quantifiable outputs. After a few minutes, students from each department went through a sectional zoom call along with their respective seniors mentioned earlier. Here the seniors helped them shortlist a variety of profiles from Internshala and LinkedIn, helped each one ramp up their resumes and conducted a few mock interviews as well. All this took a series of 5 zoom calls but at the end they were ready, not just for internships… even for final placements. Be it financial modelling, data analytics, data visualization or go to market strategy, the seniors left no stone unturned in helping out the juniors. Strong bonding and a constant hunger for excellence, these formed the two unbreakable pillars of the management department at IIT Dhanuj.

Within a span of one month, almost everyone had managed to crack some outstanding off campus internships on their own. The entire batch was excited. Rhiyan, although was still struggling a bit, was happy that the winning streak had begun for the department and for his batchmates. Because this win triggered a lot of emotions filled with enthusiasm. Instead of depending on just on-campus internships, students started focusing on off-campus opportunities as well.

"Don't worry, you will get one too", said Priyatham, as he noticed Rhiyan constantly fidgeting between browsers. "Don't know about that but I have got something interesting out here", replied Rhiyan. Seeing the excitement Priyatham joined in. "One of my friends told me about this website called Datacamp. Here we can practice both SQL and Python coding without even having to install any software", even before Rhiyan could finish, Priyatham took Rhiyan's laptop, opened a word file and typed in a series of basic SQL and Python codes with some dummy functions. "I hope it helps with the practice", said Priyatham as he returned the laptop. Rhiyan looked at his roommate with gratitude. *He wanted to say thank you but he knew Priyatham deserved better.*

The on-campus opportunities were almost over. Rhiyan was still trying for off-campus when suddenly a miracle happened. To everyone's surprise, a very renowned multinational firm had registered at the last moment to hire a few Business Analyst interns. The first call Rhiyan made was to Sam as he was the one who had cracked a full-time role at the firm. "I know what you have called for. So, without wasting any time let's get down to it", and with that Sam explained Rhiyan the entire process. Starting from fintech application development to mini case studies and guesstimates, Sam explained all that he could. "Thank you. You are a savior", smiled Rhiyan at the end of the call. "I will take that after you win", cheered Sam.

Almost everyone from Finance and Business Analytics had filled the form. First was an online test with one of it sections containing SQL Coding. *And we all know how much MBA students love being in a relationship with coding, don't we?* And that's exactly where a few geeky students were looking to take an advantage.

The test began with a basic English and Finance section. Everyone almost sailed through it but it was the SQL and Business Case Study section where the actual turbulence began. 7 SQL coding questions, 30 minutes. And then 5 business case studies, 30 minutes. Students typed in codes, wrote answers and did whatever they could in that tensed one hour. But no one knew which one was right and which one was wrong. When the results got out there were just 3 names on the board, Rhiyan's name being one. He was very surprised because he didn't expect his name at all.

Two rounds of technical interviews were all that was left. Last time Rhiyan gave an interview, it was 5 years ago. A long time had gone by. To begin, the first place he went was Google. He spent a complete hour in researching about the firm. *What the firm does? What is its main business? What is its source of revenue? Etc.* After that he opened a word file and jotted down all the common interview questions that he could scrap from the web. Based on Sam's feedback he prepared some possible questions as well. But he needed to practice it like a live interview. He opened his call list and with one glance he knew whom to call for help.

"Hello Antara, how are you?", asked Rhiyan. "I am good. You tell. Oh, by the way congratulations on getting short listed for the interview round", replied her joyful words. "Yeah, thanks. Umm…actually the interview is the reason I called. Can you help me prepare for it, live?", asked a nervous Rhiyan. "Who me?", Antara was pretty much surprised, "I don't have any idea as to what the firm even does?" "Don't worry. I have got you covered on that part. I will provide you a list of possible questions. You just got to ask me looking in the eye, that's it", clarified Rhiyan. "Okay, lets meet at the Central Library in the evening", with that Antara ended the call. Rhiyan heaved a sigh of relief. Antara too hadn't been able to bag any internship till then. Yet she didn't think twice before jumping in to help Rhiyan.

"So, tell me what do you think is the revenue model of the firm and where does a role like business analyst fit in?", shot Antara's first arrow. Rhiyan took the shot with confidence as he had already prepared it. "Hmm… good. Can you tell me how many Cadbury chocolates gets sold in India every month?", shot Antara's second arrow. That hit Rhiyan out of the blue. "What! Is that question even on the list?", asked his confused words. "No, it isn't", laughed Antara. "Come on Rhiyan. Your interviewer will not have this list in his hand tomorrow, right? You need to be ready for surprises too", scolded Antara. Rhiyan took a deep breath and started solving the guesstimate using a pen and paper and finally explained it. "Impressive. Now that's how you roll in buddy", winked Antara. This went on for another hour. Starting from mini case studies to SQL and Python based technical questions, Antara didn't leave any stone unturned in taking Rhiyan's confidence level to the highest decibel.

The next day arrived. "You look nervous", said Sushant as he walked Rhiyan towards the interview hall. "A bit maybe", came a short reply. "You know, a B. Tech graduate is much more technically sound than we are. Yet the firm had come to hire MBAs for the business analyst role. Do you know why?", his words took a pause as he looked Rhiyan in the eye. "Because it is not just technical skills they are looking for. They are looking for a person who can understand any problem, analyze it with a business perspective and finally provide a feasible solution to the stakeholders.", Rhiyan's eyes lit up as he continued, "Yes, managing stakeholders is one of the key characteristics they look for. So let go off your doubts on your technical expertise and tackle the questions with an open mind. Best of luck", with that Sushant smiled and gave Rhiyan a gentle push towards the room.

"Sir, may I come in?", requested Rhiyan. "Yes, absolutely", replied a voice. As he entered, he could see two people sitting across the desk. Rhiyan looked at the clock once to check if he is late. Mr. Desai, as the name read on the plate, laughed off. "Don't worry, we are not going to ask you any stupid clock questions. Have a seat." "So, Rhiyan, hope you are doing well. Let's start", began Mr. Singh, "Why don't you take two minutes and tell us about yourself" "Sure Sir", with that Rhiyan gave a detailed yet crisp description about himself. After a short discussion on his past experience and a few technical questions on SQL, started the actual arrows. "You know today I was trying to purchase a shirt on this e-commerce app but somehow it crashed. Was a bit disappointed. Any idea on how these applications get built in the first place?", asked Mr. Desai. With a smile, Rhiyan explained everything from front end UI/UX to backend database setup as well as payment API integrations. "Interesting. Any idea what is SDLC?", asked Mr. Singh. "No Sir, I don't have any idea about it", replied Rhiyan honestly. "Well, it stands for Software Development Life Cycle. Rings any bell?", came a small hint. Rhiyan suddenly remembered a few vague points, "Umm… I am not sure but maybe it has something to do with designing, coding, testing and deployment", replied his not so confident words. "Hmm… pretty close. No worries", Mr. Desai carried on from there. "Can you guesstimate the number of red cars sold in Delhi each year?" "Sure Sir, let me give it a try", with that Rhiyan bifurcated the Indian population with respect to demographics, income level and other characteristics to reach an approximate number. "Are you sure about that?", intrigued Mr. Desai. "More or less", replied Rhiyan. "Seems like you missed the red colour", hinted Mr. Singh. Rhiyan realized the error. He felt embarrassed. "Its okay. Excitement happens", laughed off the interviewers. *Even with errors here and there, they made Rhiyan feel comfortable at every point.*

Q&A went around for another half an hour until came the final googly, "As a Business Analyst you have to work with the developers as well as manage the stakeholders, right. Now Agile says that you can make iterative changes until you reach perfection and taking its advantage the stakeholder keeps on changing the requirements every single sprint. Naturally the developers team gets frustrated. How would you handle the situation?" Rhiyan thought for a moment and then replied, "Sir, I agree that in Agile iterative changes are allowed. But if there is a change request after every sprint then I would schedule a meeting with the stakeholder along with my manager and try to understand what goals he wants to achieve with that product. Once the final goals are clear between both the parties, that is the stakeholder and the developers, then the miscommunications as well as the frequency of change requests can be reduced." "Good, finally a sixer on the last ball, huh", smiled both the interviewers. "We will let you know the results tomorrow", said Mr. Desai. After a firm handshake, Rhiyan bid them a warm goodbye.

The results were mailed to college placement center the next day. A ping came from Shreyashi on the main group. *BA internship final select - Rhiyan.* The entire department erupted with joy. It was not just Rhiyan's but the win of the entire management department at IIT Dhanuj.

End Semester Exams

Wherever you go, whichever course you take, exams are an unavoidable part of life. So, it is better to embrace it with open arms rather than avoid it.

Starting from Operations to Corporate Finance, professors were ready with the question papers, with style and format completely different from the previous year. One thing that you will notice about IIT question papers is that they are always very conceptual. Even if you are given the entire book to cheat from, still you will make mistakes unless and until you understand the concept correctly. And this was not just for corporate finance or advanced database management, it was for all subjects.

As the end semester exams began, one after the other a series of arrows got shot. Students defended some, dodged some and even accepted some. One trick that Rhiyan always used was the power of acronym. Be it remembering 10 points of a concept or any complex formula of finance, he used to convert everything into easy to remember and recall acronyms with the starting alphabets in each point. This helped him a lot. Everyone gave their best, capitalizing on their strengths and defending their weakness. And when the results came out, a smile sketched along Sushant's face as he saw his grade sheet. His score stood at 9.21.

"What happened?", asked Rhiyan just like in the mid sem. "Some grueling sessions at the library and attention in class, that's exactly what happened", smiled back his answer.

Chapter 10 --- The Storyline Angle

It's not just a trick, it's a life saver!

Date – 2nd May, 2022

Mumbai, the city of dreams – Rhiyan knew the ride was not going to be an easy one. As his flight landed at the Mumbai Airport, he walked towards the exit stopping by to take a look around him. *Is this an airport or a shopping mall?* He was completely mesmerized by the series of glimmering outlets that covered the arena. Although his payout was quite descent back in the IT days, he had never taken a flight before. This was the first time Rhiyan had taken a flight and that too without burning a hole in his own pocket, all thanks to the tickets sponsored by the firm. After taking a few selfies he finally took an exit.

The roads of Mumbai are never empty, always bustling with cars and autos throughout day and night. Hailing one, he reached the hotel that had been booked for him by the firm. He looked up to see the flickering alphabetical lights that read as Grand Stay. He got the keys without any hassle. As he entered, he stood still. Laid in front of him was a neatly arranged air-conditioned room that had all the amenities, a corporate employee would need let alone an intern. He had no idea whether it was 3-star or a 4-star hotel, but for him it was nothing short of a 5-star. For others these might have been quite normal but not for Rhiyan. Having spent a lot of struggling days back in the past, he knew the worth of this luxury. He took a few photographs before unpacking and sent them to his parents via WhatsApp, remembering the instructions of his mother.

Kismat mein woh likha jinke, ishq unko hi milta yahan... started playing a song as Rhiyan woke up gradually. He had this weird habit of setting his favourite songs as his wake-up alarms. This time it was love ballad by Armaan Malik from a movie called Radhe Shyam. The clock had hit 8:30 am by then. *Damn, I have slept like a log!* After freshening up, he called up his parents for a brief chat and then went upstairs, where there was awaiting a buffet of complimentary breakfast. At first look, he couldn't even decide what to eat and what to leave. He was again a bit mesmerized on seeing the menu that laid in front of him. Starting from a live Dosa and Omelette Counter to chicken, paneer, fruits, juice, cakes everything laid there. After having a voluminous platter, he went to the terrace to enjoy the view of a fresh Mumbai morning. As he stepped out, he saw the one reason he had come for. The building and the logo of the firm was clearly visible from the terrace. Being the only one selected from the entire department, he knew the kind of responsibility he was carrying over his shoulders.

Next day Rhiyan reached the office where he met his fellow interns. They came from some of the renowned B-Schools across the country. Orientation and onboarding were as smooth as silk. "Any idea, what the terms Agile, Scrum or JIRA means?", began the first session. The internship period was of 8 weeks and out of those, 3 weeks were dedicated only for training. And this was a surprise for all. Usually, companies treat interns like additional resource to offload some their own work with barely any training. And here the firm was spending money just to train them for 3 weeks and add to those paid flights, accommodation, a hefty stipend and free food. Oh yes! Everyday there would be an automatic wallet recharge of Rs 180 that could be used for lunch and snacks at the office canteen. The interns were being treated like precious diamonds in there.

A day later the interns met their respective managers and buddies to learn about the project work. Terms like

Automation, Data Analytics, Machine Learning, Generative AI were doing the rounds all across the globe. And Rhiyan was fortunate enough to be assigned one such project. The firm had a flat hierarchy meaning you can approach anyone and learn from them. Rhiyan's manager, buddy and in fact the entire team was friendly and supportive in all aspects. "So, how are you liking it in here?", asked Rhiyan's manager, Anirudh. "For me this is pure heaven. Thank you for selecting me. For the first time I have got the opportunity to implement my SQL and Machine Learning skills in practice. And trust me, I am not going to let you down", replied Rhiyan. "I am sure, you won't", smiled back Sir's words. *Oh, I am so sorry!* At the firm, everyone called each other by their first name itself irrespective of their age. But having come from a background like IIT Dhanuj, Rhiyan just couldn't muster the courage.

As days progressed so did the learning modules. With time, Rhiyan and the others became more confident with the concepts. Finally, the actual project began. "Before jumping on directly, understanding the problem statement clearly is the most important task", began his buddy, Mahesh. He had been with the firm working as a Business Analyst for quite a long time now. "After you learn about the process, think about how you can do this", advised his words. After the first task was done, he guided Rhiyan on the second. Something was special about his training tactics. Every time Rhiyan completed something, Mahesh tried to take it a notch higher. And every time he did this, Rhiyan's hunger for challenging tasks increased. To satisfy it, he would deep dive more and learn more, try out multiple solutions to reach the most optimal one. After around one and a half month, the project got finally completed. Documentation and presentation were the final leg of the internship.

"We have developed a Proof of Concept to showcase how this manual task can be completely automated", fumbled Rhiyan as he stood in front of his manager. Although Rhiyan had given presentations before, he somehow lacked a bit of confidence this time. "I know what you are thinking", began his manager, "But don't think it like that. Don't think that you are giving this presentation in front the Vice President or the Executive Director. Think as if you are giving it to your best friend. That will bring the level of anxiety a bit lower. Also, you need a hell lot of practice, my friend", advised his kind words.

Time was scarce and tasks were more. So, he tried something out of the box. He approached his other team members whenever they were free, presented in front of them and took constructive feedback every single time. Bit by bit he improved. And when the final team presentation took place, he did something that no one else did. "Hello everyone, my name is Rhiyan and today I am going to tell you a story. A story that began in 1975…", began Rhiyan and with that he caught everyone's attention. "In 1975 came up a law which forms the premises of my problem statement." Once he explained the problem, he went for the solution which had two parts. The first part solved only half the problem. "So, what do you think guys? Will my story have a happy ending or not?", came Rhiyan's hook again to grab all the attention out there. "Common guys, give me some cheers!", with that Rhiyan explained the second half and solved the entire problem. By then everyone was applauding and smiling. They were happy that Rhiyan's story finally had a happy ending. Rhiyan's manager, buddy and mentors looked satisfied too. *The storyline format to keep everyone hooked till the last moment had finally worked.* After a small interview came the time for farewell. Rhiyan's team had brought a huge gulab jamun cake to celebrate with his name written in bold letters. Gifts were distributed, games were played and finally on 30th June, Rhiyan bid goodbye to one of the most fabulous experience of his life.

It was time for Rhiyan to look for his 2nd internship. Usually in B-Schools, two months internship is the norm but at IIT Dhanuj, for MBA Business Analytics students, the window of the entire third semester was open for internship. And that's where the BA students took an edge over the others, *with a chance to explore multiple roles in multiple organizations.* By the second week of July, Rhiyan had applied to almost 25 companies for a Product Management Internship out of which he got shortlisted for 3. The interviews began and so did Rhiyan's journey for the next one.

Tring! Tring! rang Rhiyan's phone. "Hey Sushant, how is it going?", asked Rhiyan's excitement. Sushant had been selected for a 6 months Product Management Internship. "Quite challenging is all I can say", sighed Sushant. "What? Why?", asked Rhiyan's curiosity. "Juggling across multiple departments to gather, convey and deliver the stakeholder's desired product is not an easy task, my friend. And add to that our thesis project", shot back Sushant. *Oh yeah! In the excitement of internship Rhiyan had completely forgotten about the only piece of academia on which the third semester grading would happen for them.* "What project have you chosen for that?", asked Rhiyan. "Something that I have never worked upon, a deep learning project. A project to find the location and percentage of damage in cars when they meet with an accident and that too directly from clicked photographs", hearing that Rhiyan fell from the sky. "Priyatham, our deep learning expert friend would help me out with it", added his words. "But what is its business application?", Asked Rhiyan's curiosity. "Who do you think needs accurate measure of car damage?", Sushant took a pause. Rhiyan was still clueless. "Car Insurance Companies, of course", clarified his words. Now everything made sense for

Rhiyan. "Well, you have taken up a huge task upon your shoulders, my friend. Wish you all the best", supported Rhiyan as he could sense the number of complexities that were coming up in Sushant's way.

Chapter 11 --- The Third Semester Begins…

Date – 1ˢᵗ August 2022

"Won't you guys be there when we arrive?", asked Parijat, an upcoming BA junior over a joint Google meet. "No. With a few extra courses spread over the first, second and fourth semester, the third one stands open for a complete six months internship", explained Sushant. "What advantage does that give?", intrigued Manjary, another BA junior. "Have you heard about candidate led vs interviewer led interviews?", asked Sushant. "Yes, somewhat", replied Manjary. "By steering the interviewer's focus towards your internship work, you can drive it towards a candidate led interview. That's where you get the advantage", explained Sushant's 8 years of corporate experience. "But don't worry we will be there for the Freshers as the date is getting clashed with our physical registration date", added Antara.

Within the next 7 days, the 2ⁿᵈ year MBA Core guys returned to the campus along with a fresh batch of junior MBA and MBA BA students. And with that arrived one of the most awaited events, *The Freshers aka the Faceoff challenge.* For those who don't know, this is one of those rituals, that help in breaking the ice and bridging the gap between the seniors and the juniors. The stage of the Grand Auditorium was set and lights at full power. For the crowd it was just a Freshers Party but for the management students, it was nothing short of a war containing a series of mini battles. "Ready to begin the game?", asked Manjary. "Absolutely", replied Ankita and Sweta, two MBA juniors as they went up on the stage. From the seniors' side, it was Megha and Antara. The boys from both the sides cheered like hell. "Who do you think will win, Sushant?", asked Rhiyan. "I don't know. But I think, deep down there you definitely know it", chuckled his words as Somanshu and Hari couldn't control their laughter. "Come on guys, stop pulling my legs. She is just my best friend", Rhiyan got defensive. "Oh! So, you do know who", continued Sushant with a laughter. For the dance faceoff the girls have chosen a combo of a few Bollywood songs. As the songs began, so did the moves. Each girl challenged the other at an interval of 20 seconds. This went on for 2 minutes and then magic happened. All the four girls got in sync and performed together for the next 3 minutes. Initially mini streams flowed but with time merged into one. Now there was no senior junior, it was just one family. Similar thing happened when Bharat came in for a faceoff with Rhiyan in singing. After some initial throw off, both sang in unison. It was the magic of these small beads that created a bond and unified all the MBA students in one string to create a unified necklace. After a day's stay, all the MBA Business Analytics students, except a few returned back to their 6 months internships at various cities in India.

The MBA Core guys on the other hand had chosen subjects according to their specializations. Some exciting subjects like Strategic Management, Computational Finance were offered in the 3ʳᵈ semester. Rhiyan wanted to study those two subjects but somewhere or the other he had to make a tradeoff. Because on the other side, after his first internship, he had managed to crack a Product Management Internship at a co-working real estate company located in Noida. He wanted to learn this trade as well. Product Management was one of the most lucrative fields among the MBA grads at that time, especially in the software application area. During 2020-2023 period, apps were mushrooming like anything. Starting from a simple door opening to making financial transactions, everything was being coded as a feature on an app. As a result, the demand for software engineers, data analysts and product managers surged aggressively. At his 2ⁿᵈ internship, more than the actual work he was enjoying the process.

"What are you working upon?", asked Rhiyan's Product Chief as he could see him fidgeting with UAT version of the app. "I am trying to learn the current workflow of the app. I want to come up with some unique features for our application that can help it stand out in the market", replied Rhiyan's excited words. *This the thing about interns. They are super excited creatures who think that they can change the world with one swipe, completely unaware of the intricacies involved in the work. And ironically that is also the reason why they are hired. To explore new possibilities irrespective of the final outcome.*

"Interesting. Trust me you are doing great but let me tell you a small story that might help you out on the way", continued his mentor as he looked at the highlighted points on Rhiyan's laptop screen, "Last year, an electric scooter manufacturing company named Zeo came up with a bike that had all the kickass features in it starting from Bluetooth connected music to Google Maps on display. And when the product was launched inspite of offering free charging, sales didn't pick up. Do you know why?". Rhiyan nodded sideways, indicating he didn't know. "Because that's not what customer wanted. They wanted a simple affordable electric scooter that had service centers spread across different locations on which they could rely upon. And Zeo found this out through an in-depth market research that they should have done before developing the product. Similarly, in our case instead of coming up with features that we think will be mind-blowing, won't it be great if we take some consumer feedback to know what they really want?", winked his mentor and left with a smile. And it was then that Rhiyan understood the importance of in-house market research. *Damn, Professor Singh had taught us about this in the Marketing class. How did I forget about this?* Rhiyan seemed a bit disappointed but was happy that he learnt the lesson at the job. *Internships give us an opportunity to try, explore, fail, re-learn and finally implement,* Rhiyan had read somewhere but now it made some actual sense.

9 musketeers at play

"Too bad you got it entirely wrong", continued Silpamoy, an MBA core student, as he tried to pull his roommate Shubham's leg for making a minor error in the last step of a finance sum. "Really, speaking as if you got it right, huh?", Silpamoy got hit with an eraser from nowhere. "Ow! Calm down, I was just" "I know. Solve the next sum", interrupted Shubham even before he could complete. *Tring! Tring!* Rang Silpamoy's phone. *"Zindagi mein sirf padhai karni hai, ya thode bohot maze bhi karne hai?",* spoke up a female voice even before he could say hello. *"If you guys wanna have fun, meet us near the stage",* ended the call. Silpamoy was stunned. "Who was it?", asked Shubham. "No idea, it just said if you wanna have fun, come to the stage", repeated his words. "Leave it, maybe a Spam call", ignored Shubham. Silpamoy took a look outside the window. It was drizzling outside, not heavily but slowly. A bird flew in and sat on a branch near him. "What if it is not?", doubted Silpamoy's words, his eyes still fixed on the bird. Shubham started getting ready. "Where are you going?" "To clear your doubt of course", smiled Shubham. With that both got ready to get drenched in the rain.

The stage is the place where usually concerts are held within the campus. It stands on an open ground with access to all. Usually on Sundays, the ground stays filled with cricket lovers but thanks to the light drizzles, it was empty that day. As the duo walked towards the stage, they saw a few waterproof portable loudspeakers blaring with music, not the hardcore DJ type but smooth yet rhythmic bollywood type. But no one was around. Shubham gave a suspicious look at Silpamoy. "What? Don't look at me like that. I didn't do all this", Silpamoy looked surprised himself. "You know what. Chuck it. Now that we are here, lets hit the beat before we head back", winked Shubham. With small steps both started grooving and started dancing to *Sooraj dooba hai yaaron* by Arijit Singh. One verse later, just as the hook line was about to hit, 4 girls and 3 boys came running from the behind the stage, circled the two and started dancing as well. The duos steps slowed down to a halt and smiles took over their lips as they saw who they were. It was their batchmates. Piyush, Apurv, Sonu, Pragnya, Megha, Pragati and even Antara. "We were overjoyed as the first rains of monsoon had arrived at the campus. And thus, the arrangement", explained Piyush. "We made some random calls to see whose hearts wanted to enjoy the first rain. Seems like you were the only one to pick up", laughed of Megha. Everyone started smiling and joined in the rain dance together. And this gave rise to a new bond of friendship. Be it any hardship or any trip to lift up the mood, they made sure to stick with each other through thick and thin.

Chapter 12 --- Losing a bet hurts!

Date – 26ᵗʰ September 2022

Things were going fine. It was again a day where Rhiyan was enjoying the Monday blues at office. His mentor had given him a task of checking the user flow and writing some relevant test cases for the firm's mobile application. Usually, people use Figma for drawing out user flow diagrams, but somehow Draw.io had caught the attention of Rhiyan owing to its simplistic UI and ease of use. Opening up one such flow, he started checking if the developers had followed the said path or not, when suddenly the sound of a WhatsApp ping distracted him. *Damn! How did I forget to silence the phone today? Thank God, it didn't happen in the meeting room.* As his fingers clicked the silence button, his eyes fell on the messenger's name, it was Antara. *Conference call in half an hour, be available!* The message read. *Strange, a conference call during office hours?* Rhiyan double checked once again if it was really from Antara. But before he could confirm, the same message dropped in again, this time from Surbhi. *What the hell is happening? Did my phone get hacked or what!* Rhiyan was a bit puzzled. The only way to confirm was to be available in half an hour. The next 25 minutes got spent in checking the app's workflow. Rhiyan took a look at his watch and then at his surroundings. The office was equipped with standalone phone booth like mini structures where one can take calls all alone. His eyes fell on one and in an instant he was inside. His phone rang. "Seriously? Who keeps a conference call in office time?", Rhiyan was quite agitated. "I can", replied a husky voice. Damn! It was neither Antara nor Surbhi. It was Sushant. Rhiyan looked at the phone screen to check the number of participants. There were 6 speakers. "Sorry, I thought it was Antara", Rhiyan got a bit composed. "Don't worry. We are here too", laughed off Antara and Surbhi from the side. "And we too", commented Piyush and Megha from the other. *What the hell is going on? This is not a very usual combination,* thought Rhiyan. "I hope we didn't disturb you, Rhiyan", remarked Sushant. "Had the user flow not been working properly, then definitely you would have", replied Rhiyan. "Good for us then that it's working fine, just the way you designed", chuckled Sushant. "Hmm… Now please get to the point", Rhiyan was getting really impatient by now.

"I'll begin. First of all, sorry for disturbing you all during office time. But this couldn't wait", started off Megha, "Guys, Navaratri starts today and with only 5 days left for the Durga Puja, we want all of you here at campus for the final four days, that is 2nd to 5th October." "But what for?", Rhiyan was still a bit annoyed for being pulled out in the middle of work. "For celebrating the first and probably the last Durga Puja together", came Surbhi's stern reply. There was a silence for a moment. "We all know that after we get into full time roles, as friends, we won't have this opportunity again", clarified Antara, breaking the silence. Now things started sinking in for Rhiyan.

"I understand but…", Rhiyan was about to speak, when Surbhi cut him off, "And we didn't call to hear your excuses, Rhiyan. Who knows it might be a one-time opportunity for us to dance it out together" *"Us?",* Rhiyan was listening more carefully now. "By us, I mean all of us together", laughed off Surbhi. "Oh!", sighed Rhiyan's mini heartbreak. "Okay. Let us think about it", suggested Sushant. *"Think?* The only thing you guys need to think about is getting your tickets booked. We want the entire MBA Business Analytics batch with us for the celebration. End of the story", ended Piyush to which Sushant just couldn't refuse. Owing to the in-campus classes, Surbhi and the 9 musketeers were already at the campus with some finishing off their internships a bit early. It was just Sushant and Rhiyan who were still far away.

As the call ended, Rhiyan got back to writing the test cases, with the conference call still hovering on his mind. "Hey Rhiyan, did you get the test cases ready?", asked his Product Chief. "Umm… yeah almost done. Give me 10 more minutes to finish it off", lied his temporary words. "Okay, I am going for lunch. We will check them after that", with that he left. Rhiyan heaved a sigh of relief. Without wasting any more time, he opened a word file and wrote down all the test cases required by the chief. After that he went for lunch himself where he met the developer's team. "Hey Rhiyan, join us. *Kabhi kabhi product features ki jagah lunch bhi share kar liya karo*", they tried pulling his leg. "Oh sure", he sat down with his lunch plate. "So, what new feature are you working upon now?", asked Rohit a senior developer of the app. "Yeah, give us a heads up on what's brewing up there?", added Kriti another developer who had joined the team recently. "Relax guys, I don't always come up with features. As of now I am working on UAT writing test cases for the app. So, it's the testing team who will get more work", clarified Rhiyan. "Really? Thank you for the break", smiled Kirti. "By the way, aren't you going home for the Durga Puja?", Rohit had just hit Rhiyan's thoughts unknowingly. "Umm… not sure yet. I mean today is Monday and we have to complete the deployment by Friday. I don't think I'll make it on time, back home for the festival. Especially when tickets are unavailable", sighed Rhiyan. "I agree. But you know what? These are the kind of situations because of which the word *'Tatkal'* came into existence", hinted Rohit back. "Hmm… that is there but still chances are pretty low", Rhiyan's spoon still fidgeting with the rajma chawal in his plate. *Damn! I am missing the hilsa fish right now.* After a few more chit chats, they went towards the foosball table. This was one indoor game people loved playing out there. "We are just three people out here. Where would we find a fourth one?", asked Kirti, her hands fidgeting with the ball. "Mind if I join in?", asked a familiar voice from behind. On turning back, Rhiyan realized who he was, the Product Chief himself. "Absolutely Sir", exclaimed all in unison. There was no question of denying.

Just six months ago, Rhiyan had no idea what foosball meant. But thanks to his previous internship, apart from analyzing problems, his mentor had taught him how to play foosball as well. For those who don't know, foosball is similar to football, the only difference being that it's played on a table by rotating two handles with mini players attached to each and a mini plastic ball flirting around. *Swoosh!* Shot the chief, his eyes straight at Rhiyan's goal. Eyes on the ball, Rhiyan defended it, slowed the ball and with the help of his goalkeeper, shot it back straight, with the Chief's goalie defending it easily. Rohit, Rhiyan's partner tried shooting as fast as possible. But Kirti, Chief's partner was not giving up too. The problem in foosball is that the handles slide in and out so swiftly, that it gets very difficult to pin point a player's constantly changing positions. And bang! The chief score the first goal. Rhiyan couldn't even see the ball. "Come on guys. Don't make it so easy for me", winked the chief. With a goal to retaliate, Rohit and Rhiyan pulled their socks and bang! Goal scored. The duo gave a high five to each other in joy. "Not easy after all, huh", smiled Rhiyan. After 15 minutes, both teams were at 9-9. Just one more was needed to win it out. "Interesting point. Isn't it?", chuckled the chief, "Whoever wins it gets a treat from the other" "Well, more than a treat Rhiyan would be happier with few days' break, I guess", winked Rohit. "What! No", Rhiyan was taken aback. "What is going on?", Chief was confused. "Nothing Sir", fumbled Rhiyan's words. "Relax Rhiyan. You can tell me if there is anything I can do for you", tried Chief's comforting words. Rhiyan was still hesitating when Rohit spoke up for Rhiyan, "Sir, actually its Durga Puja next week and Rhiyan was thinking if he could get a break for it." "Okay, so this is the matter, huh", understood Chief. "You know what, this match just got a bit more interesting", Chief started playing with words. "If you are able to score the final goal, the break is yours. But if you lose, I get what I want. So, what do you say Rhiyan? Deal?" *What I want! That means more work. Bad wager.* Rhiyan was in a fix. But then again, he wanted to take a chance owing to both the fishes and his friends. After a second thought, he nodded, "Deal."

As the shots rapid fired on each other, the race for the final goal began. Whatever random shots Rhiyan and Rohit were attempting, all were getting blocked by Chief. Suddenly Kirti's hands flipped and unknowingly the ball shot straight to Rhiyan's goal. *Damn! Rhiyan lost the bet.* "You know I tried to give you as many chances as possible, but somehow that anxiety didn't let you hit the ball in the right direction", remarked the Chief. "Anyways, as per the deal. Now I get what I want", he seemed quite happy. "Sorry Rhiyan, I didn't mean to…", apologized Kirti. "Not your fault Kirti. It's okay", supported Rhiyan. "Sir, do let me know the tasks that you want me to complete by next week", Rhiyan knew the consequences, his eyes still on the board. "Not tasks. I need you to complete just one task. And that is enjoy your Durga Puja like never before back at your place", smiled his product chief. Rhiyan's eyes lit up. "What?", he was still perplexed. "Yes, my boy. You heard it right. You must take a break next week. And that's exactly what I want", clarified Chief's words. "Thank you, Sir,", Rhiyan was still in disbelief. "I might be a strict person but that doesn't mean I don't have feelings. Happy Durga Puja, Rhiyan", and with that ended the foosball game. After he left, the trio celebrated with a mango ice cream milkshake at the café.

Chapter 13 --- Durga Puja Celebrations

Navratri, Garba and Dandiya

1ˢᵗ October, 2022

Implementing Rohit's suggestions, Rhiyan had tired a tatkal booking and by God's grace he had got a confirmed ticket in the Delhi Howrah Express. Boarding the train he informed his friends back at college about his tentative arrival time. "Why 4th. If you are on the train right now, you will reach Dhanuj by tomorrow itself", Antara seemed a bit confused. "You are right. But before I visit you, I need to visit someone else", replied Rhiyan. "Any secret girlfriend we need be aware of?", chuckled Antara. "I am a free bird as of now and would like to keep it that way, Antara. So stop teasing me", smiled Rhiyan. "Okay. But 4th October it is! Kindly don't be late", ended the call.

The train ran like a cheetah, maybe even faster. So did Rhiyan's heartbeats. The train crossed Dhanuj in front of his eyes. Yet he didn't flinch. A few hours later he finally got down. He looked up to see the board. On it was written just one word, *Durgapur.* He had arrived at his hometown first to give his parents the best surprise they could receive.

Rhiyan's parents were busy watching the television when suddenly the doorbell rang. And there he was after five long months, back home! "What! How?", his parents were shocked, surprised and happy, all at the same time. "Well, I thought why not give a surprise!", smiled Rhiyan as he embraced his parents. The next two days he spent with his parents visiting as many pandals as possible with them.

4ᵗʰ October, 2022

"Where is this bloody Rhiyan? I am going to kill him", Sushant sounded pretty annoyed, as he stood near the Durga Puja Pandal. And why won't he be? He had reasons. For starters, Rhiyan had tricked him into reaching Dhanuj from Bangalore two days earlier to his own arrival. And secondly its almost 7 pm and Rhiyan still hadn't arrived. "I guess we have to start the garba and dandiya without him", suggested Antara and Surbhi, who were draped in beautiful lehengas and were looking gorgeous. Even they were annoyed at the height of his delay. "Hmm… lets start in a few minutes, then", agreed Piyush and others.

At IIT Dhanuj, Durga Puja was getting celebrated after a long time, given the Covid restrictions in the past two years. And this time the celebration was huge. Starting from the entrance gate to Heritage Building to even the trees around it, the entire campus was beautifully decorated with lights. And on top of that was a huge music system, loudspeakers set all across the campus for the celbrations. It was Maha Navami, a day just before Dusshera. And students from all streams had gathered for the garba and dandiya near the puja pandal. Yeshita, Tania, Shilpa and a few girls had draped themselves in some iconic sarees with boys mostly in colourful kurtas. But one thing was in common. *Dandiyas,* colourful short sticks in everyones' hands. Everyone was excited to play Dandiya after the Durga Aarti.

"Where are our other friends, I am not finiding them here", asked Sushant who was himself dressed quite eligantly. "With this much crowd, its impossible to find even ourselves", laughed off Sonu, one of the 9 musketeers.

The Maha Navami Durga Aarti started as everyone stood with folded hands in front of Maa Durga. Her idol looked magnificient and so was the pandals decoration with hanging lights and a huge chandilier at the top. After the Aarti, Surbhi looked around a bit. But Rhiyan had still not arrived. He was supposed to be her dance partner for Dandiya. *Damned Rhiyan! Where are you?*

The music started for Dandiya as everyone took their position. It was the famous one from Darshan Raval, *Chogada Tara*. The lyrics started, Surbhi's sticks in the air and *bang!* Two sticks hit hers from nowhere and the steps began. Rhiyan had finally arrived and that too, just in time. Surbhi was surprised but happy that her dance partner had finally arrived. Surbhi and others had a few practice sessions a week ago. As a result, her steps were perfect but Rhiyan's were not. He was struggling with the sticks. But Surbhi guided him, helped him with the initial steps and 5 minutes down, he learnt how to repeat the steps. Everyone was enjoying the moment. Circles after circles were busy dancing to various songs with dandiyas celebrating Navaratri like never before.

An hour later everyone sat down on the chairs nearby to take rest. "Where the hell were you? And how come you tricked me to reach early, huh?", Sushant asked but this time with a calm voice. The dandiya dance had somehow managed to simmer down his anger. "Okay. First of all, not my fault. The train got delayed. And secondly, I wanted you too to spend time with your parents. So had to trick you into coming early", justified Rhiyan's tired words. "Hmm… I understood the second part better, I guess", smiled Sushant as he embraced Rhiyan with a tight hug. "Hey our part is also pending", with that Sonu embraced Rhiyan as did the others. After a few more minutes the songs started again and so did the dance. Antara, Surbhi, Rhiyan, Sushant, Yeshita, Tania, Piyush and others formed a circle and started off.

Two days later Rhiyan and Sushant were supposed to retreat back to their internships. "Thank you to all of you guys", thanked Rhiyan. "Absolutely, had you guys not taken the initiative, we wouldn't have been here. Would have missed all the fun and family time this Navaratri", added Sushant. "The pleasure is all ours", smiled Piyush and Sonu. "Next time we call during office hours, make sure to pick it up", added Antara and Surbhi together. "Absolutely", and with that Rhiyan and Sushant boraded their trains back to Noida and Bangalore respectively.

Chapter 14 --- The Fourth Semester Begins…

The fourth semester finally began. For the Business Analytics students it was going to be a roller-coaster ride because now they had seven subjects to deal with. Rhiyan's parents came along with him for the first time to see him off at his hostel, Topaz. Initially he had thought of giving them a campus tour himself, but when the load of documents required for hostel entry fell upon him, he asked Chirag for help. Everything from required signatures to his parent departure schedule was running by the clock. As a result, he didn't have any option. Chirag took Rhiyan's parents to the main canteen and helped them with the food. "Didn't know Rhiyan would get caught up with so many documentations. Sorry to bother you", said his mother. "Not at all, auntie. It is always a pleasure to give a campus tour to anyone who comes here for the first time, as for me it helps relive a lot of cherished memories out here", smiled back Chirag. After the documentation work, Rhiyan reunited with his parents, thanked Chirag and helped them head back home. "I hope you enjoyed the tour?", intrigued Rhiyan's words on the way. "Well, with Chirag as a guide, you can't say a No", smiled his parents together.

As Rhiyan started settling down on his bed at his newly allotted hostel room, he noticed Priyatham scrolling through some of the most expensive cars on his laptop screen. "Which model are you thinking of buying, huh?", smiled Rhiyan, "Or did they offer you one at the internship?", tried his over smart words. "Not at the internship. But if I am able to build this deep learning model, I can buy it myself", outsmarted Priyatham's words. "What! I don't understand", Rhiyan was literally confused by now. "Look at cars' images carefully, my friend", continued Priyatham's words, "What do you notice?" Rhiyan looked carefully but still didn't understand. Seeing his confused eyes, Priyatham decided to elaborate himself. "If you see carefully, all these cars are parked at an angle. And I am building a deep learning model that can help me find that angle directly from the image." Now things started to make some sense for Rhiyan. "Sorry, I should have known. Even in dreams you choose nothing but work." "Go to sleep early today because tomorrow a lot of surprises will be waiting for us", advised Rhiyan, which Priyatham's coding fingers chose to ignore anyway.

International Finance

Finance had always been a dreadful subject for many. But this time it came with a twist. And all this, because of just one person, Bansal Sir. *Without him the entire subject became lifeless. And with him, its magic. Let me tell you why.*

Date – 3rd January 2023

The clock had just hit 11 am. "Ready to face the wrath of numbers once again?", winked Somanshu, one of the wittiest and carefree BA students of the batch. Rhiyan was already a bit tensed, considering the volume of concepts he had to process in second semester's Corporate Finance. *"Mana ki insaan bindas ho tum, par kya yeh dar ke boondein chhidakne ka sahi waqt hai?",* ("Agreed that you are the most chilled person, but is this the time to sprinkle the droplets of fear?") replied back Rhiyan's meek voice. With that Somanshu and Sushant couldn't hold back their laughter.

Professor Bansal entered the classroom. Rhiyan had already met him once regarding some work of the Consulting Club and he seemed like a friendly person that time. As already mentioned, IITian professors never waste time. *And students get relevant examples every damn second.* Sir immediately inserted the pen drive and opened the first slide. It contained the entire list of topics for the semester. Starting from Forex Market to

Trading strategy of Derivatives, everything flashed at one go. "I know what you are thinking", started off Sir's smile, "What are all these geeky terms? Right?" Well, he was right, Rhiyan and the other BA students had never even heard about the terms mentioned. "Don't worry. All you need to do is come to the class with an open and curious mind. Rest leave it to me." Apart from the impeccable timing, this was one more highlight of the IITian professors. *Subjects might be tough; concepts might be tricky but the professors never lose faith in their students.* And with that Sir started off by explaining a few Forex Market concepts. As the class ended, everyone came out with a satisfying smile on their faces. "Yes, now I am ready to face the wrath of numbers my friend", winked Rhiyan back to Somanshu.

They say that first impression is the last impression. Rhiyan never thought that a course sounding as difficult as International Finance would leave the best impression at the start itself.

As days passed by, Rhiyan and others kept on learning, first the basic concepts and then the mastermind Risk Management Strategies like Bull & Bear Spread, Straddle, Strangle, Butterfly, Condor, Collar and Box Spread. What if the market goes up, what if it goes down? What if you want to earn money and still cap the risks? How to earn money irrespective of market movement? Each strategy had an answer to these questions. Towards the end International Finance became a drug for Rhiyan. The more knowledge he received, the more he wanted, all thanks to Professor Bansal.

Project Management

"Do not offend her even by mistake. One wrong move and you are dead for life", came a warning from Tania, an MBA Marketing student who had always aspired to become a Product manager. "And if you do chance to offend her, be ready with your apologies even before the offence reaches her table", added Yeshita, another marketing wizard, from the other side. Sushant and Rhiyan looked at each other. *Why does every course have to begin with a death threat?* Thought their thoughts. With that the first slide opened up. "What the hell is that?", whispered Somanshu. "The hell where all life began, I guess", whispered Rhiyan back.

On the slide stood a beautiful tree, with a swing attached to one of the branches, a rabbit playing around and a sneaky snake waiting to strike. "Are you ready to get an overview of the course?", shot Professor Singh's question. And the confused audience had no choice but to nod in yes. "Just like life begins from the root, similarly our course begins here", started Ma'am pointing towards the trunk. "This is our company's Portfolio, a series of broad products or services that gets offered in the market. As divisions occur, under each portfolio we come across Programs and on splitting a bit further, under each program we have Projects", continued her words as her fingers moved towards the branch and sub branches. "But we all know that life doesn't ride on a smooth road, right? There are ups and downs. The rabbit playing down there symbolizes a positive risk while the snake represents a negative risk, that we all want to avoid. Isn't it Somanshu?" Somanshu was a bit startled as to how did she know his name. "Yes Ma'am", blurted out his fumbling words. "And do you notice that swing? Even that has meaning in our course which would come later as the Project Scope." As the class ended after 40 more minutes, students started off towards their hostels for lunch. "You know today was a very weird day. All the courses that we had initially thought as death strikers turned out to be life savers", commented Rhiyan. "Never judge a book by its cover, Rhiyan. This is just the cover. Wait for the pages to unfold", smirked Somanshu.

As days passed, she covered all important topics like Risk Management, Agile, Scrum and Project Quality Management. But it was towards the end, the actual fun began. Ma'am had divided the entire class into 8 groups who needed to collaborate together and complete an Agile Project to develop a Project Management Information System. Initially everyone was going haywire. But Ma'am took charge, conducted sessions on how to install and use JIRA and finally things fell on track. Rhiyan and his team made many mistakes but with Ma'am's constant feedback, they learnt when, where, why and how to rectify themselves. "Just knowing the HOW is not enough. You need to know the WHY too", was her best advice that stayed back with Rhiyan for a pretty long time.

Consumer Behaviour

"Don't worry. I am not going to ask you about the 4Ps of Marketing today. Instead, a very simple question", began Pranali Ma'am with her eyes focused on Somanshu. "Why did you choose Consumer Behaviour?" MBA Business Analytics guys had to choose electives for the final semester and almost all BA guys had one elective as common, Consumer Behaviour. *Because I think this could be a scoring subject that can improve my grades,* Somanshu's heart wanted to answer. But his nervous words fumbled out as, "Ma'am, because I want to learn how consumers attitude and thinking affects their buying decisions." "Perfect. That's called a classic B-School answer. But I wanted a real answer. You know what I mean!", smiled Ma'am sarcasm. Somanshu's thoughts and as well as his words started trembling. "It's okay. I know the answer hidden in your heart", smiled Ma'am and let him go without any further interrogation. Suddenly a chalk from Ma'am's hand whipped past Somanshu's ear to hit its target, Shubham. "BA guys in trouble is not a giggling moment for the marketing guys", shot back Ma'am's stern words. The entire class fell silent. And with that began her words, "Today we are going to discuss about STP aka Segmenting, Targeting, Positioning."

"So, Tania what is Segmenting and why do we even need to do it?", shot her question. "Ma'am, segmenting based on multiple factors like income, gender, education, location etc. is really important. Otherwise, companies like Apple wouldn't know which segment it needs to target in order to expand its customer base", answered Tania's confident words. "Quite on point, Tania. Anyone else would like to add something?", Ma'am pushed a bit further. "Ma'am, I think Segmenting, Targeting and Positioning are all interlinked with each other. Without one we cannot proceed with the other", added Yeshita. "Examples Yeshita, examples. What did I say in the last semester, remember?", said Ma'am. "Be it Consumer Behaviour or Services Marketing no answer in your paper will be valid without relevant examples. And in Services if you give a good's example, don't come to me running for marks", advised Ma'am's preliminary warning. And with that Ma'am took charge and started explaining the concepts in detail.

Public Policy

"Hmm… seems quite a lot, huh!", Arpita Ma'am was a bit surprised seeing the number of MBA students who had opted for her course. "50 to be exact Ma'am", Rhiyan had already done the counting. "Thanks for the number. Seems like not just student count but the enthusiasm is high as well", smiled Ma'am. "You know, usually Public Policy is not a very sought-after course in an MBA program but still we offer it. Any idea why?", asked Ma'am's words. In the first instance nobody answered. "Well, it's not a rhetorical question that's self-understood. It's a question that needs to be answered", pushed Ma'am a bit further when suddenly Tamal got up and answered, "Ma'am, I think a good understanding of various public policies can help us take better decisions in the future, keeping both the profit as well as peoples' well-being in mind." "Thank God. At least somebody answered. Thank you. If I may ask what is your name?", asked Ma'am relieved words. "Tamal, Ma'am." "Well, Tamal you are almost there but to reach the exact answer can you please help me convince your friends, that a better response statistic will take their understanding to a whole new level", continued Ma'am. "See guys, I know most of you might have chosen this course thinking it's a boring theoretical subject, but let me assure you that the more you interact, the more interesting it will become. And now without any further ado lets jump into the world of Public Policy." With that began some discussions on market vs political model of society which later moved towards policy environments. By the end of the class along with Tamal, many others like Geetanjali, Sushant, Bhavay, Mayank, Apurv, Chirag, Tanmoy created a bustling web of interactions. "Loved the way the class participation happened today. Hope it will continue further", Ma'am was really happy. "Just remember one thing guys. Being right or wrong is a secondary thing. Trying it out is the primary step be it Public Policy or any other course. The more you interact the more you learn. Have a nice day everyone", with that she bid them goodbye for the day.

Advanced Multivariate Analysis

"Not again!", sighed Rhiyan even before he had met the first word of Advanced Multivariate Analysis. "What happened?", asked Priyatham. "Nothing, it's just that I am still reeling from the after effects of Stochastic Processes and now we have this. The name is itself so complex", replied Rhiyan when suddenly the door opened and Professor Mondal entered with a few class notes in his hand. "Well, the name might be complex but with time, things will become simple. Don't worry. Sorry, overheard you two at the entrance", smiled his opening words.

"If we just focus on one word, multivariate it gives a sense of multiple variables, isn't it? So why don't we start with something that justifies the name of the course itself." Picking up the chalk, Sir scribbled something on the board. With one stroke below it, Sir revealed the topic of the day, *Factor Analysis.* "Don't worry, I am not going to ask you what it is. Because by the end of this class, you will answer it yourselves", smiled his words again, this time with a whole new confidence.

"I am sure you all buy stuff from Amazon or Flipkart, right? But how many of you have noticed a section called Refurbished Goods, goods which have been initially identified to be defective but later remanufactured or repaired to be sold at a cheaper price?", shot his question. The heat of the subject's perceived complexity started to cool off because the word Amazon had already brought a smile on everyone's face. "Yes Sir, I have noticed but never bought the refurbished stuffs", answered Bhavay. "Why not? Amazon takes full guarantee of its functionality and that too at a cheaper price", countered Sir's justification. "Sir, for me it's mainly because of trust issues. It has broken down once. What if it breaks down again?", answered Bhavay. Rhiyan and others were literally enjoying the debate. "Hmm… I understand your point but that's not the only *factor* that makes the remanufacturing business infeasible." Sir's first slide unveiled a huge list of around 10 factors that actually gives the refurbish business a tough run for its money. Starting from lack of market to mindset of people, from economic profitability to hassle of returns, everything stood clear on the board. "Today, using Factor Analysis we are going to draw out a Correlation Matrix and try to reduce this entire bunch into just 3 key factors. And we will do that by assembling all information present in these 10 factors." And with that Sir helped the students understand the nature of the data, what needs to be done but most importantly why it needs to be done. Towards the end of the class, Sir ran some Python codes on Jupyter Notebook to reveal the 3 magical key factors that he had promised at the beginning. Sir noticed a smile on Rhiyan's face. "Well, seems like you have started enjoying the complexities of the course, huh", smiled Sir's parting words.

Merchant Banking and Financial Services

Now this was a subject that Rhiyan had not opted for but somehow his heart wanted to get an essence of the course. He already had 7 subjects to deal with but still his heart wanted to sneak in. And so, he did. The moment he entered, he realized that unlike others, this one didn't have B. Tech students to compete with. It was just 25 MBA Finance students, that's it. "I didn't know you have opted for this course too", exclaimed Megha as Rhiyan took a seat. "I haven't. I just wanted to learn the basics of this course", whispered his sneaky words. Half of the students were surprised. *I mean who does that. Here they were having just 4 courses and yet sailing across was difficult and this guy inspite of have 7 courses, a few technical too, had sneaked in to get a course overview!* Their looks were giving Rhiyan a lot of mixed feelings, when suddenly Professor Das entered. "I must say, some brave hearts huh! Not everyone has the tenacity to withstand the heat of merchant banking. But you guys do, so congratulations. Today we will be learning about leasing", and with that he started off and took everyone to the era of 1970s that gave rise to the concept of leasing. "Any idea why it came to the market?", asked his first question. "To avoid an outright purchase maybe", answered Nasreen. "Or maybe to bypass a high working capital initially", countered Rhiyan. Everybody's eyes fell on him. *"Oops, did I make any mistake", doubted his own words. "Of course, you did", elaborated their eyes in silence. "First you sneak in to our course and now you answer too. Do you have any idea, how high your words are taking Sir's expectations?"* Hidden conversations were going on like this when Sir decided to break the silence. "It's okay, guys. He may be right or wrong but no need to give him a death stare", laughed off his words, cooling off the environment. Sir switched on the projector and started explaining in detail. His level of knowledge was really high and so was his style of teaching, explaining in depth concepts in simple words. And the best part, at the end of each class, he used to ask one conceptual question, half of whose answer came out of the students spontaneously, giving a reality check to the professor on how well the students have understood the concepts. Rhiyan continued it for a few more sessions but owing to the pressure from his actually opted 7 courses, he finally decided to retire from the MBFS course.

Chapter 15 --- Parakram vs Srijan

Kehte hai Ishq usey jo mukammal ho jaaye, aur Aashiq usey jo barbad ho jaaye,

Mohobbat mein inkaar ho toh koi baat nahi, par khamoshi mein izhaar ho,

Toh abaad ho jaaye.

"Wow… never knew you were a poet too, Rhiyan", said Sushant as he turned the pages of a diary that laid on the table. "Come on Sushant. That's not done. You should not read someone's diary", shot back a startled Rhiyan as he snatched it back. Sushant had come to discuss a case study on International Finance. "But whom did you write it for?", Sushant was definitely not ready to let it go just like that. "No one", blurted Rhiyan nervously. *Rhiyan had a past he didn't want to talk about. A crush to whom he couldn't speak his heart out during his B. Tech college days. By the time he mustered the courage, she had already drifted away to a city far from his reach.*

"It's okay, Rhiyan. Don't worry we won't bother you about it", smiled Sushant as he looked towards Priyatham for an approval. "Yeah, but at least read out the poem to us", joined Priyatham. "I would have, had it actually been a poem", continued Rhiyan's clarifying words, "These are just the musings of a broken heart which may someday turn into a song." And with that everybody joined in to solve the finance case study. Priyatham was able to solve it to a certain extent. And the rest didn't even have a clue. As the clock touched 1 pm, they left for lunch. Although room numbers were known to all, not everyone paid a visit. It was the Topaz hostel mess, where everyone actually met. Starting from Asish, Harigaran, Bhavay, Apurv, Sudhakar from MBA BA to Piyush, Tamal, Prateek, Nandu, Yashvardhan, Aarush from MBA Core everyone used to gather up there. For the boys, mess was the adda point. "So, anything new coming up?", asked Harigaran at the table, as others settled down with chicken biriyani and raita on their plates. The veg guys had paneer and soyabean biriyani. Usually nobody likes mess food, but the cooks at Topaz play it smartly. Even though the individual items might not be lucrative but when complemented with items like gulab jamun, ice cream, stuffed paratha, the entire dish became palatable. "Oh yes, sports fest, Parakram and cultural fest, Srijan are coming up", Shubham was really excited. Usually there is a substantial gap between the two but for this year, its back-to-back. Conversations were going on when suddenly the door banged open and entered Kushagra, the Topaz hostel president. Every year a student is elected for that position to bridge the gap between the admin and students. This time it was Kushagra. He had tall and a healthy stature, had been a boxing and weight lifting champion in the past. And the aura with which he entered the mess, even the flying dust particles could tell who the Parakram champion would be. "Hey Kushagra, how is life?", asked Aarush as Kushagra settled down with his food. "Just a bit busy practicing for weight lifting and boxing", replied his aura.

Faceoff at Parakram

Within the next 7 days, Parakram began. Colleges from all across India had arrived. Students from other IITs and NITs had come in. Inspite of being busy with assignments, the MBA students had taken out some time to participate. Nandu and Aarush had been practicing basketball for quite some time now. And as the practice games progressed, they became seasoned players. Last time the participant as well as the audience count in most of the matches were low. So, this time something different had been planned. Be it Tennis, Badminton, Basketball or Chess all the matches would begin with Boys Vs Girls from different colleges, with time capped to 45 minutes per match. As this mail dropped in the students' inbox, interests started turning into excitements. The participant count jumped during the trials. Some lost, some won. And finally on the opening day, a basketball match got scheduled, boy's vs girls, Nandu and Aarush both being a part of it.

Date – 8th February, 2023, Opening day evening 7 pm

Lights were set, ground was wet and the ball started dribbling. From one hand to other, the girls had already taken a lead. As the ball dribbled across hands, one girl jumped towards the basket but was blocked by Aarush. Wet with sweat, his hands snatched the ball mid-air and passed to Nandu. As both of them landed, their feet met the ground and so did their first sight. The girl gave a stern look to Aarush. As she turned away, he read the name on her back, Anita. But what caught his eye was a small butterfly tattoo flying across her neck. A smile sketched around Aarush's face as he got ready for his shot. *He had had a few dates in the past. So at least he was not a newbie in the area of stern looks.* Nandu, completely unaware of the game within the game continued with his passes and shots. Within the next 10 minutes, both the teams had identified their opponents' shooters. Both Nandu and Anita were getting annoyed with multiple blockades. "Hey Nandu", called Aarush and signaled him something as his right index finger pointed towards the ground and drew an imaginary circle. Nandu understood. As the ball reached him, he moved towards the opponents' basket with full power. He was about to get blocked when suddenly he passed the ball to the right even without looking and enacted to throw it in the basket. *He knew who was waiting at his right.* Girls focused on blocking him. But the ball had already dribbled to Aarush by then, who wasted no time and swoosh. First goal scored by the boys. Anita, although furious stayed calm. The girls made their move towards the opponents' basket. Maira, another girl dribbled quickly through the opponents and passed it to Anita. She reached the basket and jumped knowing perfectly who will be waiting to block her. Aarush did jump to block her shot but *damn,* her hands didn't have the ball. As both landed, Maira jumped in from the side and swoosh. Before making the jump, Anita had already dribbled the ball through his flying legs to Maira. Score balanced by the girls. Anita gave a fitting smile to Aarush as she retreated back. Aarush was impressed. The music was loud and *so were the heartbeats.*

But it was not just basketball that caught the opening bid. Other courts were also lit up. In Lawn Tennis, Pragnya was sweeping one shot after the other. She had a tough opponent in front of her who was making her dance like hell. The name on the back of her T-Shirt read as Ruhi. *Swoosh!* Her 3rd shot forced Pragnya to run to the other diagonal to make a counter. Ruhi was playing one diagonal after the other, trying her best to tire out Pragnya. Five minutes in the game, Pragnya understood her strategy. In one of the shots, sensing Pragnya close to the nets, Ruhi hit a shot that went above her head and she missed. Pragnya smiled and applauded her opponent. But this time it was her turn to reply back. In the next, Ruhi hit a strong one expecting a stronger return, when suddenly Pragnya ran closer and defended the ball with a light touch. The force was just enough for the ball to cross the net and take two drops even before Ruhi could reach closer. Point scored by Pragnya. *Damn, what was that!* Ruhi was still in shock. Scores were almost at the tie. After a few more shots, Ruhi tried her diagonal strategy again. She took a shot such that the possible return shot could be at her left diagonal. Sensing her move towards the left, Pragnya played the ball with her backhand and *swoosh!* It flew to Ruhi's right and even with a jump, her racket missed the ball. Pragnya won the match. But instead of celebrating, she ran towards Ruhi and picked her up. "Are you hurt?", asked Pragnya. "A bit maybe", Ruhi got up with Pragnya's help. "I shouldn't have played that stupid shot", apologized Ruhi. "These stupid shots are the ones that makes us experienced, my friend. Come on, we should celebrate the game here, not the win or loss", smiled Pragnya, as she helped Ruhi towards the chair.

General Championship

Not all got a shot at Parakram. But that didn't deter the bustling hearts. A General Championship aka GC had been arranged internally as well. In the Sports Activity Complex, Sushant and Aditya were making one on one chess moves against each other to reach each other's king and finally on the far end, Kushagra was dabbling in punches as the area inside and outside the boxing arena heated up with excitement. Kushagra was a bit low in agility but strong in punches. And his opponent, Karan was just the opposite, high in agility and low in punches. And that's one of the reasons why this match had caught some unquivering attention from the crowd.

Swoosh! Flew one left hook from the right and landed on Karan's face. But before the left hook could take him down, Karan's agility dodged it. *Karan was floating like a butterfly and Kushagra was stinging like a bee!* With one right hook and a left uppercut, even Karan signatured that he was not far behind. This went on for another minute. Karan had a very lean body. As a result, he was able to dodge most of the punches. Even Kushagra was stubborn, waiting patiently for the right moment. Karan missed one jab and then suddenly swoosh! Came a left rear hook and a solid right uppercut from Kushagra. Karan fell down and the countdown started. The intensity with which that final punch has landed, even the audience knew that Karan was done for the day. Kushagra won his first match.

Even Rhiyan had participated to try out his badminton skills. But in front of Hyzam's shorts, he stood no chance. Was out in the first match itself. In the subsequent days, other sports also took place. MBA BA seniors and juniors had teamed up to complete the cricket team. The opposing team had scored 76 runs in 10 overs. Sudhanshu had taken 4 wickets in that match. Thinking it would be an easy win, Asish, the BA team's captain decided to take it a bit easy. But when over-confidence takes place, all else fall apart. And so, it did. With Asish and Bhavay hitting 5 sixes and 8 boundaries at the end of 9th over, their score stood at 65 with 8 wickets already down.

Sudhanshu was at the non-striker's end in the 10th over. On the other end was Suraj. He had missed three balls by now. Team's morale was down. Audience started making fun. Suddenly the striker took a single on 4th ball. Now it was Sudhanshu's turn had to face the 5th and 6th ball. 11 runs still needed. With Sudhanshu still being on zero, he told himself just one thing. *I will give it my best, this time for the honor of our entire department.* As the bowler bowled the 5th ball, Sudhanshu deliberately left the wicket open so that the bowler could see it clearly and think of taking his wicket. As soon as he bowled, Sudhanshu knew the line of the ball, checked the length and hit a six. The whole ground fell silent. Now, only one ball was left, and he followed the same strategy, hit another six, taking the entire MBA BA team to the final victory. Hailed as one of the weakest team, Asish, Bhavay, Harigaran, Sudhakar, Sudhanshu, Rajat, Suraj, Venkat went on to score the highest runs and win the trophy, with Asish and Bhavay being the man of the match.

At the end of Parakram, the IITians of Dhanuj had won gold in kabaddi, hockey, chess, table tennis, lawn tennis and last but not the least basketball with which it all began. Pragnya had won gold for lawn tennis in both Parakram and General Championship. Yeshita had won silver for Yoga, Tennis in GC. Later Shilpa from MBA HR went on to win a gold in 1500m long distance run, a silver in 800m run missing the gold by a mere 0.45 seconds, a bronze in 400m run and Surbhi a bronze in 200m race at the Annual Sports Meet.

Falling in Love with Srijan

Date – 14th February, 2023, Evening 7 pm

The cultural fest called Srijan had finally arrived. Nobody knew how, but it had definitely fallen on their favourite day. The heat that had picked up on the basketball court had simmered down as droplets of rain drizzled on the ground. Aarush had reached the podium where Mohit Chauhan was supposed to perform and along with him arrived his favourite opponent, Anita.

"I am sure by now you must have had a tour of the college but why don't you let me give you a tour through my eyes", flirted Aarush's words. "Sure", smiled her words back. With that they took off. The concert was yet to start. "Tell me what do you like best about this college", asked Anita's curiosity. "This", waved Aarush pointing towards the frontier of the Heritage building, as the decorative lights lit up in a flash and turned the entire campus into a different world. Even Aarush was surprised himself. "Who are you? A magician?", Anita couldn't hold back her smile. "Wasn't a day ago. Just turned into one, I guess", and with that both burst into laughter. As they walked towards the main gate, a series of life size artworks by Art Freaks decorated the way. There were many concepts like Jai Veeru from Sholay depicting the value of friendship, the Joker with its iconic smile but the one that caught Anita's eye was a faceoff between Harry Potter and Voldemort. "A Harry Potter fan, huh?", Aarush. "Who isn't! But I must say I have never seen anything like this. Somebody has put their heart and soul in creating this marvelous art", replied Anita, her eyes still locked on the painting. They walked further down the lane with some beautiful lighting across the branches illuminating the way. "Thank you for this walk. I will remember it forever", Anita's heart was at peace by now. "What are you thinking?", asked Anita as she could see Aarush engrossed in some thought. "You know this moment is just perfect for the words my heart wants to say and yet somehow its lacking a few drops of confidence", replied Aarush. *Boom!* A loud cheer erupted from the stage side. Aarush looked at his watch. The clock had hit 8. Time for Mohit Chauhan to begin his performance. "Well, seems like those perfect words would have to wait a bit. For now, let us head back to the concert", smiled back Anita. And with that they returned back towards the stage, this time hand in hand.

Mohit Chauhan had already begun the show with Matar Gasti song to lighten up everyone's mood. The sky lit up with revolving stage lights and the ground was filled with joyful students of IIT Dhanuj. *"Aaj Valentine's Day hai. Toh pyaar ka ek nagma toh banta hai na?"*, and with that Mohit Chauhan started off with Tumse Hi from Jab We Met movie. A few couples who had recently proposed each other danced with joy but even the singles were not heart-broken. Almost everyone was swaying with love by the end of that song, as were Aarush and Anita too. But the actual energy flowed through the veins when the final song began, Nadan Parindey from Rockstar. Everyone danced their heart out and finally the show ended. And so did the short journey of Parakram and Srijan.

"Hopefully we will meet again", Aarush and Anita bid their goodbyes to each other as Anita left to catch her train back to her college later that night.

Chapter 16 --- World within world

Around 10 lakhs Indian students attempt the Joint Entrance (JEE) exams every year with just one dream in their eyes, IIT. Be it Computer Science or Metallurgical, they don't care. The only thing that catches the eye is the legacy of the IIT brand. But why is it so? Is it because of the 1 crore packages that make it to the headlines or because of the startup unicorns that have been founded by IITians in the recent years. Whatever it is, everything starts from the IIT campus that they desire to be a part of. At IIT Dhanuj too, something similar was present. A fort within a fort, a world within a world called CDC aka Career Development Centre that forms an integral part of the entire college. It stands responsible for that one thing students rush for, the Final Placements.

CDC is a whole new world in itself with the placement faculty coordinators at the centre and the final year students as the best soldiers out there. They are called SCPT aka Students' Coordinator Placement Team and to be a part of it, you have to clear multiple levels of tests, which are definitely not easy. And from the management dept, it was time for Piyush, Apurv, Megha, Pragnya, Namrata, Bhavay and Shahsank to step up. The first round began, 3 powerpoint assignments wherein they had to complete any 2 out of 3 things in 2 days,

a) Students' skillset upgradation process
b) Convincing an HR of a firm that had never visited the campus before
c) And finally automation of the entire placement process

At first look, everything looked difficult. "Which one are you going to choose?", asked Megha. "No idea. What about you?", replied Apurv whose mind was still going haywire. "Let's team up. 7 people 2 assigments. Lets do it", spoke up Piyush's confident words, as they started taking up the assignments one by one.

"If we have to upgrade students' skillset, we have find the latest trend in recruitments", suggested Piyush as others started scribbling out the various roles that were currently in demand. LinkedIN Jobs, Naukri, previous year recruitements, they didn't leave any. They went through job descriptions of various roles and tried to map skillsets, firms want with respect to each role. Business Analyst, Product Manager, Management Consultants, Risk Managers were some of the most sought after roles as far as the latest MBA recruitment records showed. "Here. Take a look", began Megha, "Skills like Advanced Excel, SQL, Tableau are very common for the business analyst profile." "And JIRA, Agile, Draw.io, Miro and Figma, pretty common for product management", added Piyush from one side. "Knowledge of multiple industries, client interactions, guesstimates, case studies, data analysis, data visualization are common for consulting roles", added Bhavay from the other side. Like this they mapped all skills profile wise. "But these are not something that is covered in regular syllabus. Who would teach these?", asked Apurv. "What if we bring in a few externals, who specialize in these topics and can impart the knowledge and practice sessions to students on weekends", suggested Shashank. "Possible. Lets search if any such organization is there in the market who is already doing it for other colleges", Pragnya's fingers typed on Google. They got a few and after going through their details, finalized one. Within the next 1 hour, everything was consolidated in a PPT and sent. One task done!

On the next day, they took up the 2nd assignment. "Convincing HRs. Well that's a tough job", spoke up Megha. "And that too who have never visited the campus before", smiled Piyush. "Cold mailing with batch profile brochure. Would that work?", suggested Namrata. "Maybe but chances are few and time is less", said Apurv pointing towards his watch, as the time ticked in swiftly. "I have an idea. See, we know that companies that visit IIT Kharagpur tend to visit IIT Dhanuj too since both are lying around the same region. So why not check its last year placement stats and see if there is any firm that have never visited us. I have spoken to a few senior SCPTs and got to know that they ocassionally use this strategy for the B.Tech placements", suggested Bhavay's words. "In that case, let's not waste time", Shashank's fingers started on the laptop. Within a minute they identified a few firms to target. "But how to even grab the HR's attention within a few hours?", asked Pragnya. "Hmm… Do you remember our marketing case study that caught everyone's attention in an instant?", tried Piyush's words to refresh a recent memory. "We will use the same strategy." The firm they chose to target was an EV manufacturing company that had managed to capture almost 50% market share within a span of just 5 years and were trying to develop a few components in house. Withing the next 4 hours, the team collected all relevant secondary data, performed an analysis with the help of Python and showcased how the in house battery manufacturing can be turned into a profitable business for the firm. With a short message along with the brochure, Piyush sent out 5 cold mails. Megha and Namrata had already found out the email ID of the firm's 5 HRs from LinkedIN. In the last assignment they had ample time, but in this they did not. Only 2 hours was left for the clock to hit 9 pm.

Everyone was pretty tensed and the anxiety increased as they didn't receive any reply for the next half an hour. They were about to give up when suddenly Piyush got a call. "Hi is this Piyush?", spoke up a deep voice. "Yes", Piyush got a bit nervous, as he put the call on speaker. "When you know that half the world's lithium iON reserves lies with foreign countries, how can you say that our in house manufacturing can be profitable?", asked his question. First a blissful smile came on everyones' face as they received atleast one response. Piyush spoke up, "Sir, even crude oil reserves lies in the middle east countries but that didn't stop India from building the refining industries here. And then exporting refined oil and related products worth billions of dollars to other countries, did it?". For a moment there was complete silence. "Sir, I believe India can do the same with Lithium cells and who knows that in the near future, geologist might uncover its reserves in India itself. If your firm starts now, it will always have the first mover advantage", added Bhavay. "Which college are you from?", asked the voice. "IIT Dhanuj, Sir", replied Piyush. "Hmm… your answer might be right or wrong, but I really liked the positive attitude of yours. Okay… you will receive the HRs intent of recruitment letter in an hour. And by the way, I am not an HR but the CTO of the company. So whoever found my mail ID by mistake did a really good job", ended the call. Within the next one hour they did receive the letter and task 2 got completed.

The team was overjoyed. "2 out of 3 done. Now we can relax", Piyush and others were done for the day. During the final presentations and interview, they got to know how the B. Tech students have helped in the automation part. Earlier if an SCPT had to send a brochure containing the batch profile to any HR, they had to inform the faculty coordinator who would then send the brochure via CDC mail ID. This used to cause a lot of delay in replying back to the HR. So they integrated an automated google sheet with the CDC mail ID. Now the SCPTs could enter the receiver's detail in the google form which would then send the required brochure directly to the receiver in this case the HR, via CDC mail ID. After the mail is sent the SCPT needed to inform the faculty coordinator. Few more automations were done with respect to company's registration, data collection from students and distribution of that data to HRs.

After the final interview round Piyush, Megha, Shashank, Bhavay and Namrata got selected as the SCPTs representing MBA, MBA BA and M. Tech IEM branch. Apurv and Pragnya became the senior SPRs.

Chapter 17 --- The Final Placements

Time to make every second count but… in a Street Smart way!

Whenever anyone chooses a B-School to take an admission, the first thing they check out is the average and highest CTC, its students have bagged in the previous year. But all thanks to COVID, Rhiyan and company didn't have such a great privilege at the time of admission, specially MBA Business Analytics being a fresh new course introduced just a year ago. So yes, they had to take a risk and for those with 3+ years work ex, the risk was even higher.

But the entire game started changing when the 2020-22 batch took charge. Under the guidance of the then Training and Placement Co-ordinator, Sam, Prabhash, Shreyashi, Soumili and the other MBA Seniors had managed to attract some great companies with great roles and packages. Under the seniors' league, the average and highest CTC surpassed the usual threshold. And now it was upto the 2021-23 batch to carry forward the legacy.

Cracking an interview is one thing. Convincing and bringing the company on campus is another. While many were skilled in the first one, most lack skill in the later. And that's exactly where the student placement co-ordinators like Piyush, Apurv, Shashank, Namrata, Megha, Pragnya, Bhavay, Sudhakar and Sanjiv came in. They had a lot on their shoulders, infact careers of 90 students to be exact.

"What do you think? How would the placements be this time?", Apurv asked Piyush. "I don't know. But one thing for sure. We will try our best to carry forward the legacy of last year by all means", replied Piyush's confident words. Piyush and Apurv were roommates, one from MBA Core and another from MBA BA, but what united them was a strong bond of friendship and a strong grit to outperform the world. And the same held true for the girls. Pragnya, Megha and Namrata started their search for the best of the best firms but with a strategy.

"See, targeting and reaching out to the last year's recruiters is an obvious start. But not all might come for a re-hire, right?", started Piyush. "Correct and that's the reason we need a parallel strategy as well", commented Megha. "And what would that strategy be, if I may ask?", queried Namrata. "Targeting companies of the same genre", replied Piyush. "See we as students have a majority of specializations in Finance, Marketing, HR and Business Analytics aka Technology. So if we try to reach out to Banking and Tech companies, our chances of converting might be a bit higher", elaborated his words, as everyone nodded in agreement. "Hmm… and as a last resort we can keep supply chain and sales related companies too", added Apurv.

And that's exactly what the chronology was with, past companies, banking, tech and finally fmcg, sales. On Day 0 arrived a reknowned technology management service providing firm. Unlike IIMs and top IITs, at IIT Dhanuj, placements stretch out across the entire December to February. So there is less congestion in one day. Many got shortlisted but the final interviews were cracked by Apurv, Namrata, Mayank and Nihal. Some were happy and many were not. Not because only 4 got selected but because many got a skill check at the interviews that they needed to work upon.

On Day 1 no company arrived. But Piyush, Apurv, Shashank and others didn't loose heart. They kept reaching out to HRs one after the other. But just because the management department did not feature in top 20 of NIRF rankings, they had to face a lot of heat. Still, inspite of all negativities they tackled all questions like bravehearts. Apurv having a data science and analytics background explained about the various projects students have done in their thesis. Be it projects of deep learning, natural language processing or any other, he tried explaining all while relating them to latest industrial innovations like Chat GPT. Instead of using the past placement figures as a tool, they used the skills implemented by students via real time projects. With time, their efforts started bearing fruits.

Product Management

A role everyone desires

Two days later arrived an NBFC (Non Banking Financial Corporation). Antara had applied for the Product Management role, the only role her heart wanted. Sitting in front of the interviewer she felt a bit nervous. "Hmm… Your CV looks great. Since you have already done an internship in Product Management, can you just walk me through a basic workflow on how to come up with a great software product?", asked her interviewer. "Ma'am, I believe any great product starts with the basic understanding of the problem statement first. Once that is sorted, the rest of the UI/UX, database creation, API integrations and backend development are just a cakewalk for the developers", answered her confident words. "Fair enough", continued her interviewer, "You know Antara, whenever we recruit, we face a few issues with the new hires starting off with punctuality and eagerness to learn. How would you rate yourself on that?" "I know I just have a mere 3 months experience at an IT firm where timings were a bit flexible. But everything changed when I stepped into this institution. You don't have any idea how strict our professors are. If you are late by even 2 minutes, you are gone. No lecture for the day. And coming to second point, the kind of conceptual questions our professors set, eagerness to learn is not an option, it becomes a necessity. So be rest assured I won't dissapoint you in either", replied Antara. "Now that you have assured me on these 2, kindly do me a favour and assure me on the final point as well", smiled the interviewer. "I am sure you have heard about terms like moonlighting and frequent switchers, right? No offence, but this attitude hurts us like hell. See, we spent a lot time, effort and money in training you guys. But instead using that learning for our benefit, if you use it as a switching gear to another firm, it hurts us. Any views on that?", asked Ma'am. "I don't know whether switching is good or bad but one thing for sure, those people never develop a core knowledge in a particular field. They do it just for money. For me money is important, but what more is developing a core knowledge in the fintech world. So I think I can assure you on the final point as well", replied Antara. "You know Product Managers, Risk Managers etc. are very important roles but there are some other roles which are even more important. Any idea who they might be?", asked Ma'am final googly. Now Antara was in a fix. "Hmm… seems like I have finally paused your words", smiled her interviewer. "Umm… I am just thinking what to say. I want to say the CEO but not sure", said Antara. "Don't worry. I will help you out with this. In any firm, these big roles would mean nothing if you don't find any customer to sell your product, right?", hinted Ma'am words. "Sales people!", exclaimed Antara, "Yes, without them the firm would not find customers to do business with." "See, wasn't so difficult after all. These people work day in day out, in the heat, in the rain to reach out to potential customers even in the dark. And that's the reason we should always respect them. You might earn thrice their CTC, but if they don't reach the remotest of the remote, your role gets eliminated by default. Respecting ground level workers is one lesson we find the hardest to teach the new hires", elaborated the interviewer.

"Understood Ma'am", nodded Antara, "And I don't know how far will I succeed but I will try my best to pass on this lesson to me and my friends as well." "In that case I think we have a deal. Wish you all the best, Antara", clasped the final handshake. Antara got up to leave as she opened the door. "And by the way, if you ever feel that you deserve more, come to us. We will give you more hike than those competitive head hunters", smiled Ma'am's words. "Sure Ma'am. Thank you", smiled her words back as she turned and closed the door behind her.

Management Consulting

Not all solutions can be assumed!

Next in line was a multinational IT company who had come to hire a few Business Analysts and Consultants. A lot of people had applied for it. Students with experience 3 years and above were being offered the consultant roles and below 3 years, Business Analyst roles. Bhavay fell in the first category. The first round had begun and by now Bhavay had already answered a guesstimate and a logic question. "Hmm… I can see on your resume that you have done some project on NLP (Natural Language Processing). Care to elaborate on it?", asked his interviewer. "Sure Sir", replied Bhavay as a small line of smile sketched across the furthest corner of his face. *Just a few weeks ago on 30th November a company called Open AI had launched an interactive generative AI model called Chat GPT that had taken the world by storm. Bhavay's project almost alligned on a similar path. As a result his idea of higlighting that particular project to catch the interviewer's attention had worked.*

"During my internship at an Ed Tech company, I was going through multiple use cases of NLP. Earlier the teachers had to go through pages after pages to summarize a huge story that they could use as a comprehension question and also create questions out of it. So I thought why not use NLP to create a machine learning model that could solve this difficult task for the teachers", started Bhavay by explaining the problem statement first. "As I started working I realized that its imperative that I train the model on similar subjects before I can give it a test data. What I mean is if I tarin my model to summarize a history related comprehension, during testing I can't suddenly give it a scientific thesis to summarize", clarified his words. "I used many models like LSTM, BART and others to implement this project. I even created a UI/UX that could help any end user interact with the model effectively. And for the final testing I used news events as my specific test category. Now I could enter multiple pages of a particular news and the model returned a comprehensive summary", ended Bhavay. "Wow, that's quite impressive. To speak the truth the world has become a fan of Chat GPT and your work on similar lines will definitely help you earn brownie points", smiled the interviewer. "Okay, coming to my final question. Suppose I give you a truck manufaturing company whose sales have been declining for the past few months. How would you go about solving that?", came the final one. *How would you solve that? Bhavay's thoughts suddenly took him to an incident in the past where someone had asked him a similar question. For others it might have been a common question but for him it was not, because the person who had asked him that question was his own father.*

Date – 6th December, 2010

"Hey Dad, I want to ride your bike?", threw some tantrums of a 16 year old Bhavay. "I know your heart wants to but unfortunately you are not ready yet. Give it two more years and I will teach you myself", smile his dad. "And moreover this part of the engine has got damaged. *How would you solve that?*", asked his father. "Oh don't worry. I can repair it by watching an YouTube video", replied a son's confident words. His dad burst out into laughter. "I wish all solutions were available on YouTube. Would have saved a fortune on the expenses by now", with that he went inside but Bhavay did not. Somehow the heart of a 16 year old teenager didn't want to give up just yet. So he did what he said. He opened up the YouTube on his dad's phone and played with the wires as mentioned in a video.

"Tomorrow, I would take it to a mechanic. Once repaired I will take you on a ride", smiled Bhavay's father over the dinner. But Bhavay had other plans. As the clock hit 10 pm, he sneaked out, as his steps took him towards the garage. Turning on the ignition with the key he had just stolen, he tried to bring the bike back to life with repeated kicks. Woken up by the noise, his father came to take a look outside and what he saw blew his mind. As Bhavay repeatedly kicked in to start the engine, sparks started firing out. "No, don't do it son", his father rushed in to save him. He was just in time to pull him out when *boom!* A huge explosion happened which injured his father's left arm with severe burns. He was groaning in pain, as Bhavay rushed in to call his mother and an ambulance.

Present interview day

A tear dropped from Bhavay's eyes and fell on his arm. "What happened? Did I ask something personal", asked the interviewer's concerning words. "No Sir, I just remembered something tragic from the past", replied Bhavay's emotions as his fingers cleared the tears. "Coming to your answer, sales can decline due to multiple reasons. Starting from internal factors like fuel efficiency to external fators like competitor upgrades and crude oil price fluctuations, reasons can be anything. So its important to go out in the field, speak to the truck drivers who have used those trucks and find out the actual reason. Many a times the mistake that we make is assume things or sometimes be even over confident that we can solve it ourselves. But in reality, external factors are always at play even as we speak. Once the problem is identified, the solution becomes easy", ended Bhavay's answer. His interviewer looked satisfied. "Alright, I think with that we have got a hope. A hope to meet you soon after your course gets over", spoke up the interviewer after a momentary silence. "What! Does that mean?", Bhavay took a pause. "Maybe. Don't worry, we will mail the results by tomorrow", said the interviewer's parting yet smiling words.

The mail arrived a day later and in the final selects stood 7 names, starting from Yeshita, Silpamoy, Tamal, Megha from MBA Core to Bhavay, Sudhakar, Somanshu from MBA BA. Bhavay didn't waste a moment and immediately rang up his father to give him one of the best news of the day.

Pre-Sales

Be it an internship or a full time role, one word that almost every MBA grad wants to stay away from is *Sales*. And why won't they be? The reputation the word *sales* has acquired over the past 5 decades is not something worth bosting of. A highly target oriented role that adds nothing but pressure to a sane mind and more if the location is a remote place nobody has ever heard off. Similar thoughts were troubling Prateek, an MBA Marketing guy, when an FMCG company came for recruitement. In the past like many others, he too had aspirations of cracking a Govt. job. Even till the end of his MBA 1st year he had kept on trying. In one of the interviews, the HR had asked, "What is your favourite hobby?". And you will not believe what he answered. "I have just one. Solving aptitude and reasoning questions", had answered Prateek. Even the HR was in a shock for 2 minutes. Unfortunately that opportunity didn't materialize but he didn't give up. Any Govt. job opening came up, he was the first to fill it.

But now that he decided to let go of the past, the only way was forward. Forward towards using his MBA skills to crack a corporate job. "Are you going to apply for the FMCG firm or not?", asked his roommate Shashank. "Nope, I don't think so. Target based incentives is not something I am interested in", replied Prateek a bit casually. "Instead I am thinking of appying to this Analytics based firm. My skills will get better utilised there", smiled his words. "As you wish my friend", smiled Shashank back.

The first round was a written aptitude and reasoning test. Forget his batchmates even the birds that flew across the campus knew who was going to top it. *The guy whose only hobby starts with quant and logic.* When the results came, apart from Prateek there was one more name on the board, Yashvardhan aka *Yash*, an MBA Finance guy. Being the son of a Mathematics Professor, Yash had strong analytical and statistical background. Two strong contenders stood face to face with their interviewer in the same room. "What can you tell me about the 2008 Global Financial Crisis?", asked Mr. Reddy, the interviewer as his first question, his eyes on Prateek. "I don't know it in detail. Just that it had something to do with the Housing Mortgage issue", Prateek fumbled a bit. "And what about you?", his eyes shifted to Yash. "Sir, it did begin with easy credit to people, even to those with poor credit rating. But as people started defaulting on their mortgage payments, the derivatives linked to the Mortgage Based Securities (MBS) collapsed in value ultimately leading to the financial crisis in 2008", with that Yash explained everything in detail. Being a finance guy, he got an edge here. "Okay. What is the significance of p value less than 0.05?", this time his eyes on Yash. "Sir, I am not sure on this. But it related to hypothesis testing, if I am not wrong". "Sir, I agree with Yash. Just to elaborate a value of p less than 0.05 would mean that the test hypothesis is false and should be rejected", this time Prateek took the edge. Like this, it went on one on one for the next half an hour. "Hmm… Both of you are good. Lets see how you guys fair in the next round? As of now, we can call it a day", said Mr. Reddy's parting words. The next day there was an HR round where they were asked about their work experience and some behavioural questions. Once ended, both returned back to hostel. "Who do you think they'll select?", asked Prateek casually. "I think both", replied Yash with a smile. Whenever one passes the HR round, the usual thought revolves around *Ki abb toh ho hi gaya final selection*. And so did the duo's thoughts. A day later came out the results but only with one name on the board, Yashvardhan.

Damn! Sighed Prateek. But instead of drowning in sorrow, he went ahead and gave himself a good treat at the nearby café. "Don't worry. You will make it in the next", consoled Shashank. "Worried? Who me? Not at all. I am just hungry", replied Prateek as his spoon kept plucking one dish after the other. "I know rejection is a part of life. But how you handle it makes the difference. For me, I like to handle it with good food", winked Prateek with a smile on his face. "My only regret is that I didn't get to know the reason of the rejection. Had they told me the reason, my heart would have been at peace", ended his words.

Owing to an unliking for the sales role, Prateek did let go of a few opportunities when suddenly a Pre-sales role came up, not with an FMCG but an IT company. Prateek applied for it. *Even he didn't know why?* "What do you know about sales?", asked Mr. Paul, his interviewer. "Just that I hate it", replied his words. "What?", Mr. Paul was shocked and surprised at the same time, "Why did you apply then?" "Because I wanted to ask you a question and confirm something", Prateek's replies were getting weird with time. "And what is that?", asked Mr. Paul with crooked eyebrows. "Sir, in an FMCG company, sales would mean running on a taget based treadmill to receive a certain incentive at a remote location. How is it different for the IT industry?", asked Prateek's boomerang. "You know this is my first interview where instead of the interviewee, the interviewer is getting interviewed", Mr. Paul literally laughed off. "Okay. Now I understand your concern. See first of all sales in FMCG and IT stands out with a very stark difference. In IT we are either selling software products or services in contrast to FMCG where firms sell purely day to day physical goods", explained Mr. Paul. "Also, there is a difference between pre-sales and sales. Do you know what is RFI, RFQ and RFP?" "Oh yes, I know that. Professor Singh taught us about it in the Project Management class. It's a part of the Procurement Process. RFI is Request for Information, RFQ - Request for Quotation and finally Request for Proposal. After which the bidding takes place", explained Prateek in detail. "Absolutely correct. And your pre-sales role might fall somewhere around our IOT software and products", elaborated Mr. Paul. Next there were questions of Program and Portfolio Management which were well defended by Prateek. "Hmm... although our start was a bit rocky, the ending was quite a smooth one. What do you say?", reflected the interviewer. "Agreed, Sir", replied Prateek.

After a firm handshake, Prateek got up to leave when Mr. Paul asked, "Prateek, I was having a doubt. Did you really not know about what the IT firm sells or was it a trick to grab my attention?"

"Sir, I am not quite sure about that. But even if it was a trick, I think it worked out quite well", smiled Prateek and so did his interviewer.

When the final selects result came out, Prateek's name stood out on the borad along with six others.

Chapter 18 --- Business Analysts at Play

The risk finally paid off!

With time other companies arrived and students started getting selected one by one. A lot of good roles like Consultant, Business Analysts, Finance Risk Manager etc were getting offered with CTCs based on the respective years of experience the students had. Everyone was quite happy with the progress.

But amidst all these, there was one who was leaving almost all the opportunities in the anticipation of the best, the Risk Taker, Sushant. He was under huge pressure. Having already left a high paying job prior to joining the course, his heart just couldn't afford to take a random shot. And the pressure increased even more when a new of a series of layoffs floated across the news. Almost all multinational companies had begun cutting off their workforce as a part of resturcturing. And here Sushant was skipping things out with no offers in hand. "I think you should apply. I know the CTCs may not be able to compensate your experience but the roles may", advised Rhiyan to Sushant. "I understand but you know our college's policy right. One student one job. One wrong move and gone", tried his justifying words. "And moreover I have already started applying off campus as a contingency plan", smiled his brave words.

After a lot of hit and trial, Chirag had finally been able to crack a mangerial position at a retail bank. Mini celebrations were happening everyday because somebody or the other was getting placed. But so were the heartbreaks.

A few days later, one of the best news came in. It energised the entire batch. A reknowned investment bank was coming for hiring in Business Analyst role from the Management Department. And that was the exact moment Sushant was waiting for. With the clouds of recession and layoffs stretching across the sky, nobody thought that an investment bank would turn up but to everyone's surprise it did.

Sushant immediately rang up Kaustav, the only Business Analytics student who got selected in at the firm last year and had an hour long conversation regarding his approach. Everybody pulled up their socks and started preparing for the interviews. Starting from Analytics skill like SQL, Tableau to Fintech Application Development, Sushant and others left no stone unturned. Rhiyan having some past interview experience with a business analyst level interview helped Sushant with a few mock interviews as well.

The interview day arrived. Almost 30 people had cleared the shortlist round with just one interview left to decide their fates. "Hello Sushant, hope you are doing well", began Sushant's interviewer who seemed like a young person as far as the webcam could tell. "Yes Sir, I am fine. Hope you are doing well too", replied his confident words. "Yeah, I am", came an answer in reply. *'Tell me about yourself'* was a question that all interviews usually begin with and Sushant being no different expected the same, completely unaware that things were going to turn out a bit differently for him. "I hope you have gone through the job description. And if I am to draw your attention to the key responsibilities mentioned, do you think your skills tick all the boxes?", shot the first question. *Damn, where did 'Tell me about Yourself' go! thought Sushant's initial apprehentions but he didn't give up.* "Sir, back at my previous firm, being a key account manager I started off with Stakeholder Management. During the first two semesters at IIT Dhanuj, I picked up a few analytical skills with respect to data mining and visualization and finally during my internship, I had learnt a lot. Starting from how to prepare the business, functional requirement documents to following an agile process. And finally collaborate with the developers to deliver a market fit product. So yes, I think I do tick all the boxes in some form or the other", replied Sushant's first answer. Sir looked quite happy with it. As the minutes passed there were questions based on Trade lifecycle, Software development and a lot about Agile in depth. Sushant missed a few but managed to defend most of them with grit and confidence. "As a final question, should I ask you where you want to see yourself in 5 years or should I leave it?", asked his interviewer. "Sir, its completely upto you. But if I were to answer it, I would say that no classic B-School answer can actually answer it correctly. To speak the truth I would love to be at a leadership position as everyone else but as of now I strive to become a better version of myself with each passing day. Whatever I am today, I want to become a better version of myself tomorrow", answered Sushant. And with that ended the swift arrows of question and answers. "You know what I liked about you, Sushant. Honesty! Abundant in stories yet rare in reality", smiled the interviewer's parting words.

The results were supposed to arrive a day later. "Tensed?", asked Rhiyan as he could see Sushant cracking his fingers. "A bit, I guess", came the reply and before he could say anything else, *Ting!* An email arrived on his phone. Sushant opened it immediately and finally the million dollar smile apperead on his face. The final select list contained 5 names, his being one of them. "Wow! Again a single select from MBA Business Analytics. Seems like the legacy is indeed inspiring the future", smiled Rhiyan as he quoted the tagline of IIT Dhanuj. Sushant embraced Rhiyan as his tears couldn't control his joys.

Ting! Ting! Ting! Came a emails but this time on Rhiyan's phone. "Damn!", exclaimed his words as he opened them. "What happened?", asked Sushant snatching away the phone hastily. Even Sushant couldn't believe his eyes. The subject line read as, *Congratulations, you have been offered a Pre-Placement Offer (PPO).* "Seems like you have carried on the legacy a bit further, my friend", said Sushant as he embraced an overjoyed Rhiyan once again. *You know what they say about Karma… One good deed done always returns back with another.* And that's exactly what was happening. The entire department was filled with joy with selection news coming in one after the other. Everyones' mailbox and WhatsApp started filling up with just one word, *Congratulations!*

From the Business Analytics batch, Antara had bagged a Product Management role, Sudhakar, Harigaran a Business Analyst role and Bhavay a Consultant role. And Priyatham got the role of a Deep Learning Specialist at a Denmark based firm. He got exactly what he wanted. When the final placement report came out, there was a 3x ROI on everyone's paycheck.

Chapter 19 --- The Dark Horses…

Towards the end a few students were still left, one of them being Siddhi, Rhiyan's Consulting Club Co-ordinator. Being a fresher, she had to face a lot of rejections. Even Rhiyan tried forwarding her resumes to his known HRs but given the market conditions at that time, things didn't work out. Siddhi had given an interview some time ago but results hadn't arrived. A similar situation ocurred in case of Kabir, a Bunsiness Analytics guy who had a good knowledge in Analytics but just because of the fresher tag was getting bowled out every single time.

"Hey Kabir, whats up?", asked Shrishti one fine evening as she could see him sitting across the stairs of central library all by himself. "Umm… nothings up. Everything is down like hell. First the grades and now employment", replied Kabir's pent up voice. Sensing his pain, she sat beside him. "You know what they say about failures, right?", tried Shristi to initiate a converation. "Yeah, they are the stepping stone for success. But in this case, even that stone looks pretty far away", smiled Kabir. "Well for a moment even that smile looked pretty far away, but now *voila!* Its here, on your face", smiled Shristi back. "What were you doing back at the library? As far as I know, you are not a bookworm", asked Kabir. Srishti smiled a bit and replied, "Who said Library holds only books in its racks. It holds peace as well" "What do you mean?", intrigued Kabir's curiosity a bit further. "Why don't you let me show you?", with that Srishti took him upstairs to the reading section and got themselves seated comfortably. "Plug in these earphones. Close your eyes, take a deep breath and let the music sync in", suggested her words. Kabir proceeded as instructed. Five minutes in the musical world, the crooked eyes started flattening out. Kabir felt relaxed with each breath infusing positivity in him. "That felt great", said his calm words as the song got over. "Now, slowly open your eyes and observe the world around you", said Srishti. Kabir saw some busy with books, some designing logos on laptop, some turning newpapers and others almost asleep. "Hmm… now I know why you like it here. Its not just books, it's a different world out here", smiled Kabir. "And this is exactly where our minds can solve problems a bit more easily", smiled Shristi back.

"So now tell me, what kind of a role are you looking for?", asked Shristi as both came down towards the stairs. "Anything from business analyst to consulting to specialist", answered Kabir a bit casually. "Hmm, the first role that you might need is a bit of seriousness", Kabir gave a stern look to Shristi. "Come on Kabir, don't get offended. I am just trying to help you out here", defended Shristi, as both sat down on the stairs. "First thing first, send me your resume. I want to have a look." Kabir did a WhatsApp on spot. "Damn! Your resume looks like a disaster", exclaimed Shristi at first look. "What do you mean?", asked Kabir's confused words. "See I might not belong to Analytics, but have a decent idea on how to structure it out", elaborated her words. "First, your resume needs to be a one pager. Second, all your bullet points should start with actionable verbs and should reflect the outcome quantatively. For example, instead of saying that you worked upon this project during your internship, you can rephrase it as *Delivered a deep learning model that reduced the downtime by 80% and improved the automation efficiency by 60%.* You need to quantify the impact of work as far as possible", Shristi went on and on. She even opened her laptop she was carrying and refurbished Kabir's resume into a brand new model. "Wow… Who are you? A magician?", Kabir was pretty much surpised himself. "No duffer, I am your friend… in fact may be your best friend", resplied Shristi as their eyes locked in with each other. "Yes of course!" A group of bicyclists zoomed past which suddenly broke the awkward silence. "Now that you have rebranded my resume, why don't you help me apply to some off campus opportunities as well", asked Kabir. "Only after you give me a treat, my friend", smiled back Shristi.

The next day, Shristi helped Kabir revamp his LinkedIN profile with relevant details, upgrade to premium and reach out to some recruiters out there. Within a few days, he did get back a few replies but in most cases he was getting rejected. But he didn't lose heart and neither did Shristi. It was as if both of them were together in the fight. Finally a network security company gave his resume a shot.

"Well, going by your resume except for the IIT and MBA Business Analytics tag, nothing seems to impress me, except for this one thing. Your internship. Somehow it intrigued me. Even after being from such a premium branch you did sales and going by the numbers seems like you almost aced it towards the end", commented the interviewer, Mr Roy. "So tell me Kabir, why did you do it? I mean usually only marketing students go for it, isn't it?", asked his first question. "Sir, you are absolutely correct but if I may draw your attention, why do you think marketing people start their career with sales? To conduct some primary research and know their potential customers, right? Same for me. What good would an excel file with data be, if you don't know the reality?", answered Kabir. "I didn't understand", Mr Roy looked a bit confused. "Sir, whenever the term Business Analytics flashes, the only thing that gets reflected is Data. But to conduct a holistic analysis you need to be aware of all the external factors as well, isn't it?", tried Kabir's justifying words. "And that's exactly I did sales first and then went for the analysis. While doing sales, I got an opportunity to speak to customers directly, understand their perspective and include those factors in the final analysis. That's why the numbers look good", elaborated his words. "Hmm… now it makes sense. Good", continued Mr Roy,

"Coming to my next question. We are a network security firm who deals in both hardware and software products. What do you think is more important to focus on, the hardware part or the software? And please don't tell me both", came his googly. Kabir thought for a while and answered, "Sir, software because it takes a lot of time and effort to perfect the codes." Mr. Roy smiled a bit, "Are you sure?" *Damn! What to answer now? Kabir was a bit puzzled and thought again.* Suddenly he remembered something.

The day Shristi came to help him, her phone had fallen from her hand. It was not switching on. On taking it to a repair shop, the person said, "Sir, the battery got damaged badly. Seems like you have purchase a new one." "What! Are you sure? Don't you have a replacable battery?", asked Kabir. The person smiled and replied, "Sir, this is not technical glitch that I can upgrade with a new software update. Its bloody hardware, not an easy component to fetch from thin air."

"Sorry Sir. I would like to change my answer to hardware", reversed Kabir's answer as he came back to reality. "Why the sudden U-Turn, huh?", intrigued Mr. Roy. "Sir because if there is any software glitch, it can be resolved with an OTA aka over the air update but if it's a hardware fault, the replacement cost will be too high. At the end, it's a bloody hardware, not an easy component to fetch from thin air", replied Kabir's confident words. "Well, you are correct but funny too", Mr. Roy literally laughed off. "You know, I wanted to ask a few more questions, but I don't think that would be required anymore. Ususally I say that, results will mailed to you. But in your case, I'll make an exception", Mr. Roy took a pause and spoke it out, "Congratulations, you have been hired. The offer letter will be mailed to you soon. But one piece of caution. Accept it only if you have the hunger to learn, unlearn and re-learn new things in life." "Thank you Sir. And don't worry, more than the paycheck, it will be learning and feedback that I will be coming after at the end of each month", with that the video call ended.

As time passed by, the last day of the semester finally arrived, the last class infact. "So, I hope you have enjoyed the last bit of consumer behaviour and remember without relevant examples, no answer will be valid", Pranali Ma'am was almost on the verge of finishing her words, when suddenly *Ting!* Came a sound. "Sorry Ma'am, I forgot to silent the phone", apologised Siddhi. In a hurry to switch off the phone her eyes fell on the notification that had come. Without any second thought she opened the mail. *Final Selects,* read the subject line and the body had three names flashing on it, Siddhi, Shivam and Parvez. It was one of the largest steel manufacturing company in the entire country. "Yes!", Siddhi screamed with joy. Everyone was stunned. "Ma'am, I finally got selected for the HR role", spoke out her words. "Many many congratulations, Siddhi", smiled Ma'am as she bid everyone a goodbye. The moment Ma'am left, the entire class errupted in celebrations. *The dark horses had finally crossed the finishing line in the last second!*

Chapter 20 --- The Final Farewell

Time to bid goodbye…

Phase 1

The final exams were over for everyone. But still a few days were left to vacate the hostels. So as per the tradition, the juniors had arranged an extravagant farewell for the seniors. Be it any B-School, the MBA journey in itself is a tough one, hardly leaves any time for one on one senior junior interaction. But with this farewell, the juniors wanted to break all boundaries. The Golden Jubilee Hall was all set for the event. Sakshi, Manjary and Aman took over the stage as hosts as everyone took their seats. "How is the weather guys?", started off Sakshi. "Pleasant, isn't it. They say that Bangalore has the best one. I guess once in a while, they should take in a step here as well." "But with the series of events we had planned, the stage is definitely going to be set on fire by the end of the night", added Manjary's playful words. "So why waste time, let the show begin", and with that Aman pulled off the curtains to unveil a video capturing the seniors' hot and sweet moments throughout their MBA journey. The entire hall screamed with joy. Everyone received a medal along with some titles suited to their unique personalities.

"You know, inspite of being a musician I never got the opportunity to perform for my batchmates out here. And had this evening been not there, things would have gone unsung. But you guys made it possible. So thank you, thank you once again", Rhiyan got emotional as he took the stage for a performance. "Today I am going to sing a song that I had composed and written myself quite a few years back for students to use in their farewell. Never really thought I'll get to sing it on my own farewell someday." Amidst a round of applause he began his song *College Days* with a C major strum on the guitar. By the end the hall erupted with a series of applause. Rhiyan was happy that everyone enjoyed it. After that Shresth took over the stage and sang a few retro songs on friendships that made everyone emotional. The performances ended with Dipanjan performing a Despacito fingerstyle on ukelele and Sagnik singing along. After that the DJ began and so did the dance. By 9 pm everyone was tired and decided to move to dinner. Rhiyan, Sushant, Tania, Shilpa and others were quite surprised at the extravagant dinner arrangement done by the juniors. From chhole puri, fried rice, paneer, chicken, sweets to snacks and cold drinks the juniors had left no stone unturned on their part. Everyone left with nothing but happy memories by the end of the day.

Phase 2

"So, ready to embark on a new journey in Bangalore?", asked Rhiyan to Surbhi as it was their last meet in person. Surbhi had cracked a PPO at an American multinational firm by then with her posting at Bangalore. "Yeah, and what about you?", asked her reply. "I am ready too. Students who learn to tackle machine learning and ADBMS can tackle anything, isn't it?", laughed off his reply. "Come on guys. No fun without me", Antara arrived for whom the duo were waiting, "What are you guys doing here?" "Since you are the first one to bid us goodbye, we are here to say a thank you for being with us in this beautiful journey but in different ways", replied Rhiyan. With that Rhiyan took out a box of chocolate and a customized key ring, he had prepared for Antara. And Surbhi placed a brownie with ice cream in front of her. "My goodness! Wow!", Antara was a bit surprised. "Hmm, so whose idea was it?", Antara's eyes fidgiting between Rhiyan and Surbhi. "Of course, Surbhi", said Rhiyan. "Yes, before you leave us for Jaipur, I wanted to relive all the beautiful memories once again", smiled Surbhi. "Okay. That's why you organized that Garba Dance program and took me out for Dosa, Litti Chokha etc. yesterday", realized Antara, "Thank you so much guys for all the love" "The pleasure is all ours", Rhiyan was about to leave when Antara spoke up, "But one thing remains…" Rhiyan turned back to see and infront of him was a white T-shirt along with a pen and a chocolate. "Thank you. But don't you think the size is a bit different from mine", doubted Rhiyan. "No its not what you think. Its *my* T-shirt and you both need to write me a farewell message on it", laughed off Antara. Rhiyan and Surbhi both started to write a memorable message each, when loud disco sounds erupted from the nearby girls hostel. "Seems like Yeshita, Tania, Nasreen and others are rocking the dance floor", remarked Rhiyan. "And they should. After all this is our last grand party before everyone drifts away from each other", confirmed Antara with a smile. After that the trio clicked some selfies and bid goodbyes to each other.

Phase 3

But that's not where it finally ended. Sushant and Hemant had taken up an initiative to organize a grand party at a huge resort called Yamas, around five to six kilometers away from the college. With 4 cars arranged the MBA Business Analytics students set on for their party ride.

"Wow, this looks amazing", exclaimed Asish as everyone reached the spot. Everyone was greeted with fresh juice as if they were some VIPs. It was a Wednesday. With very few guests around, the entire resort belonged to the BA guys. Kabir arrived a minute later but with Shristi along. Everyone was a bit surprised as she didn't belong to BA. "I know guys she is not from BA but trust me she is here for a reason today", tried Kabir's clarification. "Its okay. Anyways we don't mind. Be it BA or Core, we always stay united", assured Sushant's words. Everyone sat down comfortably around the pool to click photographs. As the evening lights dawned upon, the DJ set the party mood and everyone's feet joined in the dance. Starting from bhangra steps to natu natu ones, everyone tried their heart out. Sushant, Hari, Bhavay, Nihal, Asish tried to replicate the exact steps of Natu Natu from *RRR* which had recently won the Oscars for the best original song that year and guess what? They did pull off the signature step with the legs. There was no stopping because the world was theirs.

"Thank you everyone for joining in today", began Sushant's farewell speech, as everyone sat down for the buffet. "Without you guys the past two years wouldn't have been as exciting. Whatever challenges came, we faced it together and that's what matters." Everyone applauded as they were reliving the moments through his words. One by one everyone spoke their hearts out. Some on the ghostly experiences of Stochastic Processes while others on the accidental encounters with people who later turned into friends. "I know there will be very rare chances where we get to meet each other after we enter the corporate world, but guys, at least stay in touch over the call", added Bhavay. Many words were spoken but every speech had one thing in common, a special thank you note for Priyatham. The way he had helped people selflessly that too in such a competitive space, no one else would have done it. Be it Machine Learning, Python codes or be it Thesis, his contribution had been commendable.

But there was one last speech that was remaining. "Personally, I want to thank all of you for your constant support. Being a fresher, things were tough but with you all beside me, I learnt", began Kabir. "Although I was poor in many things, fortunately lucky in some", his eyes took a look at Shristi, "But there is one thing I have hid from you all. Any idea what that might be?" "Secret night outs", guessed Rhiyan. "Or maybe some secret crush, who knows", added Bhavay as everyone laughed out.

"Funny, huh", smiled Kabir. "No, none of that. The secret lies on the table itself. You just need to have a look", everyone looked confused. "Shristi, would you like to help out a bit", asked Kabir as she looked even more confused. "What Kabir! Even I don't know", exclaimed her voice. "But your plate does", replied his tricky words. "Seems quite normal to me", Shristi looked at her plate. "Look carefully", persisted Kabir when suddenly she removed the plate to find a piece of paper beneath it. She opened it and took a look. Her eyeballs and pupils dilated like huge spheres. She couldn't believe it. Sushant snatched it and read out, "Congratulations Kabir. You have been selected for the Product Specialist role at our network security firm." Everybody looked up at Kabir and there was a moment of silence. "I am going to kill you. Why didn't you tell me earlier?", spoke up Shristi, "I am so happy for you." "You didn't understand Shristi. He wants to get beaten up first. That's why he hid this till the last moment", with that Asish and Hari chased him down and gave him a nice time with punches. "Come on guys, it was supposed to be a surprise not a kick boxing invitation", screamed Kabir as he defended himself. After that everyone congratulated him along with Shristi. "Thank you so much for all the help in the world", Kabir thanked Shristi himself once. "You deserved it", replied Shristi. "But not without you", smiled his words back.

Finally the grand dinner began. It was a complete buffet. Table set with paneer and chicken items, polauv and special raita. There was ice cream and sweets as well. Everyone ate to their hearts content. And before the clock could hit 10 pm, everyone returned back to their campus and on the next day back to where everyone's journey began from, their repective homes.

Part 2

Chapter 1 --- Paranthon ka Samrat

Time to follow your heart, I guess!

Date – 10ᵗʰ June 2023

The clock struck 6 pm. Rhiyan looked out of the window. Light drizzles were gliding down along his window. A cold coffee stood firmly beside the laptop he was typing in. He had almost finished jotting down a few key points that he wanted to touch upon in his journal. After all its very rare to have such a thrilling journey in academics specially in the MBA domain. While finalizing upon which characters to use, he was going through the students' list in his batch, when his eyes suddenly fell on one name *Samrat.*

Samrat was a marketing student who had joined the course as a fresher. Quite familiar with various marketing strategies but lacked interest in others. But that was not the reason why Rhiyan's eyes stood fixed on his name. The reason was something different. Because of consistently poor CGPA grades throughout the semesters, his resume had failed many shortlist criteria. And at the end he was the only one who remained unplaced in the batch.

Rhiyan's heart felt a pang of pain. He had tried helping him with a few off-campus opportunities but none of them worked. Picking up the phone, he scrolled through to find his number. He stared at it for a minute, still in dilemma whether to hit the call button or not. His thoughts started wandering towards the day when he first met him.

Date – 8ᵗʰ February, 2022

"Hi, I am Rhiyan and today is my birthday. So contrary to usual college traditions here I am with some chocolates for you", smiled Rhiyan as he extended a pack full of Cadbury Perks towards a guy, he had just met in the Finance class. "Hmm… And here I thought we left this tradition back in school", laughed out Samrat as did the others. "I would have loved to leave this tradition back at school had it not been such a great initiator to new friendships", replied Rhiyan's witty words. Samrat smiled as he took two Perks from the pack. Rhiyan went on to distribute the rest to others.

As the class ended, everyone started to leave when Samrat's hand fell on Rhiyan's left shoulder. He turned around and spoke up, "Trust me, I am done with my Birthday bumps." "No brother, I just missed saying a few words to you", said Samrat. "And what would those be?", Rhiyan looked a bit confused. "Happy Birthday, wish you many many happy returns of the day", shook the hands in exchange.

After that they met quite often, sometimes at the hostel but mostly during the lectures. On usual days, Samrat spoke very less but when it came to marketing lectures he had a very intriguing mind, constantly fidgeting around as to how could those age-old strategies be made better. Once when the professor was teaching about the Poter's five forces, she asked a question, "Which one do you think should we focus on more? Threat of substitutes or threat of new entrants in the market? I will take a vote with your hands raised" Half the class chose the first while half the second. Ma'am smiled, "Thank God, I didn't ask for your opinion on an open book vs a closed book exam. Otherwise, there wouldn't have been a common decision." "Ma'am, I think it depends on whether we are talking about products or services", spoke up Samrat. "Care to elaborate?", Ma'am sounded curious. "Ma'am, in services it's very easy to replicate the offerings of a firm because unlike products, execution is the key in here. So new entrants can pose a threat here", continued his words, "But in case of products, it's not easy to replicate them considering patents on their designs. Here substitutes can play a major role", tried his justifying words. "I appreciate your try but here I beg to differ a bit", countered Tania's words, "I mean Samsung and Nokia were already in the product market. But that didn't deter new entrants like Redmi and One Plus from capturing a significant market share. They were not substitutes." The debate started heating up with counters from each other when Ma'am decided to end it. "Guys, I appreciate the debate but it's not a question of right or wrong. It's how we look at it. Anything in the market can be disrupted by either of the forces. And be it product or service, we need to keep an eye out for all these five forces. You never know which factor slips you out", ended Ma'am's words as the environment cooled down a bit. "Ma'am, sorry for the heated-up argument. Actually, in classes like Finance or Statistics, you can't debate on anything. Its either right or wrong. But in your class, we can put forward our perspective out quite easily", commented Samrat. "Maybe that's why sometimes things turn from a simple discussion to a heated debate", added Tania. "I understand", smiled Ma'am herself.

Present Day

As Rhiyan got back to the present, his fingers were still waiting to hit the dial button when his mother called him out and his fingers hit it involuntarily. "Yes Mom, I will be there in an hour", he replied as Samrat picked the call, "Hey Rhiyan, long time. How are you?" "Yeah, I am good. You say, what's going on?", Rhiyan sounded a bit awkward. "Nothing much. I am still applying off campus with a hope to crack something soon", replied his words comfortably. "Glad to hear that", came a relaxed reply. "Had a chat with others recently?", asked Rhiyan. "Yeah, a bit with Sushant and Antara. To speak the truth, I am really happy for you guys. Business Analysts, Product Managers big posts, huh!" "Hmm…but you know what they say about big posts, right? With great post comes great responsibility", chuckled Rhiyan. "That reminds me of the Spider-Man dialogue", both of them laughed together.

"You know this job thing is great. I am trying to get one but somehow my heart wants to do something different", paused Samrat. "Different, as in?", intrigued Rhiyan. "Different as in a startup. Now I know you might rub it off with current examples of companies losing valuation, struggling to become profitable and even shutting down. But…", his words paused again. "But if IITians like us don't take risks, who else will", Rhiyan completed the statement. Samrat's eyes lit up with hope. "I am listening. Tell me what is going on in your *khurafati* mind", Rhiyan was curious by now. "Do you remember how you used to crib about not getting tasty parathas in and around the campus, the lack of variety and all", Samrat tried to pull out a string from the past. "Yeah, I do. And I am sure the situation hasn't improved much yet", replied Rhiyan. "That's exactly where I want to build my brand, *Parathon ka Samrat*", shot Samrat. "Oh! You have thought of a name as well. Quite pro-active, I must say", Rhiyan sounded a bit surprised. "See, we all know how much we all love Parathas, especially Paneer and Matar Parathas (Green peas parathas), right? So why not set it up into a full-fledged business?" "Woh woh, hold your horses' brother. Before you jump in there are a lot of factors to research upon starting with market size, competition, initial investment etc", shook up Rhiyan. "Well, you and the others have almost 3 months in hand before you join the corporate world. So why not help me out set it up?", proposed Samrat. Rhiyan paused to think. "And in return I give you 5 percent equity each", continued Samrat. "The company has not even been formed yet and you have started distributing equity", laughed off Rhiyan. "But okay, let me have a chat with others on this and I will get back to you", replied Rhiyan's corporate words. "Thank you for understanding", replied Samrat as the call ended.

Chapter 2 --- The Journey Begins

"Hey Antara, what's up? Received your joining date", asked Rhiyan as he called up the would-be product manager, a few days later. "Nope, still waiting. Meanwhile I was going through some products the firm had built till now", replied her busy words. "Somebody is gearing up quite aggressively for the joining, huh!", exclaimed Rhiyan. "Nothing like that", laughed off her words. The call was progressing quite well, when Sushant called up. Rhiyan tried to ignore it when a message popped up. "I know you are busy. But pick mine first", threatened the words of the one-liner. A feeling of anger tried to surge through Rhiyan when his finger accidently touched the merge icon and all three got merged in a conference. *Damn!* sighed Rhiyan. "Hmm, seems like we have an intruder here", smiled Antara. "Yup. I hope I didn't interrupt a cozy conversation", smirked Sushant. "If you consider a discussion on software products as cozy, then yes Sir, you did", laughed off Antara.

"May I know the reason for this intrusion?", Rhiyan still holding off the surge of anger. "Yes, the reason is something that you have forgot completely", continued Sushant's voice, "Parathon ka Samrat!" The surge came down in an instant. There was a moment of silence when Antara spoke up, "Yeah, he called me up too." "Sorry, completely forgot about that", replied Rhiyan's meek voice. "But what can we do to help him. This is not a college project where we can just conduct some internet analysis and tell him, hey this is the market share, these are your competitors and here is a Zomato App that can help you sell the parathas", argued Rhiyan's thoughts. "At least we can begin by supporting him", shot back Sushant. "I agree.

Let's meet him and hear him out. Who knows the value of that 5 percent equity might surpass out corporate income by a few millions?", smiled Antara. There was pin drop silence. "Come on guys, I am just joking. Let's do this for our friend, Samrat." With that the conversation ended and a trio trip got planned to the city which never sleeps, *Mumbai*. Because that's exactly where their friend was.

Date – 20th June 2023

"I am so glad you all came in here", Samrat was so happy that he hugged all the three together. "And so are we", smiled the trio back. Keeping the bags down, Antara walked towards the window and looked down, where her eyes fell on something that looked like a sparkling necklace with beads moving towards a common destination. "I know what it seems like but it nothing but the cars' headlights that's forming the glittering beads of a beautiful necklace", clarified Samrat. "I thought the house would be filled with people", commented Sushant. "It would have, had my parents not gone to our native place", replied Samrat. "So, when and where do we begin?", Rhiyan sounded a bit restless. "Oh ho, somebody is in a hurry", continued Samrat's smile, "But coming to your question, we begin tomorrow by visiting the best paratha restaurant along the western line of Mumbai." "And do what? Taste one paratha of each type?", asked Rhiyan's playful words. "Exactly", answered Samrat's shocking reply, "I am sure you guys are dying to explore the city. So why not start from the same point where everyone begins, *The Gateway of India*, but with a different agenda." With that, everyone settled in for the day at Samrat's cozy 2 BHK.

Chapter 3 --- Hurdles on the way

Although Sushant had spent a few years of his corporate life in Mumbai, the scene was a bit different for Rhiyan and Antara. The internship journey being a flight one, Rhiyan hardly explored the *life line connections (railway lines)* of the city. For Antara the city that never sleeps aka *the city of dreams* was quite new too. And that's the reason when the conversations moved from Mumbai's Central Line to Western Line, their minds got jumbled up. "Mumbai is one city right. Then why this bifurcation of Central and Western?", asked Antara's words with her mind still in a confused state, as they stood on the railway platform waiting for their ride. "Actually, the word should be trifurcation if you take Navi Mumbai aka the *New Mumbai* into account", laughed Samrat's even more confusing reply. "Let me explain", began Samrat. But before Samrat could even start, the blaring horn of the incoming train silenced his words. As the train stopped, Rhiyan attempted to board it but failed miserably as the crowd's hastiness made sure his feet remained on the platform. All his attempts went in vain. Sushant and Samrat stood by the side smiling at their friend. Irritated by the unfriendly reaction, Rhiyan shouted out, "What's there to smile? And why didn't you guys attempt the boarding?" "That's because this is a *Fast Train*, which stops only at a few stations and as a result remains jam packed. We need to wait for the *Slow Train* which has a stoppage at all stations and remains a little less crowded", explained Samrat's calm words. "And coming to your previous question regarding the trifurcation, I think we should leave that to your upcoming experiences", chuckled Samrat's words. Boarding the next slow train, the quartet moved towards their first location, the Gateway of India.

After an hour's ride, the quartet's feet landed at the Gateway. As Antara's vision expanded, a huge monument in the shape of a gate came across. "Magnificent. Isn't it?", exclaimed Samrat, as the four stood in front of it. "Indeed, it is!", exclaimed Antara back. *Erected to commemorate the landing of King George V and Queen Mary on their visit to India in 1911*, read the lines etched at the top of the gate. On moving a bit forward, Antara's eyes fell on a fleet of ships and small ferries that moved across the mammoth Arabian Sea. "Some of them take tourists for a ride to the Elephanta Caves, others busy with import and export business", replied Samrat as he could see question flickering across Antara's eyes. "Guys, let's not forget the reason we are here for. *Parathas*, remember?", Sushant's words tried to bring everyone back on track. "Yes, and I think we are on the right track", replied Samrat as he turned around and pointed towards a huge palace-like structure overlooking the Arabian Sea. "Well, just by the look of it, I can clearly say that its beyond our reach", said Antara. "Umm, are you sure? That's the Taj Mahal Palace hotel. Just a cup of coffee could cost us a fortune out there", Rhiyan had seen the building in magazines before. "No guys, not that. I am talking about that", Samrat's finger pointing towards a sign beside it that read as *Paratha Life*. "Okay, that!", Rhiyan heaved a sigh of relief.

As the quartet entered the restaurant, Sushant's fingers literally burnt as he picked up the menu card and saw the prices. The starting point was Rs 400. "Damn! It's too costly", exclaimed Sushant. "Exactly and that's exactly what we will address first. *Affordability*", said Samrat, "I know what you are thinking. An aloo paratha starts off from Rs 40 anywhere in India. Then what rubbish am I talking about. Isn't it?" "Yes, my friend, you read my mind", Rhiyan waiting for a reply. "I am talking about a world class standard quality serving across any outlet in India", smiled back the answer. "And how are we going to do that?", asked Antara. "Antara, if I knew all the answers, you guys wouldn't be here. We need to explore and find that answer out together", replied Samrat. Meanwhile Sushant was busy going through the menu, when Samrat snatched it and closed it, "Come on Sushant, I am not that rich you know." "I am bloody hungry. So, you better have a plan B for the lunch", Rhiyan was furious. "Woh ho, relax guys. It's time to enter platform (9 ¾), if you know what I mean", winked Samrat as he led them towards an unknown alley. There was nothing but shades of buildings that covered the path. Light of the Sun barely reached there. They kept on walking until they hit a dead end. "Wow, and here I thought you to be a good guide", Rhiyan was about take a U-turn when Samrat pulled his hand and pushed the wall, a part of which opened like a door. "Don't tell me we are about to enter the world of Harry Potter", Antara and the others were quite surprised. "Not exactly Harry Potter but maybe the world of Parathas", smiled Samrat.

Slowly and steadily the quartet progressed, completely unaware that they were about to discover a plethora of variety they had never thought about. "Woh, hey Samrat, brought some friends I see", spoke a voice from behind. As they turned around, a clumsy old man appeared. "Yes. They are here to help us", replied Samrat. "Help us in what? Making parathas", reacted a rough voice. An old woman appeared from the other side. The quartet was about to get crushed from both sides when a sweet voice saved them, "Come on guys, let's not bother our guests." And there she was, a young lady with an unbaked paratha spinning across her fingers. "You know what Samrat, sometimes you should try the front door as well", added her voice. "Next time for sure", replied Samrat, his fingers busy scratching his head. "Sorry guys. Didn't mean to scare you. For starters, this is the back door of one of the busiest mini meal outlets around here. And these are its owners", Samrat pointing towards the trio they had just encountered. "Hi, I am Emily and these are my grandparents, Mr. and Mrs. D'Cruz", spoke out the lady, extending her hand for a handshake. "And we are Samrat's friends, here on a mission to make him the

Samrat of Parathas", laughed off Sushant as he shook her hand. Samrat literally coughed off as Emily gazed towards him. "Interesting. I did not know he wanted to become a chef", reflected Emily's crooked eyebrows. "Not chef exactly but the owner of a business that involves parathas", tried Samrat's clarifying words. "Trying to put your MBA learnings at work, I see. Anyways, I suppose you guys are hungry. So, what would you like to have?", asked her courtesy. "Parathas", spoke up the quartet unanimously. Everybody laughed off.

As Rhiyan moved towards the front, his eyes fell on the name, *Feast On* which means eating quickly in hunger. It was a mini restaurant with a small seating area. "I know what you are wondering? But trust me, land is more costly than oil out here in Mumbai. That's the reason we mostly function as a quick service outlet rather than a full-fledged restaurant", came Emily's voice as she brought some delicious looking parathas for everyone. "And that should give you some leverage on the operational costs related to waiters and stuff", smiled Samrat. "Come on Mr. Analyst. This is the time to Feast not analyze operations", smiled Emily back. And with that everyone started tearing off the paratha pieces. And the moment they tore, surprises jumped out. Each paratha had a different stuffing. Be it aloo (mashed potato), paneer, veggies or cheese corn, all were out there. "Wow, I don't know about Samrat becoming the king, but you are definitely the queen of parathas", Antara spoke up. Others nodded in unison. Mr. and Mrs. D'Cruz were busy serving a few hungry visitors at the shop front. But even they overheard Antara and managed to steal a smile away. "Maybe but my reach is limited to this area only. And as far as I remember, Samrat promised to help me build a brand out of it two years ago", commented Emily. All eyes moved curiously towards Samrat. "There is nothing to look at me like that. I promised and I am back here to fulfill it", fumbled his words. "So that's the reason you took marketing as your major, huh", commented Sushant. "Yes, you are right. And now that you guys are here, you will help as well", replied Samrat, this time a bit more confident. "With this kind of a taste, surely we will", Rhiyan still drowned in the delicacies, "Emily, you should have a nickname called *Imli* aka tamarind. The way you have used the tamarind flavor in some of the mix parathas, it feels like sweet tooths like me are going to have a time of their life."

"So let me get this straight. You guys already have some lip-smacking recipes with you but not the reach. Right?", asked Antara. "We are also lacking trained staff who can replicate our specialties, I guess", added Emily. "Hmm, now that's a tough problem to solve", pondered upon Sushant. "It's okay guys. We will figure out something", hoped Samrat. "Let's hope so but as of now let's devour the delicacies in front of us. By the way, do you serve non veg parathas as well?", asked Rhiyan. "Only Egg Parathas. We have not explored the chicken part yet", replied Emily.

"I hope you guys had a good time", said Mrs. D'Cruz as the quartet prepared to leave. "Definitely", replied Antara. "And we are coming back pretty soon", added Rhiyan. With that everyone bid their goodbyes.

As the Sun moved towards the west skyline, the four moved towards the Marine Drive aka *The Queen's Necklace*. "So now that we know you have a prospective girlfriend, how do you suggest the split of your precious equity", teased Sushant mischievously. Samrat literally coughed off. "Here, have some water. Some interesting questions are coming your way, I guess", chuckled Rhiyan as he handed over a bottle to Samrat. "Guys, she is not my girlfriend. We are just good friends", replied the most cliched line the country has ever heard. "Yeah, we know", chuckled Antara back.

"Now that you guys have tasted our queen's paratha, don't you think it's time to have a look at the Queen's Necklace?", Samrat tried to create a diversion. "We know what you are trying to do. But since this place is new to us, we will let you go", said Antara. "Queen's Necklace, huh. I can see nothing but sea waves striking the rocks out in here. The breeze is good, though", Rhiyan was getting restless. "Give it a moment", Samrat. As the dusk set in, all the street lights glowed up and as Samrat guided the trio towards a central point on the Marine Drive, the scenery revealed a curve of sparkling lights from one end to the other, which indeed resembled the pearls of a necklace. "How long is it?", asked Antara. "3.6 km to be exact", replied Samrat, the trio's eyes still mesmerized.

Within the next few minutes, people started coming in. Most of them seemed like couple with a few singles in between. "I think we should give Emily a call. I am sure Samrat is feeling lonely out in this beautiful arena", chuckled Rhiyan. "Stop it", Samrat was about to surge with anger when a voice spoke out, "What to stop?" Everyone turned back in an instant only to find out that she was none other than Emily herself. "Nothing… nothing Emily", stammered Samrat. "Today the rush is a bit less, so thought of joining you guys. I hope you don't mind", smiled Emily. "We are more than happy. In fact, Samrat was just speaking about you and your parathas", chuckled Rhiyan. "All good things, I hope", laughed off everyone.

"You know Shah Rukh Khan, our favourite actor once stood exactly at this point and said, *I want to rule this city* and today he is the king of Bollywood", reflected Emily. Samrat gazed at her longing eyes across the sea and spoke out, "And today we stand here. We are going to rule as well, but with Parathas." Emily looked back at Samrat as if she could trust him with her life. Rhiyan coughed off to break the moment, "Not to break the moment, but how exactly are we going to do that?" "By creating a distribution chain", spoke up Sushant. Everybody sat down to hear. "See, with Emily by our side we already have a world class product. The only issue is the replication and distribution", continued his words, "For replication and standardization, we can find and train chefs at each outlet, but we will have to figure out the distribution part." "Yeah, even if we think the KFC way, we don't have the capital to set up so many quick service restaurants aka QSRs across the city. Real estate is damn costly in here and the scenario is almost similar in other states", added Emily. "That leaves us with the Cloud Kitchen concept where in you prepare at a city's central location and distribute via Zomato or Swiggy", invoked Antara's insight. "But then the reach will still be limited and the brand that we will be building will be that of Zomato's not ours", added Samrat. Everybody was engrossed in deep thoughts but nothing innovative came out. "Let's not burn out today. We still have some time. For now, let's call it a day", suggested Rhiyan. Everybody agreed and set out for their respective homes.

Chapter 4 --- Some Discoveries on the Way

The next day, the fantastic four set off to taste parathas of local shops along other areas of the western line. "Today, we are in the Malad Goregaon region. Let's see how the place treats us in terms of paratha delicacies", started off Samrat. "I am sure the city has more to offer rather than just parathas", said Rhiyan, his eyes gazing across the metro skyline unaware of the heavy traffic traversing across the busy roads. "Careful my friend", exclaimed Samrat pulling Rhiyan to avoid an accident, "This is not Durgapur, this is Mumbai. One wrong step and you land up at hospital." "Hmm, will be careful", Rhiyan.

Taking help from Google Maps, the four tried to track down some local shops that served paratha but the result brought up just two in their vicinity. They tried both and needless to say, were not very satisfied. "What was that? One, so spicy and the other no stuffing at all. No wonder Google showed us just two shops. With this the demand would never grow for parathas", Antara sounded quite disappointed. "I am really missing Emily now", sighed Rhiyan. Samrat gave a hard look at him. "I mean her parathas", clarified Rhiyan. Sushant and Antara literally laughed off.

As the Sun moved towards dusk, the four strolled across an alley to find a park where they could take some rest. Upon entering the main gate, Rhiyan stood still. His eyes gazed across its length and breadth as if he had seen the park before. "What happened? Mesmerized with a simple park?", smiled Samrat. "Not mesmerized, but flooded. Flooded with a whole lot of memories", Rhiyan stood still. "What memories? Have you been here before?", asked Sushant. The other three stared at him, when Rhiyan finally spoke up. "It was 2020, I guess. And this feels like a similar place where I played my last show before the Covid hit", continued Rhiyan's words, his eyes still flooding with memories, "It was a solo performance of 2 hours. It was arranged to promote products of a company that wanted attention of local people around. Today I am back, at a similar spot where it all ended with the last strum of my guitar." Rhiyan was badly missing the days of his live performances back in 2019-20. "It's okay brother. I am sure you can start off again", consoled Sushant. "Sorry guys, I think we deviated from our main topic", apologized Rhiyan. "Not at all. In fact, your nostalgia might have just given us a way to promote our parathas", smiled Samrat. "But before that we should find out a way to produce them, I guess", suggested Antara. "Oh yeah, having tried so many outlets, we have realized one thing for sure. Not everyone is perfect", hinted Sushant, "Some might have the best spot and yet the oiliest parathas, while others may have the best stuffing but not the real taste." "Fortunately, we have the taste", Samrat sounded excited. "But not the rest", added Antara with a pinch of salt.

The quartet spent another half an hour and started departing towards their home. Apart from Samrat, the other three got drowned in the well-lit sparkling city amidst the crowd's hustle and bustle. They kept on scanning each and every signboard their eyes could catch hold off. Food stalls and malls thrived in that area. "Hey guys, do you see what I am seeing?", poked Antara. The other three turned around and the board across the street read as *Paratha King*. "Damn! Somebody has already stolen the trademark of king!", exclaimed Antara. Rhiyan immediately took out his phone and started googling about it. "What does it say?", asked Sushant. "It says that someone named Pankaj Prakash started off this venture back in 2006. But it also says that his major focus remains on Dubai market rather than India." Samrat heaved a sigh of relief. "What if he has started experimenting with mini outlets like this in India. We have some tough competition coming in", hinted Antara. "In fact, we already have a lot in this over saturated market", sighed Sushant. The team morale was half down by now. "But inspite of that, entrepreneurs like Nidhi and Shikhar managed to generate an annual turnover of crores in a saturated market like Bangalore", spoke up Rhiyan, his fingers pointing to the store just beside the Paratha King. "Giants like Haldiram have been making samosas since ages and yet a venture set up in 2016 managed to sway some of its customers away", added his words. "How do you know all this?", asked Antara. "Do you remember our final MBA innovation project? This was one of the companies, I was researching on", replied Rhiyan. "And what innovation did they exactly do?", pestered Antara a bit more. Rhiyan looked at others with a smile. "I think we can taste that ourselves", with that he took them directly to the stores and ordered samosas. With each bite, the folks realized the efforts the founders have put in. Each samosa had a different filling and it was not just samosa. They served a lot of complimentary items as well like sweet lassi, lemon soda and halwa. "Hmm… now I am getting some idea on how to please customers", commented Samrat. "I am sure you did", added Sushant.

After a lip-smacking experience, the four departed towards their only abode in Mumbai, Samrat's home.

Chapter 5 --- Food and Music goes hand in hand!

"Hey guys, what's up", Emily called up early next morning. Samrat had put on the loud speaker. "We are good. You tell, did you discover a new recipe?", asked Antara. "Nope. But I thought of inviting you guys for the Food Festival to be held near the Colaba area over the next 2 days. We are setting up a stall as well", Emily was excited. "Wow! You know sometimes I feel as if Mumbai's life revolves only and only around food", exclaimed Sushant. "And music. There are musicians coming too. Rhiyan, if you know what I mean", winked Samrat. "Umm… I don't know. Let's see", replied Rhiyan hesitatingly. "Come on Rhiyan. I have a spare guitar here. Let us strike some chords out there", hinted Samrat. "Again, let's see", persisted his hesitance. "Meet you at the food festival, then. Bye", with that Emily rushed off as she had a lot of work to do in setting up the shop alongside Mr. and Mrs. D'Cruz.

Later in the evening, the four reached the Colaba area, where the food festival was. The entire vicinity was decorated with lights. Stalls and trees were glowing as if the Sun has decided to visit them again. Most of the stalls were designed in the shape of tents with some in the usual squared ones. At the entrance stood a detailed guide, directing visitors towards their favourite delicacies. "I hope you guys are not lost", screamed a voice from behind. As the quartet turned around, they found themselves amidst an area that was surrounded by pizzas. The name on the board read as Mozo Pizza. "Hello, my name is Firoz and if you are looking to have some lip-smacking pizzas, you are at the right place. We have the veg and non-veg sections completely separate. So, no issues there", Firoz's charm was attracting customers from everywhere across the vicinity. "We would love to, but as of now we are here to support our friend. So will have to move in there", apologized

Samrat on everyone's behalf although not everyone wanted to leave. Sushant and Rhiyan were ready to dive in. But Samrat managed to cut their way out. "And who would that be? Because talking of friends even I can become one of yours", persisted Firoz. "Umm… would love to stay back but Emily would be waiting out somewhere", persisted Samrat back. "Oh, Emily huh… I know her. She is the Paratha queen, right? Her stall is over there", Firoz helped by pointing towards the right. "By the way, what did you say your name was?", asked Firoz. "Samrat", replied a confident voice. "Oh, so you are the one who has promised to help her out with the distribution and expansion, huh!", exclaimed Firoz. "Oh yes, absolutely. So much so, that he even managed to steal her heart away in the process", commented Rhiyan. Samrat literally coughed off when Firoz gave him some water. Samrat turned to give Rhiyan a sharp look. "Just wait buddy, my turn will come too", shot back Samrat. "Yeah, we shall see", laughed off everyone.

As the four moved on, they reached the other end where stood a tent shaped stall with *Feast On* written on a board atop it. "Hey guys, where have you been? Its already time", Emily seemed a bit nervous. "Time for what?", asked Antara. "That!", pointed her finger towards a stage. "The show is about to begin!", announced the host draped beautifully in purple colored saree. "Are you ready to bleed blue? Because Darshan Raval is here!"

All eyes moved towards the stage, especially Rhiyan's. The singer he had always adored was finally in front of his eyes. Darshan looked quite dashing in his white jacket and trousers. With a mic in hand, he started off with everyone's favourite, Chogada Tara song. The whole area just got filled with life as everyone swayed along with the beats. "I didn't know they call such famous singers at food festivals", Samrat was a bit surprised. "They don't. But this year they wanted to attract a larger crowd base. So, the organizers arranged for a half an hour surprise this year", clarified Emily. And she was right, people started live streaming the event on Instagram and Facebook and the crowd increased gradually. As the show ended and Darshan left, people started flocking in for food at the food stalls. As for *Feast On*, all hands-on deck were full. Even the four were busy helping out Mr. and Mrs. D'Cruz along with Emily. "I wish we could sell like this on all 365 days", wished Emily. By the end of the day, all the stalls were out of stock. Motivation and happiness flooded the entire region in there.

The next day was no different except that there was no celebrity performance that day. The crowd was still there but was scattering out pretty fast. There were some who had anticipated this and had stocked their stalls accordingly. But most didn't. They were still in trance of the previous day. *Feast On* was no different. "Damn! Seems like we are really overstocked for today", Samrat sounded worried. "No live music, no crowd", added Emily. As Sushant's eyes moved across the arena, he could see a few loudspeakers blaring at their highest decibel, yet failing to attract the crowd. "I thought food and music go hand in hand", spoke up Antara. "They do. But more with Live Music, I guess", added Sushant as his eyes moved towards Rhiyan. Their eyes locked with each other. "Why are you looking at me like that?", Rhiyan was a bit lost. And then Sushant looked at the Guitar that they had brought along, guiding Rhiyan's view towards it. "No. No way. You are thinking it all wrong, Sushant", hesitated Rhiyan. "Yes. And I am thinking it just the right way", Sushant literally held his hand so that he can't run away. "Rhiyan, look at these people. If the stock doesn't sell, they will be in deep loss", tried Sushant's convincing strategy. "But I am not Darshan Raval, come on", defended Rhiyan as the picture started to clear out for the others. "Maybe not. But a try doesn't harm. Does it?", persisted Sushant, their eyes still locked with each other. There was a moment of silence when Rhiyan finally spoke up, "Fine, but just one try. That's it." Smiles took over the worrisome faces.

Rhiyan picked up the guitar and tuned it properly. Meanwhile Sushant and Samrat rushed to have a talk with the organizers. "This is a crazy idea, Antara. People won't even listen to me", blabbered Rhiyan's skeptical words. "Rhiyan, as long as you don't believe in it, people would indeed remain unaffected. But if you believe in it, people will listen", advised Antara. By then, the loudspeakers had gone silent. Emily took over the stage as a host. "Hello everyone", started off her sweet voice, "Today we don't have any celebrity to entertain you but we know for sure that you guys are hungry. Yet your hearts are waiting for that one trigger that would sway a smile across your face. So why don't you give us a chance? A chance to make you sway with a few songs, live. Presenting before you a musician from the unknown, Rhiyan!" *Aankhein khuli ho ya ho band, Deedar unka hota hai…* started off Rhiyan with a strum on the guitar. *Kaise kahun main o yaara yeh, Pyaar kaise hota hai… Tu ru ru, rurururu rurururu…* As the song progressed, people started joining in for the humming part. Although he didn't know a single person, he tried to involve them as if they were his own friends. Although for a moment, but still a light string of attraction started forming, people stayed put and listened to him. And then he did something strange. Rhiyan kept on playing but moved across the different stalls out there making sure the people moved along with him. Some people stayed, some moved on to the next. Rhiyan played near *Feast On* and took up a few song requests from the crowd as well. Gradually people started ordering and food stocks moved like crazy across the region. Many a times Sushant even switched to recorded songs to give Rhiyan a break. Sushant and others took it a step even further and invited people to sing along with

Rhiyan on the stage. The crowd loved the gesture and started interacting more and more. By the end of the night, almost all stalls were stocked out.

"Thank you Rhiyan, for performing today. Couldn't have done it without you", thanked Emily. "On the contrary, I couldn't have done this without you guys. So, all thanks to you", countered Rhiyan.

The clock struck 1 am. "Today was just crazy", laughed off the fantastic four as they sat on the Marine Drive taking rest for the day. "Yeah, it was indeed a long day", reflected Antara. Emily was quiet, drowned in her own thoughts. "What happened? I thought you were happy", said Samrat. "I am. It's just that from tomorrow it will be normal again. No more crazy sales", replied her meek voice. "Don't worry. We will find a way soon", supported Samrat as he took her hand in his. "Oh yes, definitely we will", smiled the others.

Chapter 6 --- An Idea!

The next morning, the fantastic four woke up pretty late, owing to the hard work done last night. Samrat made coffee for everyone. "Thanks brother, what would we have done without you", said Sushant as his fingers turned the pages of the newspaper. "For your information, that paper is two weeks old. We have stopped the subscription now, thanks to the digital media at the palm of our hands", commented Samrat. "I see. By the way, did you see this? The sale of electric vehicles is shooting through the roof in India", Sushant sounded excited. "Only till the Govt. subsidies continue. Once it falls, so shall the sales", Samrat sounded a bit pessimistic. "Maybe but new launches are happening across segments. For example, this, a Tata Ace EV launched in the mini truck segment. And here I thought only scooters, bikes and cars dominated the EV market", reflected Sushant.

"Hey guys, I had enquired about some re-sale cloud kitchen equipment for our paratha king. Would you like to visit the shop?", asked Antara. "You already began?", Rhiyan was a bit surprised. "Yup. At least someone had to take some initiative. Emily and I thought of taking a step forward", replied Antara. "So, are we going with the cloud kitchen concept, so to say?", asked Samrat. "Not exactly. But starting off at one location won't hurt", Antara persisted. "Okay, lets pay the shop a visit at least", suggested Sushant.

As the four reached the shop, they were joined by Emily. The shopkeeper showed them the entire set that they would require for starting a paratha business but what blew their mind was the cost. "Even if we shell out all our savings, we won't be able to afford it", sighed Samrat. The cost was in lakhs. "Yeah, I agree but if you see carefully, we don't need so many things. We just need a few crucial items like the dough kneading machine, the multi burner gas stove and a few small stuff", suggested Emily. "And the best part, you guys don't need to buy these upfront. You can lease and pay on a monthly basis", added the shopkeeper. "That's great", Rhiyan felt excited at the proposition. "But where will you set it up? I mean do you guys have a place where I can deliver these?", asked the shopkeeper. There was pin drop silence for a moment. "Damn! I didn't think about that", spoke out Antara. "Neither did I", continued Emily, "I mean for *Feast On* we already have stuff in place which can act as a cloud kitchen in itself. But what about the second location? We don't have one", added Emily. "Well in that case, you are screwed. Without a place, you cannot open a cloud kitchen and going by your condition, I don't think you guys can afford the rent of such a place", the shopkeeper's words sounded very demotivating. With that, everyone started retreating back to pavilion as they realized the kind of hurdle they have in their way. "Had we joined our firms by now, we could have helped but our joining is still a month away", sighed Sushant, Rhiyan and Antara. "It's okay guys. Even *Feast On* hadn't had consistent profits, otherwise we could have used that", Emily felt the pang too. They were walking towards the metro station when Samrat stumbled against a tyre that laid ahead. "Sorry guys, my mini truck had a puncture. Was just replacing the tyre", spoke out a middle-aged man who seemed to carry bags of vegetables in his mini truck. Samrat looked at the truck. And his worrisome face suddenly turned into a smiling one. "Guys, I think we have stumbled upon an idea", spoke up his words. "What do you mean?", asked Emily. "That is exactly what I mean", Samrat's hands pointed towards the truck.

"Sushant, do you remember the Tata Ace EV you were talking about today morning? What if we purchase it on a loan and convert it into a food truck? A paratha selling food truck. Renting of a fixed place, logistic issues, fuel cost, reaching out to a new customer base every other month and building a brand. All problems will get solved in an instant. What do say guys?", Samrat's mind was erupting with ideas. "Yeah, but still, we will need some capital to make the down payment and who will pay the EMI?", asked Emily. Rhiyan started googling to find the current price of the vehicle and the EMI amount for a 5-year loan. "I think we can take care of that. Considering the required modifications and equipment the EMI would be Rs 30,000 per months. Sushant, Antara and I would be joining the corporate world next month and can easily contribute 10k each per month", suggested Rhiyan. "Yeah, we can do that", added both Sushant and Antara, with double the excitement. "Thank you, guys, thank you so much", Emily was almost in tears. "Anything for our Paratha King and Queen", smiled everyone. "But we are forgetting a few more things like licenses, billing software and a pair of extra helping hand. Samrat cannot do everything all alone, right?", pondered Antara. "I agree. Starting from the food license aka FSSAI, Fire Department NOC, GST, Local Municipal Corp NOC to even Insurance and RTO NOC, we will be in for a hell lot of paperwork", Sushant listed out some of the basic licenses required. "Yeah, regarding that, I have already done my homework with the help of Mr. and Mrs. D'Cruz. So, no worries about that part. That will be sorted", replied Samrat's confidence. "The only issue lies in finding those two people who can be trained not only to become expert chefs but also good drivers", added his worrisome words. "I think I can help in that part", spoke up Emily, "Back at *Feast*, we do have Sameer, who knows our recipes like the back of his hand. We just need to find one more." "In that case I think it's time to split. Samrat and I are going to take care of the vehicle purchase, modifications and licenses, Emily, you will be helping us with the equipment setting and grocery planning, and you two, Antara and Rhiyan will find our second master chef. Take Sameer's help if required", Sushant managed to chalk out a rough plan for the upcoming venture aka the upcoming adventure. "Also, one more thing. Let's not forget, we have just one month to set and roll Feast on Wheels", added Sushant. "What? What did you say? Repeat again", asked Samrat's curiosity. "Are you not listening? I am talking about our limited time, my friend", Sushant sounded anxious. "No, not that. The last three words… *Feast on Wheels*. Yes, that's it. That can be our Brand's name", Samrat sounded excited. "But we thought you wanted to keep it as *Parathon ka Samrat*", Rhiyan seemed a bit confused. "Yeah, I did. But I want to include Emily as well", replied Samrat as his eyes moved towards Emily. "Moreover, strategically speaking Feast On already has a sizable customer base. We can tap into it the moment *Feast on Wheels* sets rolling", added Sushant. "By the way, what about the initial capital? We will require money for all this, you know", reflected Antara. "Yeah, I was coming to that. So, I have around 50k with me, saved it for a trip after college", spoke up Sushant. "Same here", spoke up Rhiyan and Antara in unison. "Me too, but for a different purpose", Emily and Samrat joined hands. "Great, in that case we have 2.5 lakhs in hand", concluded Sushant and with that the squad of 5 set out on their respective paths.

Chapter 7 --- Search for the Master Chef begins

Antara had been a foodie since childhood. So, whenever the *taste* factor comes into picture, she hates one word specifically, *compromise*. "So where do you want to begin from?", asked Rhiyan, as the duo were joined by Sameer in the hunt next day. "Given the fact we are in a city like Mumbai, finding a chef won't be difficult. What will be difficult is convincing that person to join us and stay for a long period. You know how fast switching happens in the corporate right?", smiled Sameer. "True. If I may ask, what motivated you to stay with Feast On for the past 3 years. I am sure you received better offer", asked Rhiyan's curiosity. "Sure, I did but there were two factors, one was the location and the second was the freedom to handle things on my own. I hate to carry an annoying boss at the back of my work", replied Sameer's to the point answer. "What about the location? Didn't understand that", Antara was no less curious. "Would have been an easy answer had I put it all the scenic beauty I get to see across the sea every day, but the truth is my mother kind of loves that place. So yeah, really couldn't just move", clarified Sameer. "Interesting, to speak the truth, I love both the reasons", smiled Antara. "But you didn't answer my first question. Where are we exactly heading?", interrupted Rhiyan, seeing the increase in the duo's coziness. "Just like in Delhi, you have Paranthe Wali Galli, here in Mumbai we have something called Khau Galli in here. And that's exactly where the seasoned players are", a smile of confidence sketched across Sameer's lips, as the trio progressed towards their destination.

After an hour's ride, the trio reached the Churchgate Khau Galli. The dusk had set in and thus the entire place was lit up with lights. But not just any lights, each and every shop and even the trees were decorated with mini bulb lights that is mostly used in Diwali, the festival of lights. "Damn! It feels as if we have entered the Diwali Galli", a feel of cheerfulness spread across the trio's face. As they progressed, they were welcomed by mini shops set up on both sides of the road, each trying to sell something unique to its customers. Freshly grated cheese covered almost anything that could be found, be it pizza or a paratha or even kebab. Crowd of youngsters thrived like anything. And youngsters of similar age were busy spinning roomali rotis and parathas on their fingers. Few experienced hands were busy cooking the delicacies that goes along with them. The road seemed to be endless. In fact, the twists and turns along with it, turned the place into a maze.

"Hey boy, do you know where the Foodie Hoodie is?", asked Sameer as he managed to snatch the hands of running kid. "A right from the left", shot his reply back as he dashed into the crowd. "What?", by the time Rhiyan managed to utter the word, the kid had already vanished. "What did he mean by a right from the left? Is that a direction or a puzzle?", Antara was quite perplexed by now. "Well, for outsiders it's definitely a puzzle. But if you don't want to get lost, follow me", winked Sameer. The duo had no option but to follow. They moved forward to find the first left turn, proceeded ahead to find the next right and finally their feet landed in front of a shop that read as *Foodie Hoodie*. "Searching for someone or looking for something to quench your thirst", spoke up a voice behind the counter. "What if we say both?", shot Sameer. "In that case, you are at the wrong place my friend, because I sell none", shot back the voice, the torso of which stood up to reveal a young lady somewhere in her 20s. "Hello sunshine, what's up?", Sameer looked a bit cheerful. "Nothing's up. Everything is down. Be it sales or be it life", replied her confident words. "What brings you here, Sameer and who are they? Friends or foes?", Mrs. Sunshine seemed a bit skeptical. "Friends of course. Who would bring enemies for a dinner?", laughed off Sameer. "Guys, this is Jaanvi, our master chef and they are

Rhiyan, Antara, friends of Emily", explained Sameer. "Emily? How is she? Haven't met her in quite a long time", pieces of nostalgia hit Jaanvi as her thoughts dived in the past. "She is good. Misses you a lot. But so do you. Isn't it?", asked Sameer's attempt to invoke her nostalgia a bit deeper. "Really? What makes you feel that?", Jaanvi was taken aback. "Your hoodie of course. This is the same one she gifted you when you decided to leave, remember?", smiled Sameer. "Not at all. This is a different hoodie", retaliated her words back. "Yeah of course, a different one and yet having the same friendship band attached to the hood. Come on Jaanvi, even you know how bad a liar you are", replied Sameer, pointing to the pink band attached like a ring to the hood. "Come inside, you all", Jaanvi guided the trio towards the backdoor that led to a room. "Damn! What is this place?", Antara and Rhiyan stood mesmerized as their eyes spread across to find a bunch of hoodies lined neatly across its borders. "It's exactly what the shop name says, *Foodie Hoodie*. It's a shop with two different products, selling across two bifurcated hubs within the same shop", elaborated Jaanvi.

As the trio took the seats, Jaanvi brought a few parathas along with a cream like paste. "This is a peanut garlic chutney. Hope you will like it", offered Jaanvi. "Thank you", and without wasting anymore word, Rhiyan and Antara jumped in to Feast On, all thanks to the hunger that had managed to linger upon for the past few hours. The parathas were neatly cut, proudly boasting of cheese corn mixed with spices along its sides. The duo took their bite and the word that came out in unison was *Wow… Just Wow!*

"Where were you till now? We were searching just for you", Antara just couldn't hold herself together anymore. "I guess, just here in Khau Galli", smiled Jaanvi's reply. "In that case, it's time to move on", added Rhiyan, still busy devouring the delicacies lying in front of him. "I wish I could but seeing this I hope you can understand why I can't", Jaanvi's hand moved across the shop. "Is this yours or do you work in here?", asked Antara. "I think inherited would be the correct word. My scene is quite similar to that of Emily, the only difference being that she still has her grandparents with her and I do not", Jaanvi's tearful eyes moved across a family picture that stood hanging on the wall. "We are really sorry to hear that", sprinkles of sadness spread across everyone. "In that case, why don't you join us? We are starting something called Feast on Wheels, a food truck concept to sell parathas across regions", suggested Sameer. "Wow, new concepts huh! You guys are going just right", exclaimed her excitement which soon got drowned in thoughts. "You know Sameer, how much my parents loved this shop. And to speak the truth, even I want to continue the legacy", tried her words to reason things out. "Hmm… we understand", Antara sounded a bit disappointed. "Gave up so easily? How will you guys run a business. Never heard the word persistence or what?", teased Jaanvi's words. "What do you mean?", retaliated Rhiyan. "What I mean is that I may not be available but someone else maybe", the words came as a ray of hope from Jaanvi. "Who?", even Sameer was curious. Jaanvi took a pause, smiled and finally spoke out, "My brother, Aarav." Sameer's eyes sparkled with hope. "Exactly, how did I forget him. Where is he?", blurted out his question. "Somewhere you can get lost quite easily", winked Jaanvi's words. "Damned", Sameer shook down his head, he knew that tone.

The next day, the trios' feet landed at one of the busiest railway stations of Mumbai. "Welcome to Dadar, guys. It's time to get lost", spoke up Sameer as they stood on the main bridge, crowds of people running like their lives are at stake. One line here, one line there and Antara literally got lost. Rhiyan pulled her back. "Woh… let us find Aarav and get out of this place fast", screamed her words, as the trio moved to some safety. "Where is he exactly? I am sure he doesn't work here?", gasped Rhiyan. "We don't know exactly where he works or stays. He moved in somewhere in here after a nasty fight with his grandfather last year", even Sameer's words were not helping. "What about calls? Doesn't he call his sister?", hinted Antara at the obvious possibility. "I wish. But he has literally not called anyone in the past one year. That's the kind of grudge he holds, I guess", sighed Sameer. "So how on earth would we even find him?", Antara sounded frustrated. "Same way we found his sister. Khau Galli", replied Sameer, but with some confidence lesser than the previous venture. "There is a Khau Galli here too?", she was surprised. "Well, there are Khau Galli spread across multiple regions in Mumbai with Ghatkopar, Mahim, Carter Road, Dadar, Churchgate being some of the famous ones. You can't have just one Khau Galli for a population of 2 crore in a city like Mumbai, can you?", clarified Sameer. "Hmm, got it", continued Antara, "So, do we have any guide out in here who could give us directions like *a right from the left*", chuckled Antara. "Glad to see you smile. But to break your heart, we don't have any guide in here, except…", paused Sameer as his eyes fell on something familiar. "Except what?", persisted Rhiyan. "Except that… we have him just in front of ourselves", Sameer dashed like a cheetah without even uttering a word more. "Wait what?", Rhiyan and Antara followed the chase, although completely clueless. Climbing down the stairs at the end of the bridge, Sameer jumped to board a running train, but in vain. His suspect had already slipped away by then. Meanwhile Rhiyan and Antara struggled through an insanely incoming crowd, somehow managing to reach Sameer. "What was that?", Rhiyan was panting quite heavily. "Are we here to find a chef or a thief", the scene was no different for Antara. Sameer turned back and answered, "Both."

The trio moved out of the crowd and took shelter in a nearby dhaba, a roadside restaurant across the street. "You know we are really getting confused here. Can you please give us some background or context?", asked Rhiyan, as they sat down for lunch. "What would you like to order?", interrupted the waiter. The trio had got so engrossed in thinking about Aarav that they had forgotten about food. "Yeah, completely forgot about that", Rhiyan literally snatched the menu card that seemed like a 4-pager document. "I think Kulcha and Matar Paneer should do the trick. What do you say guys?", asked Rhiyan. "Add masala chaas to that", added Antara. Rhiyan was about to close the menu card when his eye fell on something unusual. "Green Apple Cooler, huh? You serve that too?", Rhiyan was a bit surprised. Taking a break from Aarav's thoughts, his eyes ran across the place. The name's a dhaba but with one look he realized its more than that. Beautifully decorated with wooden architecture, it was actually a mini restaurant that was built on the concept of a dhaba, to sprinkle a feel of Punjab and Delhi among the diners. "Yes, we do serve it, Sir", the waiter's light and husky voice broke the trance Rhiyan was in. "Well, in that case, cancel the chaas. We'll all have the green apple cooler", smiled his closing order. Penning down everything, the waiter moved on to the next table.

"So, coming back to Aarav, what is the story?", asked Antara. "It all started with *Foodie Hoodie* a year back. The Foodie part was always there, all thanks to Jaanvi and Aarav's grandfather, Mr. Singh", began Sameer, "Hailing from a city called Jalandhar in Punjab, Mr. Singh settled in here to create one of the demanding paratha stores of Mumbai. To a certain extent he was even successful, thanks to his passion towards innovation." "Innovation, huh? What kind of innovations can you do with parathas? Experiment with the stuffing part?", Antara was curious. "Yes, and many more. Remember, at that time *Hoodie* had not come into picture yet. So, it was not just parathas, he was experimenting with dishes like you just ordered Rhiyan, your Green Apple Cooler", elaborated Sameer, his palm pointing towards Rhiyan. "In fact, he loved tweaking with ingredients here and there to find a unique taste in literally everything he served the customers. But no chemicals. That was his core. He used everything natural. Yes, it did take effort, maybe even a higher cost. But the customers loved it, never hesitated to pay off a bit higher", paused Sameer, his thoughts had gone beyond the past. "That reminds me of someone", interrupted Antara. "Emily", spoke out Rhiyan. "Some traits of a teacher passed on to a student", Sameer continued as the two looked confused, "Come on guys. I am sure you can connect the dots."

"Sir, here is your order", interrupted the waiter, his hands filled with Kulcha and Matar Paneer. Another one brought the Green Apple Coolers as he placed the food on the table. "Thanks. We will serve ourselves", said Rhiyan, still busy connecting the dots. "Okay. So, Aarav, Emily and Jaanvi were the students of the same teacher, Mr. Singh", Antara connected the dots. "And that's the reason Emily too has the knack of experimenting. Remember the tamarind flavored paratha, we tasted at Feast On?", reflected Rhiyan, connecting a few more. "Yes. And they learnt it well. Emily even trained me on some special recipes. But things started falling out when *Hoodie* came into picture", continued Sameer, as the trios' hands moved simultaneously with the food at hand. "Why, what happened with that?", Rhiyan's eyebrows crooked a bit. "Didn't you notice something unique back at the Foodie Hoodie shop?", smiled Sameer, trying to give a hint. "I don't remember, must have missed it", nodded Rhiyan. "There was one section which read as Customized", spoke up Antara. "Thank God. Somebody paid attention", Sameer and Antara cheered with the green apple cooler. "Hmm... by the way this tastes delicious. Thanks for ordering it Rhiyan", thanked Sameer's words, as he continued, "Coming back. Who do you think wanted to start the hoodie business?" "Aarav of course. That might have been the reason of quarrel and his exile to Dadar", attempted Rhiyan. "In fact, just the opposite. It was Jaanvi who wanted to start… *Hoodie*", countered Sameer, "But there were two problems. On one side Jaanvi's maximum time got devoted in the hoodie customizations, the market of which was picking up rapidly at that time. And on the other side, the increase in *Foodie's* customer base", explained Sameer's words. "Now the only solution was either hiring more people or franchising the brand out. In fact, they did both. But the lack of passionate cooks and standardization across the other three outlets literally killed it even before it could become a brand. Entrance of competitors aided the downfall a bit further. Quarrels kept on happening between Aarav and his grandfather owing to how poor Aarav was in terms of management skills. And one day, he left never to return back", elaborated Sameer. "Hmm… expanding a food business is tough indeed", reflected upon the other two. "But you said that he stole something as well. What was it?", asked Antara's curious words. "Blames. That's all he stole", sighed Sameer. The two looked a bit confused. "The idea of *Hoodie* was of Jaanvi's, not Aarav. Had Jaanvi helped, the fall wouldn't have been so bad. But she chose her passion and moved on with it. Aarav took all the blames for the fall on himself. Later Jaanvi realized it too, but by then it was too late. Mr. Singh passed away a few months later and Aarav never returned back", concluded Sameer's words. For a moment there was pure silence. Nobody knew what to say, when Rhiyan spoke up, "I understand. Must have been tough for the entire Singh family. But let us not lose our focus. Where can we find him, remains the question?" Sameer reached out to his back pocket and brought out a piece of paper. As he opened, it revealed something that looked like a map. "Are we going on a treasure hunt?", asked Rhiyan. "Read the lines below it", hinted Sameer. The lines read as *Mega Fair, Shivaji Park, Dadar at 6 pm on date…* "Oh dear, the date is of today!", exclaimed Antara, as she understood Sameer's hint. "Yes, Antara. You guessed it just right", smiled Sameer.

Chapter 8 --- Time to Gamble

As the dusk set in, the trio moved towards their only hunt, Aarav. But this time in a different arena, Shivaji Park, Dadar, an area that had the capacity to host millions and is also known as the cradle of Indian cricket, because that's the ground that has produced several international level players for India, including our beloved Sachin Tendulkar. But on few occasions like Ganesh Chaturthi and Durga Puja, Shivaji Park becomes the hub of celebrations. People flock in like anything just to enjoy the grandeur of the pandals and decorations. A similar kind of feeling surged through the trios' hearts as their path led them to a world filled with lights and crowd. The first thing their eyes fell was on an illuminated statue of Shree Chatrapati Shivaji Maharaj, one of the greatest rulers of India, whom everyone in Maharashtra worships like a God. In the statue he rode on a horse with his hands pointing towards a certain direction. "I think I have seen this somewhere", muffled Rhiyan. "Yes of course", Sameer unfolded the paper and there it was. The statue's image pointing towards the entrance of the fair. "Wow. That's interesting. I have never seen someone utilize a statue like that", spoke up Antara. "Let's hope we find him here. Aarav had not missed this fair even once since childhood. This is our only chance", pondered Sameer. "But where are we supposed to even begin? I mean, this place is huge and filled with people", Antara looked a bit puzzled. "He is a chef. He will be exactly where the food is", suggested Sameer. "And that's literally everywhere", Rhiyan's hand moved from the left straight to the right.

The trios' feet moved on. On one side circled the carnival rides with people screaming their hearts out in excitement and on the other circled round up rides, where people screamed even more. Rhiyan and Antara were quite baffled by the scenic beauty of the lights but Sameer stayed focused on a special aroma that had caught the wind moments ago. "Come on guys. I think we have hit a trail", as they moved behind Sameer, a new world opened up. As the trios' eyes moved, the words read as, *"Welcome to the world of Foodie Hoodie."* "Damn! Do you guys see what I see?", Antara's mouth was wide open. "I bet Jaanvi doesn't even have a clue about this", even Sameer's feet turned cold. The trio moved on. On one side apparels' stalls and counters thrived and on the other, lined up the food stalls. Unknowingly Rhiyan's feet hit a placard that read as – *Win a hoodie, if you are a foodie.* People were flocking to the food counter like anything. "Hey brother, what is going on here?", Sameer caught hold of a passerby who looked a bit disappointed. "It's called the Foodie Hoodie game. Be it in the pictures or in the placards, they show you a variety of food that you need to finish off within 5 minutes and in return you win a hoodie and pay nothing. But if you can't, bang bang! You pay double the price. In short, a gamble with your appetite", explained the stranger's short answer, "And I just lost it", walked away his feet with hints of disappointment. "That's the problem with people like us. The only word that captures our mind is *Free* and we jump in like frogs in a well", sighed Antara. "Hey you, wanna try the Foodie Hoodie game?", a person dressed as a waiter called out Sameer. "Sure, but only if your boss serves me himself", answered Sameer casually. The waiter laughed it out. The trio were about to retreat when a voice spoke out, "Agreed. But if you lose, you pay triple the price." The trio turned around to find an old gentleman standing with a stick by his side. "Fair enough", said Sameer as his bold steps moved towards the counter. The old man served him a huge plate filled with delicacies that were difficult to finish off at one go. Sameer started eating, his eyes constantly fidgeting between the timer and the food on his plate. Sameer was eating but somehow it didn't feel normal. Rhiyan and Antara paid some real attention on seeing this. Usually, people start with starters.

But he started off with the sweet. Then he went for the main course. The clock was ticking. Beads of sweat started forming on his forehead. But he went on. He attacked the starters at the last and bang! He was done. The timer still had 10 seconds left in it. Rhiyan and Antara jumped with joy as if their happiness knew no bounds. "How did you do it? I mean you are a perfect food runner", asked Antara. "That's because the appetite suppressors were added in the starters, not the deserts. Isn't it Aarav?", Sameer caught hold of the old man's hand and pulled him towards himself. This time the beads of sweat started forming on the later's forehead. "What do you mean?", stammered the old man. "What I mean is this?", in an instant Sameer ripped off the fake beard to reveal the one person they have been looking for, their Master Chef, Aarav. "What do you mean by appetite suppressor?", Rhiyan and Antara looked baffled. "Will you tell that or should I elaborate?", Sameer's eyes still fixed on Aarav. "Guys, let's take a few steps aside and then we can talk", whispered Aarav, fearing on the public wrath. Adhering to his request, the trio moved inside a tent that laid beside the Foodie Hoodie's main counter.

"What the hell, Sameer? Your words could have busted me out to the public", said the young man who didn't seem a day beyond the age of 22. "Did you think, you could fool me with that old trick?", burst out Sameer. "Cool down brother. I agree, shouldn't have underestimated you. My bad", apologized Aarav. "But can someone explain what is this appetite suppressor?", Antara was still curious. "I am sure Sameer had given you some context on my food experiments. It's nothing but a chemical, mostly used in medicines that can reduce your hunger instantly. But mind you, I didn't use any chemical. I used natural and organic suppressants which will not harm the human body in anyway", tried Aarav's justifying words. "And still that would fall under the broad category of Cheating", Sameer had calmed down by now, "How long do you think you pull these tricks off, Aarav?" *As long as people could be fooled,* thought his answer but didn't blurt it out. "Do you have any idea what kind of an image of *Foodie Hoodie* you are putting out there? People will start referring it as a gamble hub instead of a food hub", explained Sameer, "I think it's time for you to return back." "Nope. Not at all. Not after what happened…" "What happened after your minuscule quarrel is Mr. Singh left for his heavenly abode leaving your sister completely alone. I am sure you know all this", burst out Sameer before Aarav could even finish. And this time Aarav didn't have a comeback. "See Aarav, you want to grow big and continue experimenting with food taste. We get that but this is not the right place", suggested Rhiyan. "So where is it then, *Foodie Hoodie*? I don't like staying at one place, keep on selling the same stuff till the day gets over. It feels like a 9 to 5 job", burst out Aarav's frustration. "Agreed. But what if we give you the option to explore, travel, experiment, sell and make money, all via single mode?", hinted Antara. "And what would that be?", Aarav seemed a bit curious. And with that, the trio looked at each other and smiled.

Chapter 9 --- The Deal

On the other end of the spectrum, struggled the trio of Sushant, Samrat and Emily, not with the licenses or equipment, but with the main chariot itself, the Tata Ace EV, that the bunch desired to turn into a food truck.

"Sir, as you can see, we have just graduated. Although placed, we are yet to join the firms. And in a situation like this, a down payment of 3 lakh rupees becomes tough", tried Sushant's justifying words, the panel still busy going through the first page of his offer letter. Two people constituted the esteemed panel. One, the owner of the showroom and the other, loan manager of a reputed bank. "First thing, you should consider yourself lucky that you got to visit our loan partner's manager in the showroom itself. Lucky day, I must say", smiled the owner Mr. Sunil. "And second, to even sanction the loan, we need a minimum of last three-month salary slip. I mean, what is the guarantee that you would even join the firm?", countered the manager, Mr. Devesh. "Sir, *Feast On* has a legacy of more than 30 years. We have been serving customers across the length and breadth of the southern Mumbai, with 90% customer retention and 25% year on year growth. I am sure we can repay your loan within just 5 years", tried Emily, not willing to give up just yet. "Woh ho… This is not the audition for Shark Tank India guys. We can't give a loan based on old metrics, we need collateral in place", retaliated Mr. Devesh, as he returned the offer letter to Sushant. The trio felt pretty much helpless. Their hearts didn't want to give up but the numbers spoke otherwise. Sushant sighed heavily and got up to leave. The other two followed. "Giving up so early huh?", shot Mr. Devesh's words. "Are you sure you did your MBAs from IIT Dhanuj?", continued his words, "Because as far as I know, Pranali Ma'am and Bansal Sir never taught us accept defeat that easily." The trio turned back with their eyes wide open. "Who are you?", asked Sushant, still unable to believe what he just heard. "An Alumni of the same college, batch 2010", smiled an answer back. "Come on Samrat, you said you are from Marketing, right? If numbers don't play out in a deal like this, what else would?", triggered Mr. Devesh's words. "A strategy", spoke out Samrat's words involuntarily, as if the words came out on their own. "Good. So, if I may ask, do you have a strategy to crack *this* deal?", persisted Mr. Devesh as if he was hinting something out. The trio sat down again; this time deeply engrossed in thoughts. But nothing came to their mind. "You don't just make profits when the market is going up, you can also make it when it goes down. Forward, Future, Options. International Finance 101. Remember something?", spoke the final hint. "Of course. Damn it! Why didn't I think about this?", sparkled Samrat with light, "If we don't have an existing collateral, what if we can offer a future one?" "What do you mean?", asked a perplexed Emily. Samrat looked at Emily and simultaneously at Mr. Devesh. "What if we offer your bank a share in our profits?", offered Samrat. "Now you are speaking the way I like it", smiled Mr. Devesh, "10% of the annual profit and maybe we can have a deal." Samrat thought for a bit. "What do you say guys?", his eyes moved towards Sushant and Emily. "Let's do it", replied both in unison. "Great. It's a deal then", Mr. Devesh was overjoyed. "But what about the down payment?", Sushant was still concerned. Mr. Devesh looked at Mr. Sunil and spoke up, "Maybe we can bring it down to the industry norms of 10% aka 1 lakh rupees, right?" Mr. Sunil nodded in agreement. Although the deal was sealed, the trio didn't seem much happy. "This is business guys. Sometimes to take a leap forward, you may need to take a few steps backward, remember?", Mr. Devesh's ability to quote Pranali Ma'am at the right time was just amazing. "But since you guys look so gloomy, let me add a cherry on the cake", this time Mr. Sunil spoke up. "We already have a modification process streamlined for the customers. So, cheer up, you will get your food truck completely ready and equipped by next week. By the way, I hope you have the food licenses cleared." The trio cheered up at the proposition, "Thank you so much and yes we do have all the required licenses in place." The trio shaked hands with the panelists, signed some documents and finally left.

"Did we make the right deal?", Emily was still thinking. "Yes, we did", affirmed Samrat's voice, as his eyes met hers.

Chapter 10 --- Time to set Feast on Wheels

A week later, everyone met near *Feast On*, where Emily along with Mr. and Mrs. D'Cruz were preparing to welcome their first food truck, Feast on Wheels. "Hey, where are Samrat and Sushant?", asked Emily as Rhiyan and Antara arrived. "They have gone to take the delivery of the food truck. Oh Sorry! I mean *Feast on Wheels*", chuckled Antara. "But seems like you guys are fully ready for the inauguration", said Rhiyan as his eyes moved across the place. The dining area as well the preparation area sparkled like anything. "We are ready too", spoke up a familiar voice. "Hey Aarav, can't believe you are back!", exclaimed Emily. "Hey, what about me?", Jaanvi tried to feel a bit offended. "You too, my friend", Emily sealed the long-lasting friendship with a tight hug. "So, Aarav, how did they manage to bring you back?", asked Emily. "Just a little persuasion was needed I guess", spoke up Sameer, as his shadow emerged from the door. "Yeah, quite the persuasion I must say", confirmed Aarav with a smile.

Honk! Honk! Came the sound from behind. Everyone turned and what stood in front of them blew their mind. One of the most beautifully designed food trucks stood in front of them, the side panels on both the sides of which read *as 'Feast on Wheels."* And to add to that, there stood a smiling cartoon that looked like, "Is that what I see it is?", asked Emily. "Yeah, that's our mascot, Bugs Bunny", replied Samrat. On the panel, Bugs Bunny stood with a paratha spinning across its hands. "But…", Emily seemed a bit concerned. "I know what you are thinking. But don't worry, we have acquired the license to use him as our mascot in return for a small monthly fee", affirmed Samrat's voice. "Really? I didn't know you had some contacts in Warner Bros?", even Rhiyan was surprised. "I didn't. He did", Samrat pointed towards Sameer. "Yeah, I knew a few people at their Mumbai office. Took some help to make sure

Bugs Bunny becomes our mascot at least for the next five years", smiled Sameer's words back. With that, everyone dashed to check out the interiors that looked like a loaded gun. Complete with multi burner ovens, a mini fridge, utensils, water supply and most importantly, a gas line protected by fire safety measures.

The team looked overjoyed with their first victory. "So, when are you planning to set it out on the Marine Drive?", asked Rhiyan, his eyes fixed on Samrat. But the answer came from a different direction. "You can't set it on the Marine Drive. Nowhere even near it. Didn't get a permission for that", sighed Mr. D'Cruz. "Yes, neither roadside stalls nor food trucks are allowed on the actual stretch", commented Emily. "Understood, but why are we even targeting the Marine Drive? Shouldn't we try out the place people actually go for their favourite fast food? Come on guys, am I the only one thinking about it?", Samrat looked excited. "Umm... maybe", Emily looked a bit clueless. "Church Gate Khau Galli, guys", blurted out Samrat unaware of the upcoming consequences. "What? But that's exactly where *Foodie Hoodie* is! *Feast on Wheels* will be in direct competition with us", Jaanvi looked concerned.

"Unless we have a second spot that can grab the visitors' eyeline?", spoke out Aarav's thoughts. "What do you mean?", people around him looked a bit confused. "Let me show you", with that Aarav took the wheels and drove it to Church Gate Khau Gali and parked it at a spot that looked like a blind spot at first glance. But when looked from the passerby's angle... *Bang!* It fell straight in their eyeline. And the best part, it was carved out in such a way that only the food truck could fit in, not any permanent stall, completely ruling out the possibility of anyone setting a brick-and-mortar shop in there. "This spot falls almost on a different lane all together. So, *Feast on Wheels* will attract a completely different set of fan base than that of

Foodie Hoodie. And moreover, with *Foodie Hoodie* nearby, menu and grocery co-ordination will become efficient", suggested Aarav. Things somehow started to make sense even though the execution was yet to be tested. "How do you know of this spot?", asked Jaanvi's curiosity. "Well, it was not just you who took the tour with grandfather, I did too", winked Aarav's reply. "In fact, people knew about this spot even back then, but the lack of an ability to set up a physical shop here drove away most of them", added his playful words.

"Now that we have a place, when do we start?", Emily sounded a bit impatient. "Tomorrow itself", replied Samrat with a confidence touching the skyline.

The next day was a tough one. Starting from Rhiyan, Antara, Sushant everyone had to pour in their heart and soul to get things ready. Be it groceries, utensils or decorations, all hands were at deck. And by evening, the lights glowed up, with Bugs Bunny spinning a Paratha on his fingers.

People returning from their visit to Gateway of India and Marine Drive flocked in. A young couple came in first and started scanning the menu that had just 5 items on it. "We would like to have the Chef's special, Khatta Meetha Paneer Paratha", came in the first order. And Aarav knew exactly what he meant. He set off the burners and the frying pan. He already had the dough and filling ready. Huge filling portion went in, oil spread out on the pan and flew in the raw paratha. Five minutes into the music and the couple had it on their plate. An attempt to tear off the first piece literally burnt the couples' fingers, given the amount of heat the paratha had just absorbed while cooking. "Give it a minute guys and then tear off", suggested Sameer as he took care of the other burner in an attempt to serve the second customer. Meanwhile people were busy taking out their phone and scanning the payment QR codes set on all four sides of the food truck. The couple finally managed to tear the paratha apart and set in for the devour. They literally closed their eyes as the tiny bits of *imli* aka tamarind melted in their mouth. "Wow!", exclaimed the first word from their mouth. "One more please", added the girl's voice. "Sure", smiled Aarav and set in for the next round. The clock ticked on and so did the flow of customers. Meanwhile Samrat with the help of Jaanvi had already taken care of the place's rent that housed the food cart. "Thank you, Jaanvi, without your trusted source it would have been difficult to secure the place", thanked Samrat and Emily's words. "Formality, huh?", laughed off Jaanvi, "Anything for you guys." Sameer and Aarav rolled on without a break. Samrat helped with the billing part. Rhiyan played on the guitar and the rest sang on chorus to some of the popular Bollywood songs, leading to more footfall at the place. By the end of the day, everyone had just one thing on their faces, *a huge smile of satisfaction.*

As the days passed by, the word of mouth started spreading along with social media posts leading to increase in daily footfall. But along with that came in the days nearer where the trio of Sushant, Rhiyan and Antara had to return back. "Seems like the time has finally come for us to join the corporate world", began Sushant as everyone stood at the airport awaiting the departure of the 12 o'clock Mumbai-Kolkata flight. "So, are you guys returning home or going somewhere else?", asked Aarav who seemed a bit confused. "Yes, home first and then to our respective base locations", affirmed Sushant's words. "Well in that case, do let us know about the possibilities of suitable expansion in those locations", chuckled Samrat. "Of course, my friend, would love to see our 5 percent equity grow as well", laughed off Rhiyan's words, as the trio walked towards the boarding gate. The flight took off after a few hours and the trio went back to the pavilion aka their home.

Chapter 11 --- House Hunting

Date – 20th August, 2023

Rhiyan having received a Pre-Placement offer, had got his location as Mumbai. Although he had Samrat and others for any support, he wanted to give it a shot on his own. Last time the trio had Samrat's place as a safe haven but this time not. Finding a place to stay in Mumbai is like find a pearl in sea full of oysters. And Rhiyan being no different faced similar challenges. Having stayed at other places in the past didn't seem to help him much when it came to the heart of Mumbai, the Western Line. Not having any brokers' contacts added to the difficulties.

But fortunately, as a ray of hope he managed to grab in an Airbnb from the depths of the Internet. Tring! Tring! Rang the bell and the door opened. In front of Rhiyan stood a middle-aged man who passed on a smile and asked, "Yes?" "Hi, this is Rhiyan. I had booked…" And even before he could finish, "Oh yes! Welcome Rhiyan… welcome to my humble abode", smiled the host, this time a bit wider.

As his steps took him forward, the hall seemed quite dark and as he turned around, he realized why. In front of him stood a 60-inch screen but not that of an LED but of a huge projector screen, on which rolled on a Netflix movie. On another side stood a wall covered with mirrors from end to end with two ring lights at the corners. "Wow, who are you? A prince?", blurted out Rhiyan. "Nope. Just a Product Manager who wants to live his life on his own terms", laughed of Mr. R Suresh, the host. Rhiyan had often wondered why do most south Indian names had these initials in front of them. Even Priyatham, his college roommate had a few. In fact, his full name was BNS Priyatham, where BNS stood as Bhaskara Naga Srinivasa. Rhiyan not being accustomed to the format, initially felt pretty odd. But then when Priyatham explained the significance, things started to make sense, Bhaskara being his actual surname and Naga, Srinivasa named after God's name.

"This is your room and required amenities. I hope you enjoy the next few days", said Mr. R Suresh as he guided Rhiyan on the basics. "Sure", Rhiyan settled in with a smile. As he looked out of the window, he could see a money plant twined neatly along the window grills, as the droplets of rain drizzled on its leaves. But the one thing that was drilling down his stomach was a really heavy Hunger. The journey had completely drained him off his energy. Although he had seen a Dominos while coming, he was in no mood for pizza. He needed a proper meal. He opened Zomato to check out the menu but closed it straight away on seeing the prices. Rhiyan's low bank balance didn't quite support him either. *Tring! Tring!* Rang his phone. "Hey brother, reached Malad?", asked a familiar voice. "Yes, I did. But given the heavy rain, food delivery charges have shot up, you know", replied Rhiyan. "I wish I could send the *Feast on Wheels* to you right away", sighed Samrat. "And I wish I could have been in Church Gate", laughed off Rhiyan. "By the way, why don't you try Rebel Foods?", suggested Samrat, "I know they are our competitors, but trust me they serve well." "Woh! So, our entrepreneur has started tracking competitors as well", Rhiyan looked quite happy, at least that what his smile expressed. "When you are in Food Business, I guess you should not only track but also learn from the best", smiled Samrat in return. "Anyways, I got to go. Sameer and Aarav are waiting for me. Let me know if need anything. And if you don't find a place, my home is always there. I hope you remember the address", winked Samrat. "Absolutely my friend", winked Rhiyan back.

Rebel Foods, was a company that came in just 2011 and took the cloud kitchen concept to a whole new level within a few years. But Rhiyan was particularly impressed with its bifurcation strategy, a concept wherein it sold different items under different brand names. It was like Tata, a huge umbrella giving shade to multiple sub brands which grew bigger in themselves. Rhiyan downloaded the Eat Sure App from the Google Play store and started scrolling through the menu. It was perfectly designed. Easy to scroll across, the sub brands horizontally and the menus vertically. But the one section that caught Rhiyan's eyes was the 1+1 section. It was exactly what he needed at the moment, quality along with affordability. Without a blink he ordered two chicken rice bowls along with a jeera soda.

After a nice warm bath and a heartful meal, Rhiyan dozed off straight to the land of dreams. Feelings of anxiety as to how his first day would be did manage to crawl down among his thoughts but more than that was the anxiety of whether he would get a decent place to stay or not. Being in an unknown place, although he had an address to the office, but for a place to stay nearby, he didn't have any. After a nice nap, Rhiyan freshened up and joined in Mr. R Suresh, his host for a light chat. "Feeling fresh?", asked his courtesy. "Oh yeah! It was one hell of a sleep", laughed off his words in return. "What are you watching?", asked Rhiyan as his eyes fell on the 60-inch projector screen rolling in some action sequence. "Inception, a concept that lets you live and explore dreams within dreams", smiled Suresh's words. "I see. Well, seems like I just had an experience similar to it", smiled Rhiyan back.

After a little more chitchat, Rhiyan went on to explore the nearby market. But with one step outside, he realized how heavy the traffic was. *Damn! There is hardly any place to set a foot in here, forget about exploring,* thought his thoughts. *But that's how the Mumbai life was! People super busy in their lives, in a constant race to achieve something or the other.* Yet Rhiyan braved the incoming traffic to search for some food outlets nearby. As he walked down the street, his eyes fell on a huge building that looked like a corporate office at first glance. But as uniformed students came out from the exit, he thought it to be a school. But on a deeper look at the boards, he realized it was not just a school, it had a college too which was offering hospitality management courses and others. A few minutes later, young boys and girls came out from the exit confirming the same. *Damn! I didn't know Mumbai is so crunched for space that it had to house a school and a college in the same building!* Rhiyan's eyes were wide open. *Thank God, they didn't house a coaching center here as well.* Spacious and open areas that housed his childhood days flooded across his memories. Exploring down the lane further, he did find a mini restaurant that could satisfy his hunger for the next few days.

Coming back at the room, his fingers started scrolling a few housing websites that could help him find contacts of PGs aka Paying Guest apartments. "Hello, umm… I have called regarding the PG listed here", began Rhiyan as he dialed the first number. The pictures on the website had shown him a decent double sharing room to begin with. "Yes, it is available. To visit, you will be requiring a visiting card that would cost around 2000 rupees. When would you like to come?", replied the voice on the other side. "What? 2000 rupees. I have not yet seen the flat and I have to pay money?", Rhiyan was literally confused. "Yeah, that's how the system works in here", confirmed the voice. "Okay, I will let you know soon", with that Rhiyan hung up. Scrolling down the list further, Rhiyan made a few more calls. The responses were quite similar. Rhiyan hung up again. And finally, Rhiyan called up the last one, which looked decent but had a triple sharing in a room. "Hi there. I am looking for a PG near Malad West and your location seems close by", began his words with not much expectations in return. "Sure. Come in and have a look. I am sending you the location on WhatsApp", replied a husky deep voice. "Really? Do I need to pay any visiting charges?", Rhiyan sounded apprehensive. At first instance the voice laughed off and then replied, "No, you don't. And try to hang up calls which asks for so. Come on in and I will explain."

Following the Google Map, Rhiyan reached the place that housed the PG. "Come on in. First let me show you the room and then I will solve the mystery behind the visiting charges for you", said the host. As he guided Rhiyan into a neat and clean room, a lot of amenities like air conditioner, washing machine and a fully furnished kitchen came into picture. Rhiyan met one of his roommates who seemed like a quiet guy, self-absorbed in his laptop. "Rs 12000 is the rent and electricity charges separate. And coming to the visiting charges, its nothing but a Scam that has recently spread across the area, all thanks to the increasing demand for PGs in and around Malad, Mumbai", continued Rhiyan's host, "And I am glad you didn't fall prey to it. But some are not that lucky, you know. Some do fall in prey, lose money until they finally reach a trusted source like me."

Rhiyan's heart was beating like hell. *Where have I come? A place of work or an abode of scamsters?* Thought his anxious thoughts. But he was happy that he finally found a trusted source. Two days later he shifted to the PG that was 2 km away from his training office according to the Google Map.

Chapter 12 --- The Corporate Ride Begins

Date – 25ᵗʰ August, 2023

The D-Day finally arrived. Earphones plugged in, suited in formals Rhiyan took an auto to reach his training office. The song Aashayein by KK had always served as an inspiration for him, be it starting a new day or playing his first song on guitar. The clock on his watch ticked 7:45 am. The street was filled with autos and cars, but fortunately not enough to cause a traffic jam. That was reserved for the 10 am slot, he guessed. After a 10 minutes ride, he finally reached. Taking out his smartphone, he paid the fare using Google Pay, thanks to the wide adoption of UPI payments across the country.

As he got down, in front of him stood a tall building with Qrian's emblem shining at the top. After a thorough scan of bags and a Govt. ID, Rhiyan finally stepped in. The first person he met at the reception brought a huge smile on his face. No, this was not any high official or any would be colleague. He was the chief security officer, the same person who had welcomed him just a year back for his internship. "Hi, my name is Rhiyan and I am here for first day", spoke out his voice in an attempt to introduce himself. "First huh? Are you sure? Because from where I look you have already spent a good two months here, somewhere last year maybe", came the words in reply, that left Rhiyan surprised. "You still remember me?", blurted out his excitement. "Of course, I never forget faces", winked the officer. "Come on, lets click a good photograph for the ID card and complete the formalities", with that both of them walked inside. And there a whole new bunch of faces welcomed him, some of them whom he had only seen in Zoom meetings.

"Hey Rhiyan, how are you? Recognize me?", spoke out Satyendra, one of the 12 Business Analysts selected across the country. "Of course, my friend. Just because your internship happened in Bangalore, doesn't mean I forgot your quirky questions over the zoom meetings", smiled Rhiyan as both embraced each other, after which he met the other 10. But apart from them there were B. Tech guys as well who had been selected for the software development role, one being from the same team he had worked with in his internship. "Hey champ, how are you?", Rhiyan moved towards Sujit, the only Bengali he knew around the batch. "*Aami toh bhaloi, tumi kemon achho? (I am good, what about you?)*", replied his Bengali words. "Same here. By the way, many many congratulations on cracking the PPO", Rhiyan sounded cheerful. "Well, he is not the only one", spoke up a female voice just behind him. "Forgot to introduce. This is Srinipa, my batchmate", Sujit introduced. "In that case, congratulations to you too", shook the hands. As Rhiyan left for the formalities, the duo got into an interesting discussion over the available Tech Stack available at the firm.

As the clock ticked 9 am, the 12 BAs visited the cafeteria and the thing that blew their mind were the prices. *Damn! Its costly,* I know given the city Mumbai, that's the first thing that comes to the mind. But here it was just the opposite. *Damn! It's cheap,* that was the reaction that came first in Rhiyan's mind. Nowhere else could he have got a full meal at just Rs 25. He was damn happy, completely unaware that it was a thoughtful strategy for employees to come office regularly. Within 10 minutes the breakfast table was laid with steam hot Cheese Uthappam, Masala Dosa, Cheese Grilled Sandwiches, Chocolate muffins and many more. "What do you think they will be training us on? I mean given that we are in Technology division, I hope they don't start training us on Java or Python", began Manav, an MBA Finance Grad. "I don't think so. But SQL and Power BI would definitely be there", added Rhiyan. "And I have heard that they take tests as well, failing which your offer letter might be at stake", Satyendra never missed a chance to mix a flavor of horror along with humor. "Come on guys. It's just our first day. Let's not drown ourselves in the pool of anxiety", reflected Garima, another finance grad who knew exactly when to take out the chill pill and lighten the mood. With that the conversation moved towards Mumbai accommodations, in short, the PGs and Rhiyan had a lot to talk about it, thanks to all the scamsters in and around the region.

As the herd of developers and BAs took their seats at the training room, they were greeted by their training managers. *"Kasa kai, guys? Tumcha Mumbai Madhe Swagat Aahe.* (How are you guys? Welcome to Mumbai)", began Priyanshi, one of the managers in Marathi. That one line was enough to cheer up the entire batch in an instant. "Now that you are in Mumbai, it's time to get used to some of its popular greetings? What do you say guys?", added Deepali, another manager. "Coming to us, we are your training managers, who are here to make sure when you step into your project the first day, you are completely ready", spoke out Priyanshi. "So be it a difficulty with courses, fear of exams or sick leaves, you come to us first", added Deepali and with that began the first day.

It all began with the usual HR sessions of Dos and Don'ts but later moved towards the Dos and Don'ts of even Investments. "Yes, you heard that right. We do monitor your LinkedIn Profiles. And we do prohibit our employees from mentioning anything related to the work they do at the firm", commanded the speaker. For a moment there was pure silence. "But why?", spoke out a voice with a raised hand. "Because even though Chinese walls exist within the firm, there is a chance that you may get exposed to some confidential information and indulge in something that is strictly prohibited, Moonlighting. Ever heard the term? If not, I suggest, you take a look on Google.

But overall speaking, we have spent some real time and money in hiring you and we can't afford to lose you to petty corporate head-hunters. Can we?", explained the speaker. Silence of sadness crawled across the room. "I know I have given you a sad pill but what if I can give you a smile pill as well", continued the speaker. Eyes rose in hope. "All of you will receive your relocation bonus in the first month itself." A sea of smile took over the gloomy faces that laid around. Suddenly the silence disappeared in the excitement of mini chit chats, because that was not a small amount. It was huge. "See, that's the reason I love my job. Even if I have to pour a drop of sadness, I make sure to bring with me a sea of happiness", smiled the speaker.

As the day progressed, the herd of 12 got introduced to their courses which included a plethora of technology as well as finance. Concepts of Agile, DevOps, SQL and Data Visualization tools like Power BI dominated from the basic angle whereas concepts of Cloud, GenAI dominated from the advanced one. Being exposed to almost all the concepts back at IIT Dhanuj, Rhiyan heaved a sigh of relief, *completely unaware on how the course was about to take his peace through a roller coaster ride.*

Back at his previous firm, Rhiyan had dealt with Indian clients, most project being on the Indian front themselves. But this was for the first time Rhiyan was interacting with a foreign person. The guy was from Europe and in the first interaction itself he made everyone feel comfortable. "Guys, this is not a college. We are not here to compete. We are here to learn from each other, help each other and progress with each passing day, making sure that we are ready for our first project", tried his comforting words. With that began the first course.

As days passed by, people started becoming comfortable. And the best part was in person reviews, wherein the tutor met with each one individually to understand if they were facing any difficulties. And if they were, guide them in the right path. But the part that Rhiyan and others enjoyed the most were the Practicals, wherein they had to use their brain and come up with flowcharts depicting the possibility of feasible solution to some indirect problems. Closing the days with delicious food at the office cafeteria was personal favourite for Rhiyan.

Chapter 13 --- A moment with Finance

Date – 16ᵗʰ October, 2023

By now, Rhiyan had figured out the cost-effective outlets in and around Malad, that could provide him some decent food. Coconut water served well in preventing any kind of dehydration and its nutritious kernel provided the required fiber and minerals. He had also set in a good tuning with his PG mates, especially in terms of AC temperature and washroom timings. Things were going well, until 16ᵗʰ October hit the calendar. That was the day Rhiyan and his friends could never forget. No, it was not any pandemic. Neither was it an earthquake. It was a cyclone. A cyclone of Finance that was about to enter their lives and take them off their feet in an instance.

"Good morning, guys. I am sure you enjoyed your Tech Presentations last week", began Deepali with some memories from the past week. "From today, your financial training would begin. So, are you ready?", she could see some enthusiastic smiles floating in and around the room, when a voice spoke up, "I am sure they are." The half-opened door slid to unveil the tilted shadow of a middle-aged man, who looked very experienced at first look and friendly in the second. "Let's welcome Mr. Rajeev, who is going to cover some finance essentials for you. He has an impressive corporate record as Business Analyst, Manager who now has chosen the entrepreneurial path with his own educational consulting firm", elaborated Priyanshi. "Thank you for the warm welcome, Priyanshi and Deepali. I am sure we are going to have some fun in the next 2 weeks", thanked Mr. Rajeev's courteous words, as the duo went back leaving the BA cohort in safe hands.

"So, why don't we begin with some introductions? And going by Qrian culture, you can address me with my first name, Rajeev. No Sir, please", began his words, "But before that, you must be wondering as to why you are getting trained in Finance, right? To answer your question, Qrian is on the verge of branching out a Finance Consulting section this year, apart from its normal IT ones. And that's why it's important for you guys to know at least the basics", continued his words, "Umm… What I need you guys to do is, use the white A4 sheet and marker near you to create a nameplate and place it on your desk. I keep forgetting names, you know. And yes, along with your introductions let me know about a country that you would like to visit someday." The cohort followed the instructions and then began. "Hi, my name is Satyendra and I have recently graduated from Pune with an MBA in Data Science and Data Analytics", started off Satyendra. "Wow. Data Science and Analytics, huh? Eagerly waiting to learn a few tricks from you, then", smiled Rajeev. "Not sure about that but the country that I would love to visit someday is UK", smiled Satyendra back. Within the next few minutes, the rest of the cohort was completed. "Great, now that we have your favourite countries in hand, it's time to begin with their financials. What do you say guys?", started off the winds of a probable cyclone, "Let's open our favourite website. Tradingeconomics.com, which is a publicly available website that will take you almost 25 years down the memory lane." Everyone typed in and a lot of tabs starting from GDP to Inflation Rate came up. Be it commodities or the money market, indicators popped up like hell. "What the hell is this?", murmured Rhiyan. "The hell that we are just about to dive in", smiled Rajeev, as he overheard his whisper. "No, I didn't mean…", fumbled Rhiyan. "That's okay. What did you say your name was? Oh, yes, Rhiyan", interrupted Rajeev as his eyes fell on his newly created nameplate. "So, Rhiyan, you chose Bangladesh, right? Why so?", asked Rajeev's curiosity. "Umm… I have heard that it's one of the world's largest apparel exporters. Wanted to explore how. And moreover, it wouldn't be an expensive affair since its close to my state", replied Rhiyan. "Hmm, so why don't we hit its import export tab and do some analysis with respect to its employment rate. Maybe you will get your answer to how?", and with that began forming the first layer of analysis that revealed the huge percentage of women participating in the workforce, almost 42% as the numbers revealed. "Interesting. Isn't it? But that's not the only reason. As you move ahead, each financial indicator will reveal a new story. And nothing but persistence can get you there, my friend", advised Rajeev's calm yet focused words.

"Oh nice. I see you have opened up the Balance of Trade for Bangladesh? How much is it down?", asked Rajeev as his eyes fell on Satyendra's screen. "No, I was just exploring", fumbled his words. "Yes. That's exactly why we are here for. Now come on, what does that graph say?", persisted Rajeev. "Umm… it has a consistently negative balance of trade", Satyendra was still a bit nervous. "And what does that mean?", Rajeev was not letting him go just like that. But unfortunately, only silence seemed to fill the gap. "You know, 99% of the time, the answers lie in the words themselves. For instance, Balance of Trade. Which trade?", continued Rajeev, "Import and Export. So, if it is talking about some balance, it must be some expenditure subtracted from income, right? So going by your graph Bangladesh is a net…" "Importer", completed Satyendra's words. "There you go. This is how words help discover their meaning themselves", smiled Rajeev.

The class got over by 4 pm. Everyone had smiles on their faces. They were almost ready to pack up and leave for the day, when Rajeev spoke up, "I hope you guys have received the schedule." "Yes, we have but…", spoke up Satyendra. "Forgot to check it out", completed Rajeev as he brought it up on the projector and what it revealed got the folks a bit nervous. "Come on guys, what good would a session be if it doesn't test you with assessments. And mind you, these are not just finance questions, these are case studies that would test your abilities to combine Finance and Technology in a run to become the Business Analyst you are supposed to be", smiled Rajeev as the rest of the smiles faded away.

Rajeev pulled in a white board and created a table with the markers that laid on his table. On the left-hand side, stood some factors like Root Cause Analysis, Probable Solution, Feasibility, Flowchart, Hygiene etc. and on the right-hand side a hell lot of Zeros. "Today, you guys are at this. By the end of the next weeks, you better increase it to a minimum 8 or else…", he preferred not to complete it. Heartbeats were pounding like thunder across the room. *"Or else what?"*, everybody got thinking. "Today's assignment has been sent to the common folder and I hope to see some good analysis tomorrow", smiled Rajeev's words as he took a break and left for the cafeteria.

"What did he mean? Or else what?", whispers turned into chit chats across the room. "We better start working now itself or else tomorrow we would face that *or else* part", suggested Satyendra as everyone opened the assignment and started reading it. Even 10 minutes had not passed when a voice spoke up to break the silence of terror. "Guys, this looks interesting. *Par Doobki lagne se pehle kuch pet puja toh ho jaaye* (But let's eat something before we dive into it)", Trisha seemed a bit more confident than the others. "Yeah, that's important too", with that everyone moved towards the cafeteria to feast on some Masala Dosa and Sandwiches.

As the 12 sat on the table, discussions popped up from multiple corners. "You look pretty confident Trisha on this? Care to explain how?", Satyendra was curious. "Umm… I won't say confident but you saw the problem statement, right? Don't you think we have an obvious solution in front of our eyes?", replied Trisha, her hands busy tearing up the Cheese Uthappam from the side. "What do you mean?", Satyendra was still not convinced. "See, the problem is that the senior management had to repay a loan but didn't have a visibility over the payment schedule. So, if we build an automated system that can trigger a notification 30 days prior, won't the problem be solved? I mean 30 days is good enough time to arrange the money", elaborated Trisha. *And damn!* Everyone's thoughts moved in that direction. "Hmm… good catch Trisha", praised Neetu who looked a bit more cheerful than a few minutes ago. Rhiyan still looked unconvinced. "What happened? Don't you agree to her solution?", asked Satyendra as his eyes fell on Rhiyan. "No, nothing like that. I am just thinking. How could a personality like that craft a question whose answer is so obvious?", pondered upon Rhiyan. "Maybe because, this is our first assignment and he didn't want to terrify us?", laughed out Trisha. Curves of smile flew across each face, as the mood lightened up. Gradually the conversation moved towards the Navratri plans which was due in just a few days. From Garba to home visits, topics took a completely different turn leaving the problem statement at a corner far from their thoughts.

The next day arrived. "Good morning, everyone, I hope the problem statement treated you well yesterday. So, who is coming up first?", asked Rajeev. At first no one volunteered. "Seems like I will have to make the choice. Trisha, why don't you start?", Rajeev seemed quite cheerful. "Sure", and with that Trisha pulled up the slide she had designed last evening. Everyone's eyes were wide open. It was huge flowchart that not only showed a detailed process but also included databases from which the required data could be fetched automatically. "As a part of my solution, I have designed a fully automated system that will trigger an alarm, in this case notifications whenever there is an upcoming payment from the firm's side. But not on the payment date but 30 days prior. This would give the finance team ample amount of time to arrange the funds", explained her confident words. "Interesting", said Rajeev, his eyes busy scanning each and every flowchart element in detail. "So, who is next?", Rajeev wanted everyone to finish their individual presentations before commenting. Satyendra, Rhiyan and others followed the line. Everyone's solution kind of followed the same path as Trisha's but with minor changes. Some introduced chatbots while others automated payment systems. Rajeev heard each proposition with keen interest. Within the next one hour, everyone managed to wrap up with their solutions.

"Bravo guys, bravo. First of all, I loved the amount of effort you folks have put in. That resolves at least one of my worries. That you guys are not lazy", smiled Rajeev's opening words, as everyone laughed off. "But the worry of something else still remains", and that line was enough to snatch that laughter back. "I love the way you guys designed the notification and payment system, but no one spoke about the money", paused his words briefly. "Where would that come from?", questioned his smile. Everybody fell silent. "See if you are repaying a loan, you need to think about the money as well, right? Building a pipeline without having the oil in the first place, doesn't make sense, does it?", persisted his words. "But we thought that payment was the issue here", defended Trisha. "Well in that case, I suggest you go through the problem statement again", smiled Rajeev as he continued, "The problem was never the payment or for that matter even notifications. All these things will be taken care by the bank where you have your account.

So where did the actual problem lie in?", Rajeev still hoped for a spark as he had already given a hint. But no one spoke up. Rajeev had no choice but to explain it himself, "The problem laid in the cashflow management. For any organization to function, there will be debts, there will be investments. But to track the amount and timing of the cash inflows and cash outflows is the main thing. Had the higher management kept a track of this part, the problem would have never occurred in the first place." "So instead of build an automated payment system, your time and effort should have gone into building the cashflow management system. Do you agree?", asked Rajeev's words, as everyone nodded in agreement. *Damn! How didn't I get that?* Sighed Rhiyan's thoughts. "It's okay. This was just the first assignment. Don't worry, you will get many more opportunities", tried Rajeev to cheer up the cohort, as they moved towards the next topic for the day.

As days passed by, the cohort learnt some tough Lessons. Lessons wherein they stopped jumping into the solutions without analyzing the problem first. Lessons wherein they stopped designing complex flowcharts where simple ones can do the task. It was not easy. With the volume of content packed in, each day felt like two days packed into one. But at the same time, the cohort learnt their lessons for a lifetime. The students stopped mugging up to pass an exam, instead started applying their own intellect to solve real time problems. And that was the beauty of the entire program.

By the end of the two weeks, the BA cohort managed to crawl up to a fair 6 points in each of the section that was drawn out on the white board the first day. The cohort looked a bit dull. "I know 6 feels a bit low. But don't worry the projects you are going to join will teach you some further lessons to make sure that number reaches 10 someday", tried Rajeev's cheering words as the cohort smiled back.

"Now come on. Get ready for your program completion convocation. I don't want Priyanshi and Deepali to come and scold me for holding you guys up. And by the way, many many congratulations on completing this 2 month of rigorous training. I know it was tough but I am glad you made it through", congratulated Rajeev as he clapped for the cohort for the first time. "Thank you, Rajeev. We enjoyed your sessions a lot. But more importantly learnt a lot", thanked Trisha as the others joined in. And with that Rajeev bid goodbye to everyone as he left for his home.

Chapter 14 --- The Actual Project Arrives

Date – 1ˢᵗ November, 2023

By now, projects had been assigned to each of the Business Analysts and they were about to step into their first day. On a usual note, the folks should have been a bit nervous but instead they were excited. And particularly for Rhiyan, it was even more. Having done a summer internship a year back at the same place flooded in a hell lot of memories as he stepped into the building once again. *(For those who might be a bit confused, the previous one was where the training happened, but this one is where the actual project took place. The firm had 3 different offices in Mumbai.)*

Without a second thought, Rhiyan headed straight towards the bay where his team sat. "Good afternoon, Sir, how are you?", addressed his voice to a middle-aged person busy scheduling a meeting for the next day. "Good afternoon, Rhiyan. I am good. You tell me, how are you?", replied Anirudh, his manager, "I hope the finance projects didn't trouble you much back at the training. Rajeev and I curated them together." "I see. That's the reason they were so mind boggling. I should have figured that out", Rhiyan was surprised. "Hey champ, welcome back. Ready to trek again?", cheered up his internship buddy, Mahesh, who had taught him how to approach things stepwise. Be it a problem or a solution. "Absolutely", smiled Rhiyan as both embraced each other. "I know you will take a day to reminisce on the internship memories. But before you get flooded with them, let me introduce you to your upcoming project, *GenAI Config* and its team", Mahesh took Rhiyan towards the next bay, where awaited two more familiar faces, Pawan and Dhruv. Both were experienced Business Analysts, with Dhruv even becoming a Scrum Master for the team. "Welcome back, buddy", Dhruv looked cheerful, "Seems like you will finally get the taste of GenAI, huh!" Last time although allocated a mini project, Rhiyan had a keen interest in learning about the other teams' work as well. At that time, the words GenAI didn't make much sense to him, but now it does. Thanks to his college professors and the exhaustive training by the firm. "I am sure you know who he is, right?", asked Mahesh as he pointed towards Dhruv. "Of course, I do", replied Rhiyan. Dhruv had just joined the firm around two years ago. And now Rhiyan was just about to find out how having spent more than two years at the project had taken his expertise to a whole new level.

After having met a few more people, Dhruv, Pawan and Rhiyan sat down for a joint meeting in a room, where they explained him in detail about the project and their scope of work. At first instance, the volume of information felt overwhelming and Dhruv could sense it. "Don't worry. It will take time for details to sink in. As of now just focus on the overview", advised Dhruv. "More than coding, this project deals a lot in stakeholder management. There will be roadblocks, yes. There will be delays, yes. But as a Business Analyst, it will be not yours, but OUR task together to analyze the problem and figure a way out. So never think that you are alone", winked Pawan.

That's the thing about Qrian. It hails Work Culture as its top most priority. Supporting each other, helping each other has always been a key factor to its growth. Add to that an easy access to higher authorities. Be it the Vice President or the Executive Directors, doors are always open even for a fresh starting level employee. Rhiyan spent the rest of the day meeting a few more familiar faces, raising the access requests and getting accustomed to the place and cafeteria.

The next day when he arrived, he was greeted by 50 emails at one go. *Damn! What is this?* Rhiyan looked a bit perplexed until he actually opened them one by one. The first started off with a welcome mail from his manager, Anirudh. It had nice template describing about Rhiyan, his educational background and his interest in music. A curve of smile appeared across Rhiyan's lips. The mail had been sent to the entire fleet. Here fleet didn't mean ships. It meant actual people. Concepts of Agile was followed all across the firm. And as a result, terms like squad, fleet and chapter were something Rhiyan was about to get accustomed to. As his fingers scrolled through the following mails, he understood why the number shot upto 50. They were not just for him; they were for the entire team to be kept in loop of what is going on where. Rhiyan tried reading them in an attempt to decipher the meaning, but all in vain. Nothing made sense.

"Hmm… champ has already got into work, huh?", flew in Pawan's voice as he took his seat beside him and placed a steaming cup of coffee beside his desk. "Yeah, but unfortunately quite clueless where to begin", sighed Rhiyan's meek voice. "And isn't that how it's supposed to be?", winked Pawan. "What do you mean?", countered Rhiyan. "This is an ongoing project, in short, a spinning wheel. You can't understand its spinning strategy unless you know why and how it started spinning in the first place", elaborated Pawan as he took a sip of his coffee. "This project started of two years ago when Dhruv came in. It was Anirudh and him, who realized the possibilities of GenAI applications in this project and thus formed the team. We are not only developing AI products but making sure that whatever we do or the path we take, is in full compliance with respect to technical risks, functional risks and most importantly compliant with Qrian norms. Because without that, our applications might get exposed to cybersecurity threats leading to loss of data, business and goodwill", completed Pawan's words.

"Wow… Didn't know this team is so crucial", Rhiyan looked a bit surprised but happy that he got to join it. "Hey, what is that?", Rhiyan got a bit distracted with the certificate that laid across Pawan, "What? I mean congratulations. Didn't know you got an award for being the most dependable Product Analyst." "Thank you, Rhiyan. But this is not the time to get distracted. It's time to dive into the world of GenAI Configurations", and with that began the KT aka Knowledge Transfer sessions.

As days passed by, Rhiyan learnt more about the business and along with that the risk factors involved. He started getting comfortable with the work. But there was something that was about to get him into the uncomfortable zone, a zone which he didn't think could even exist.

Rhiyan by birth was not very rich. He belonged to a middle-class family. His mom being a simple housewife had spent most of her life in the vicinity of a known neighborhood back at Durgapur, a city in West Bengal. She was happy amidst the Bengali community she was in but after having spent a full month as a residential in Mumbai, the charm of the city started fading away. Rhiyan's father had to return back owing to his work. And the moment that happened, *damn! The zone of loneliness crept into his mother's world.*

With just a handful of Bengalis available, most of them busy with work, Rhiyan's mother could hardly find someone to talk to. And even if she did, the language barrier made things worse for her. The moment Rhiyan left for work, she felt as if she has been locked in a cage. And one night she was literally in tears. As she explained her woes to her son, a decision to return back took a stand. Rhiyan's convocation was still a month away. She decided to wait and return back along with her son.

The next morning as Rhiyan sat on the bench waiting for the metro train to arrive, some strange feelings started creeping in. Although he had stayed alone in the past as well, but this time his heart was just not ready to let his mother go. His heart wanted to hold her back, stop her from going away and yet he couldn't, given the fact on how the lack of familiar faces made his mother feel lonely. The timer showed one minute for the train to arrive. His eyes stared on the opposite side platform, where a tall figure stood waiting for his train. And the moment Rhiyan got up to look a bit further, *whoosh!* Two trains crossed each other in an instant, settling down on their respective platforms a few seconds later. Without a second thought, Rhiyan boarded the train. In local trains, the way it moves you usually get the feeling of a horse ride at a steady pace, but in metro trains, it feels as if you are gliding through the sky from one place to the other. Rhiyan loved the pace but what he liked more were the tall skyscrapers that formed a scenery along the way. Crossing the bridge his eyes fell on the heavy traffic that moved along the highways. He thanked God for saving him from the woes of traffic in his daily commute. And even more so, since his rented flat and office, both stood at a walking distance from the respective metro stations. Not all were fortunate to have such a smooth communication. For instance, the other grads who had their homes in places like Navi Mumbai and Thane, a struggle through a 2 hours traffic was a day-to-day affair. Rhiyan kept on walking until he reached the main gate. "Someone is looking a bit gloomy, huh?", spoke out a voice from behind. Rhiyan turned back and a curve of smile replaced the sadness he was absorbed in. It was none other than Pawan. "You know your parents have kept a perfect name for you. Wherever you go, you carry along the winds of happiness", smiled Rhiyan. "Really? I am glad you thought so", smiled Pawan back as they both walked together inside. "But tell me, what was the sadness about?", asked Pawan. "Umm…

nothing. It's just that my mother has decided to return back owing to the loneliness in which she feels captive. And the moment that happens, I will be lonely again", sighed Rhiyan. "See Rhiyan, Mumbai is a very busy city. People struggle all day to make a living out of it. In fact, time is money out in here. And if you expect people from other states to adjust easily, trust me that's not a fair expectation", spoke up Pawan's thoughts. "And moreover, how long do you think your mom would have stayed along, leaving your father behind in West Bengal? These are life transitions that we need to accept and move forward." "Hmm… I think you are right. There are indeed some phases, where moving forward is the only solution", agreed Rhiyan as both switched on their systems and got down to work.

Chapter 15 --- Thief of Cards

Date – 8ᵗʰ November, 2023

Work is something everyone gets used to after a point of time. Money keeps the kitchen ovens burning. It even acts as a motivation for switching companies, sometimes in a higher profile or maybe even the same. But neither work nor money builds a culture. It gets built when people come along. And the corporates know this well. Maybe that's why they never miss the chance of incorporating celebrations and festivities in their culture to keep the folks motivated. Qrian was no different. With the upcoming Diwali festival at hand, some celebrations had to make their way through. But Rhiyan was unaware of how they do it.

A ping pooped up on his screen. It was from the Executive Director himself. *Welcome to the firm Susmit. I know you might be feeling a bit overwhelmed. So here is a chance to let all of it go. Would you like to become the SPOC for the Diwali Celebrations? It might help you get familiar with the folks around,* read the message. Instead of typing back an answer, Rhiyan dashed towards the ED's cabin. For an instance, even Pawan was clueless as to what happened? But even before his hands could prevent the fiasco, Rhiyan flew far from his reach. *Damn! What is he going to do?* Pawan got perplexed.

"Sir, may I come in", asked Rhiyan as he knocked on the ED's door. The ED, Mr. Jay had not even left the message window where he was waiting for Rhiyan's reply and to his surprise, Rhiyan stood at the door himself. "Yes, tell me", fumbled the ED for a second. "Sir, is there any music event involved? I can be the SPOC, sure. But along with that I would love to volunteer for a musical performance if something musical is there", Rhiyan sounded excited. *Huff!* Jay heaved a sigh of relief. "Of course. We would love to hear you out. You could have typed that out in reply, no?", Jay sounded excited too. "No Sir. That would have snatched away my opportunity to meet you in person", smiled Rhiyan as Jay laughed off. "I see. Go on. Begin the preparations. Let's see how you do it", signed off Jay's words. Happy with the response Rhiyan went back to his desk and joined the team that was making the overall preparations.

Date – 10ᵗʰ November, 2023

The roof was all decked up with Diwali lights, some hanging in the form of stars others in the shape of diyas. Desks were decorated with mini rangoli diyas depicting the festival of light. The decorations looked elegant, but so did the people. Each one dressed in their traditional attires walked down the aisle like a pro. The ladies were all dressed up in colourful sarees with men mostly in kurta pajamas. Dressed in a peach-coloured kurta, Rhiyan entered the bay. It seemed as if he had entered into a fair, not an office. EDs of all the teams were quite happy with the joint effort put in place together.

The event began with something called Beg Borrow Steal. The entire floor was divided into 4 teams, 10 members each headed by a leader. Rhiyan came to know about it at the firm itself. Neither had he heard nor experienced the game before and that's where the twists were about to take place. Each team were given a list of day-to-day items that they had to find and whoever brings in all the 10 items first, stands the winner. The four leaders were handed out the list and as the bell rang, 40 people dashed out in different directions to collect those items. The cyclone had already set in when two beautiful eyes locked in with Rhiyan and vanished in an instant. *Who was she?* Wondered Rhiyan's thoughts. "Come on Rhiyan, we need to help the core team with the counting of items", screamed Namita, who had volunteered as well. "Yes coming", Rhiyan's thoughts broke away from the spell. He was about to swipe his card at the door, but *alas!* There was none to be found. Last time he checked it was attached to his belt loop, near his waist, with a hook. *Damn! where did it go?* Rhiyan's desperate eyes started looking here and there in an attempt to retrieve the lost ID card. And then suddenly something struck him. An item on the list, two ID cards with same surname. And then he realized how those beautiful eyes stole it like a pro. *Damn it! Now where do I find her?* Rhiyan was clueless. "Hey what happened?", asked Dhruv, "You look tensed." "Yeah, two beautiful eyes managed to steal away my ID Card without a blink", Rhiyan explained his ordeal as Dhruv couldn't stop his laughter. "Come on Dhruv. This is serious", defended Rhiyan. "Not as long as the game of Beg Borrow and *Steal* is going on", Dhruv was still laughing, "Don't worry, you will get it back once the game gets over." Rhiyan was about to give up when his eyes caught hold of that mysterious girl dashing across the bay. Without a second thought, he blocked her way and she slipped, eventually falling in his arms. Their eyes locked with other. She was draped in a purple-coloured saree with the borders sparkling with golden embroidery. For a moment there was silence, when Rhiyan decided to break it, "Hey princess, going somewhere?" "Yeah, I was, until you blocked my way", replied her voice as she got up and stood up straight. "Who am I to block your way, unless of course you stole my card with those beautiful eyes", shot back Rhiyan. "I see. Well, I don't have it but be rest assured you will get it back once the game is over", assured her sweet voice. "But I want it now", retaliated Rhiyan. "In that case you should have had a different surname", smiled her reply as she flew out again. Rhiyan had no option but to stand quite helpless.

Within the next 30 minutes, items like bus tickets, lipsticks, caps and even books poured in from different teams in an attempt to win the game. But only two teams managed to bring in all the items. And there Rhiyan saw his ID card hanging along with the girl's ID card that had the same surname. He heaved a sigh of relief. After the counting was done, the mysterious girl's team won the game. She jumped in excitement, her fist still clinging on to Rhiyan's ID Card firmly. Cadbury Celebrations were distributed to the winners. "Here you go. Sorry for the trouble but had to steal it beneath your eyes", apologized her words as she handed over his card. Rhiyan was still thinking whether to accept the apology or not, when her hands offered him a Cadbury Chocolate and he decided to finally forgive her. "And by the way, my name is Ruhani, not princess. Thanks for the compliment though", flew in her parting words, as she joined her team for the celebrations.

"Seems like someone is about to fall in love", tried Dhruv's words, in an attempt to pull Rhiyan's legs, as he observed a light smile across his face. "Not at all", exclaimed Rhiyan's reply with a surprise. "Well, you never know when a Thief of Cards turns into a Thief of Hearts", smiled Dhruv as he left to join in the celebrations.

Next in line was the ramp walk show, wherein men and women dressed up in traditional attires took the stage. First in line was Anirudh, dressed up in a Rajasthani attire with a turban and a vintage dagger in his hand. His look was quite unique. Even Rhiyan couldn't take his eyes off him, given the fact that he had never seen his manager in nothing except formals and that too with a different coloured tie on each day. But even Dhruv was not far away. He was himself dressed in a golden coloured Manyavar Kurta along with a dhoti styled pajama. Others gave a tough competition too, with Punjabi and Marathi style attires making the way. And the ladies were not behind too. Ruhani, draped in her purple saree led the way with others draped in Marathi and Bengali styles themselves. Each of them used a signature style to end the ramp walk. The crowd literally burst in excitement. As the judges chose 3 from each group, the winning shot came down to a very simple question, "What does Diwali mean to you?" Some came in with obvious answers like festivals of light, celebrations with family and triumph of good over evil. But what struck out was Anirudh's answer, "Yes, Diwali is indeed a festival of light, but for me, it's more of finding the light within yourself rather than just in the outside world. If we are able to find that, no roadblocks could stop us from overcoming any hurdle in life." Sounds of clap surged across the room, as the winner was declared.

And finally came the turn for Rhiyan's performance. As he sat down on a chair with a guitar in his hand, his eyes moved across the hall in an attempt to feel the audiences' vibe. Without wasting a second, he began the song *Dhunki,* a Bollywood favourite from a 2011 movie. Many a times during the chorus, his eyes did strike Ruhani's but his focus remained on the chords and the scales of the song. The show ended with a huge round of applause. Words of praises flew in from all corners. "Hmm… didn't know the person I stole from had such a lovely voice", smiled Ruhani as she approached Rhiyan. "Even I didn't know the Thief of Cards had an elegant taste in music", smiled Rhiyan back as the duo moved towards the food counter in order to devour out the delicacies lying out there.

Chapter 16 --- Elephanta Caves and Peace Pagoda

Date – 11ᵗʰ November, 2023

The next 4 days were a holiday for Rhiyan, thanks to the weekend falling in conjunction with the Diwali holidays. And this was the perfect moment for Rhiyan to take his parents out on a Mumbai tour. Oh yes, owing to his mother's loneliness, his father did come back for a few days. "Oh! Thank God, you are here", Rhiyan embraced his father, as he landed at the airport. Having explained the ordeal his mother was going through; his father understood the situation. "To make her feel better, I have planned out a two days tour to two of the tourist spots around", said Rhiyan. "In that case, let us not waste time", winked his father back.

The next day, the trio started off with the journey. A journey that flooded in a lot of memories for Rhiyan. It was the same platform from where Rhiyan, Sushant, Antara and Samrat had begun their journey to *Feast On*. And yet he stood there again but this time with a different destination. Boarding the train on the Western line, the trio reached where it all began from, The Gateway of India. Rhiyan went straight to the ferry counter and purchased 3 tickets that costed him around 800 rupees. *Wow, that's costly,* Rhiyan felt a pinch on his wallet. Last time he was there, his feet stopped at the grandeur of the gate itself but this time they moved further. Just behind the gateway, stood a fleet of ferries waiting to carry people towards the *Elephanta Caves.* As they moved forward, their eyes fell on another set of fleets, that travelled towards *Alibaug,* another coastal town of Maharashtra that served as a weekend gateway for most of the Mumbaikars, thanks to its beautiful beaches and sea rides.

The trio boarded the ferry and started off with the ride. Many thought the scenery was ahead but instead it fell on the back.

As the ferry moved further, a look back at the Gateway of India revealed the entire city in one frame. Taking the smartphone out, Rhiyan did manage to capture the scenery in a few clicks. As the ferry moved forward, a huge ship appeared. The name on the deck read as *Cormat*. A few seconds later its full form came into view with Rhiyan realizing it to be a Cargo ship, mostly used for import and export purpose. On the opposite side, floated some oil tankers as well which were huge in size. Rhiyan had never seen ships so close in life. His eyes remained wide open. The cool breeze on the both sides of the ferry added an extra layer of comfort in the journey.

"Hey look, whales", screamed a tourist, as her eyes noticed some grey-coloured mini whales taking one dive after the other but at a distance far from the ferry. On a closer look, everyone realized them to be Dolphins. Rhiyan's parents felt quite happy with the view. Seeing their smile, Rhiyan forgot about the pinch on his wallet completely.

The ride went on for another 20 minutes, where a few speedboats managed to cross their paths. At a distance of around a kilometer, appeared a huge mountain covered with trees with some clouds trying to circle the top. The scenery was breathtaking. Meanwhile Rhiyan's mother had already started off with chit chats. Oh yes, they were fortunate enough to find a Bengali trio on the ferry itself, a young couple with their son. For her, it felt like an icing on the cake, completely unaware that the party was yet to begin. After a couple of minutes, the ferry took rest as the tourists deboarded it to begin their journey towards the Elephanta Caves.

Walking past the bridge, Rhiyan noticed a mini rail line which revealed the presence of a toy train, carrying passengers from one end to the other. Since the site was just a kilometer ahead, the trio decided to take a walk. In ten minutes, they reached the entrance where a series of steps awaited them to make their way along the hilly area. Shops of artifacts like mini buddha statues, artificial daggers, bangles etc. formed their lines on both sides of the staircase. A few air gun pistols caught Rhiyan's eyes but his feet decided to move on, until they finally reached the main entrance of the *Elephanta Caves*. At first look, it seemed like a park, thanks to the staff who had maintained it so well. But as they entered the first cave, appeared a 7-meter-tall statue of a 3 faced God. The board near it read as *Trimurti Sadashiva,* where Trimurti represented three aspects of God Shiva: *The Creator, the Preserver, and the Destroyer.* Rhiyan and his parents stood there for almost five minutes trying to understand the significance and history behind it. Thanks to the board, most of their questions were answered. They moved on to the next cave. The island consisted of seven caves in total surrounded by the Sea of Oman. Most of them were in a broken shape. But that's what gave them the ancient look, tourists were looking for. A few of course argued on the how the govt. could have done a better job in restoring the fallen pieces. As the trio moved ahead, they were welcomed by different kinds of broken sculptures, that reminded Rhiyan some pictures from his class 7 history books. Having finished the tour, they returned back towards the ferry, which helped them reach the Gateway of India. After having food at Bademiya, one of the most popular eateries near the gateway, the trio finally returned back to Malad.

Date – 14th November, 2023

The next day, Rhiyan and his parents started off their journey towards the Global Vipassana Pagoda also known as the Peace Pagoda. For this they had to take a ferry ride again but this time from Borivali Jetty. Contrary to the previous day, this was a short ride. Took around 15 minutes to cross and reach the Golden Shrine. At first glance it looked like a golden palace shaped in the form of a Buddhist shrine but as the trio entered, it revealed two men like structures holding a horizontal shaft from which hung a huge bell, with tourists trying to ring it with the help of a wooden log. As their steps moved forward, a statue of Buddha and a huge circular dome came to the forefront which had the capacity of holding 8000 people in meditation. Rhiyan's vision went upwards, when his eyes fell on the Ashoka Chakra, residing at the center of the dome.

Coming out they went towards a park like area where a few artificial deer structures had been created with a revolving Ashoka Chakra on the wall. It did manage to attract a few tourists for photography purpose. On another side, a tourist guide stood busy explaining the significance of the place, the structures and the meditation hall to a few keen tourists around. But one thing was for sure. Pick up any corner of the place and take a seat. You will definitely find Peace. The trio explored each and every corner of the place, even clicking a few photos themselves. After an hour, they decided to return back via the ferry.

In the evening, they enjoyed a firecracker show next to their building. All homes including their rented one were decorated with colourful lights and diyas. For the trio, Diwali got spent really well. A few days later Rhiyan's parents went back to Durgapur, together, with his mother finally at peace.

Chapter 17 --- World of Scamsters

With Rhiyan's parents back in their hometown, feelings of loneliness started creeping in for him. But what crept in more was the pinch in his pocket, thanks to the high house rents in Mumbai. Coming back from the office, Rhiyan looked at the entire flat which seemed too big for him. Not that the thought of bringing in a flat mate didn't come to his mind, but the societal rules of not giving homes to bachelors did pose a hindrance to his masterplan. The only way left was to leave and move to a smaller place with lesser rent.

Without wasting time, he stood in front of the broker who had helped him get the house. Oh Yes! It's very difficult to find a decent place to stay without a broker in Mumbai. One month's rent as a brokerage is what they earned in return. In this case, Rhiyan had gone beyond his means to secure a fully furnished 1 BHK flat for his parents to stay, but as fate would have it, the hustle and bustle of the city failed to impress them. "So, you are telling me, you want to leave, huh? Where to?", spoke up the 60-year-old Gujrati shopkeeper who does the brokering as a side business. "And moreover, you have a hard lock in period of six months as per the agreement", added his grumbling voice. "Umm… yes, I understand that. But now that my parents are not here, the rent of 30k is literally pinching a hole in my pocket", pleaded Rhiyan's voice, "I am sure you can find a way out." For a moment, there was silence, when the grumbling old man finally spoke out, "Hmm… Maybe I can do something or… you can do it yourself", Rhiyan looked a bit perplexed. "A replacement, Rhiyan. A replacement", exploded his voice, "You find me a good family as a replacement and I help you break the contract." *But isn't that your work?* Rhiyan wanted to say but given the ball laid out of his court, his words couldn't. "There is just one catch", rolled up his eyes. "And what is that?", asked Rhiyan. "I get to keep all the brokerage, not you. But don't you worry, I will help you with the search as well." *Damn it!* Sank Rhiyan's heart. *I will lose the 30k brokerage,* realized his logical chain of thoughts. *But paying 30k for the next four months…* Rhiyan's dilemma kept on increasing. He could even feel the rumbling noise brewing down in his stomach. His tensed eyes stared straight into the broker's heart. "I know what you are thinking. But this is Mumbai, son. Fortunately, or unfortunately, the only thing that speaks here is money. Not feelings", sighed the broker along. Seeing no choice on any side, Rhiyan had to give up. "Okay. At least it will save me from the extra rent from next month", signed off his voice with a lost trade-off.

The next day, Rhiyan started off by posting an advertisement on a few renowned real estate websites. At first, he could not believe that he was having to do the task of a broker. But this time he literally didn't have a choice. The next one hour got spent in doing a few household chores and preparing a decent breakfast. *Tring! Tring!* Rang his phone. *Really, you get response that fast?* Rhiyan got thinking, his hands busy slicing off a boiled egg into half. Reaching the charging port, he picked up the call. "Hi, main Rhiyan se baat kar raha hoon? *(Hi, am I speaking to Rhiyan?)*", started off the voice in Hindi. "Yes, you are", replied Rhiyan's voice.

"I saw your flat advertisement. Is it still available?"

"Yes, it is"

"Great, this is Maninder Singh from Delhi. I work in the Indian Army and have recently got my posting at Mumbai. I am looking for a flat where I can shift along with my family", elaborated the voice over the call.

Indian Army, huh? For a moment even Rhiyan got convinced.

"I have sent you a Hi on WhatsApp. Kindly send me the flat's pictures", requested the voice. "Yes, I will", Rhiyan didn't speak much as his fingers decided to hung up. Rhiyan immediately copied the phone number and pasted it on True Caller. The name was indeed Maninder Singh. This confused him even more. Somehow his intuition didn't feel right. He decided to block the number, inspite of nothing being suspicious. He went back to his boiled eggs. Having a hearty breakfast, Rhiyan decided to watch a movie on an OTT. He was about to get cozy in the sofa, when his phone rang again. "Hello, is this Rhiyan? I wanted to speak about the flat for which you posted an advertisement", spoke up the voice. "Okay, if I may ask, where do you work?", asked Rhiyan casually. "I am from the defense, the Indian Army. I recently got my posting in Mumbai and…", started off the voice. "And you want to settle down here with your family", completed Rhiyan, but this time with a devilish smile. *Caught you… and your trick,* Rhiyan's intuition was correct. His number has fallen in the hands of scamsters. He cut the call and blocked it immediately. In the next one hour he received five similar calls, some even from brokers but not actual tenant. Without wasting any more time, he deactivated the advertisement from all websites. Although he was worried that his phone number had fallen in wrong hands, he was at peace that he was able to identify the scamsters at the right time. But then his phone rang again. *Tring! Tring!* Clouds of worried thoughts came down circling again. He was about to cut and block it, when his fingers touched the green button in a hurry. "Hello, is this Rhiyan?", spoke out a vibrating voice. "Yes. Did you call regarding the flat?", asked Rhiyan, expecting the same reel to wind again.

"Yes"

"Where do you work?"

The Indian Army, Rhiyan was smiling as he expected the answer. But instead, he spoke up, "A fintech consulting firm." Rhiyan sat up straight. "Okay, and where are you right now?", Rhiyan got a bit curious. He was expecting the answer as *Delhi,* but the reply came as, "Malad East. Can I come and visit you once?"

With that, Rhiyan knew that it was a genuine call. "Yeah sure. I am available. You can come", replied his voice. In the next one hour, a young man stood at his doorstep. He looked like somewhere in between 28 and 30, but not a day more. Rhiyan welcomed him inside, offered him a seat and some water. "Thanks. I was indeed a bit thirsty", smile the guest. "So yeah, I was searching for a 1 BHK flat on this website, when your number popped up", began his words. "Yes, even I am looking for a replacement. Do you mind telling me a bit more about yourself?", Rhiyan wanted to enquire a bit more thoroughly. "Umm… yeah. I am Harshit, currently working at a fintech consulting firm, here in Goregaon East itself. I did my MBA from IIM Rothak. As I getting married next month, I am looking for a place to shift next month", elaborated his answer. As the conversation progressed, Rhiyan heaved a sigh of relief. He had finally got a genuine person. And fortunate for him, Harshit liked the flat, thanks to its amenities and its spaciousness.

Within an hour, the duo stood in front of the broker. "I have found my replacement", spoke out Rhiyan, but with a heavy heart, knowing fully well that inspite of his hard work, he will lose out the brokerage. "Great. Let me talk to the owners and we will get your deposit back", promised his assuring words. Harshit got into a detailed conversation with the broker, following which the duo left in their respective directions.

Rhiyan settled in as the dusk settled into a quite evening. But soon realized that this was just one side of the equation. The other side was still left. A place to stay for himself after he vacates the current abode. *Damn it!* Sighed his worried thoughts as he dived into another set of websites with a hope to stay clear of the scamsters.

Rhiyan could have hired another broker to find him a cheaper place, maybe a 1 RK. But this time he wanted to test himself, a test to find it out all by himself. Scrolling down the list, he did find one advertisement that was posted a few hours ago. But inside his heart was rumbling with fear. A fear to fall in another trap of scamsters.

In the first ring, nobody picked up. Thinking it to be another scamster, Rhiyan gave up and started scrolling again. He shortlisted a few, but unfortunately there seemed to be a brokerage component attached to each. Rhiyan couldn't help but smile at his bad luck. The clock struck 11 pm. His yawn signaled him towards the bed. *Fine, lets try it out tomorrow,* thought his thoughts as his sleepy eyes drew him towards the bed.

Tring! Tring! Rang his phone as the morning dawn threw in some sunlight through the window. *Not again! Didn't I delete all the postings?* Rhiyan was still asleep. As his fingers grabbed the phone, the name read as Lead 1. Without a second blink he picked it up. "Hello", spoke up a light voice. "Hello, hi, yes. It was me who called you up last night. I am looking for a 1 RK. Is yours still available?", asked his sleepy voice. "Yes, it is. If you can come down to Kandivali East, Lokhandwala Complex, maybe I can show it too?", replied the answer in return. "Okay. I will be there in an hour", replied Rhiyan. After seeking a few more details regarding the address, he hung up.

With a light breakfast of an apple, banana and a glass of milk, Rhiyan set out on another adventure, hoping it to be a good one. The closest metro station for Kandivali Lokhandwala

Complex was Akruli, just two stations after Dindoshi, where Rhiyan currently stayed. Travelling towards Akruli, his eyes fell on an artistic work. It seemed as if while creating the path for metro, the authorities had to cut through a rocky area, with squared shaped rocks neatly arranged on either side of the pathway. But Mumbaikars being creative in nature, painted it like a fort and placed artificial Marathi soldiers' cardboard cutouts with ropes passing down, as if the soldiers were climbing up a hilly area to capture the fort. And since the stones were kind of protruding outwards, it gave a 3D feeling. With the metro train moving at a uniform pace, the scenery looked beautiful. As the train moved forward, high rise buildings popped up on both sides of the line, some very old and some newly constructed. Mumbai's real estate demand was growing like anything, thanks to the corporate hub and film city nearby.

Ting! Opened the door, as Rhiyan stepped out in Akruli station with no idea where to go next. Taking some help from the helpdesk counter, he moved towards a bridge that connected both ends of the highway below. The Kandivali Police station laid just in front. Remembering the cue over the call, he kept on moving. He switched on the Google Map for some help but was still clueless from where to get a direct auto. Seeing the misery and confusion he was in; a policeman offered to help and guided him in the right direction. Thanking the policeman, he took a sharing auto, which led him straight to Garden Tower, the building he was supposed to reach. He called the owner but no one picked up. *Damn! Don't tell me I came this far to fall in another trap of scamster.* Rhiyan was indeed a bit tensed. He decided to explore the nearby area. Starting from grocery shops to food outlets, daily need items did fall in his eyes. *Hmm, the place is fine but where the hell is the owner,* tension was brewing inside his stomach when his phone rang up. "Where are you, Sir? I was just about to leave", burst out Rhiyan. "Yes, sorry I was in office. Give me just 5 more minutes and I will be there", hung up the owner even before Rhiyan could even react. Finding a place in Mumbai had always remained a challenge for countless migrants who shift to the city of dreams, in order to fulfil theirs. The same is with Bangalore, another IT hub that had become the Silicon Valley of India. The process always starts with braving the home owner's ego, proceeds with an interview round and depending on whether the society allows bachelors or not, you might get a place at a feasible rent. *Oh, did I say feasible? Scratch that. It always remains high.*

After a few more minutes, appeared a middle-aged man who appeared to be in his late 30s. "Hi, are you Rhiyan?", asked his husky voice. "Yes, I am", Rhiyan had shredded his anger by now. "Hmm… So where are you from?", started off the interview on the footpath itself. "Oh, I am from a city called Durgapur in West Bengal. And currently I am working at a firm in Goregaon East", replied his confident words. "West Bengal, huh? I thought *Sarkar* was a Marathi surname", the owner looked a bit disappointed. "Oh no Sir. We Bengalis have a lot of Sarkars in our community", defended Rhiyan. "Okay. Come on. Let me show you the room", finally the duo started walking. With one look upwards, Rhiyan realized it to be at least 25 storey building. The lift buttons' numbering confirmed the same.

Moving across the 5th floor, the duo entered a narrow pathway which opened into a room with a window wide open. Rhiyan took out his phone and opened the digital compass to confirm it's the East side. Not that he was looking for an East facing flat but he had a personal liking for Sun's rays coming to his room in the morning. As the needle moved towards East, his thoughts were in peace. It was a one RK flat with a room, kitchen and a washroom, that's it. But fortunately, it was semi furnished with Beds and Wi-Fi already set up. Rhiyan looked around a bit more to find a decent kitchen, a piped gas oven and a spacious washroom. His heart was at peace. "Umm… if I may ask. Where do you stay?", asked Rhiyan's curiosity. "Oh! Here itself", replied the owner's husky voice. "What?", Rhiyan looked confused. "Not here, here. But beside you", with that owner guided him towards another entrance that opened into a hall and then into a room. "This was a 3 BHK flat. We separated out the one RK with the thought of converting into an office. I am an advocate, you know. But since that plan didn't pan out, we converted it to 1 RK and decided to rent it out", explained the owner's words. "I see", Rhiyan was relieved. Although the room was devoid of the lavish windows and cabinets that his current flat had, it still seemed like a suitable place to take a ground for at least another 2 years.

"So, you like the place?", asked the owner, "Sorry, I didn't tell you, my name. Its Pradeep. Nice meeting you", extended his hand. "Nice to meet you too", Rhiyan had a firm handshake. "Yeah, I kind of like the place. But seems like the window installation is left and the washroom ceiling needs a repair", Rhiyan's eyes did manage to scan a few shortcomings. "Yeah, I know. But don't worry. It will be done within seven days. Anyways you are not coming before 1st Dec, right?", Mr. Pradeep was quite confident. "Yes, that would give you around 10 days to complete the work", nodded Rhiyan. "So, what about the rent?", Rhiyan turned to negotiating mode. "The advertisement showed the figures. Didn't they? 15k it is with 50k in deposit", the owner was nowhere to budge from the figures. "Yeah, I did read that. But as you can see, I am not a very rich guy", Rhiyan had purposefully worn very simple clothes, a plain light-yellow T-Shirt and a cotton black trouser, "I have recently completed my MBA from IIT Dhanuj and have shifted in this city. So…" "Did you say IIT Dhanuj?", interrupted the owner. "Yes, IIT…" Mr. Pradeep's eyes lit up. "And earlier I used to work at Zunith…", continued Rhiyan.

"Zunith huh? I have heard they pay a lot. Don't they?", interruptions kept on coming. "Umm… not as much as you think. For the first 5 years, the increment was really a bit slow", defended Rhiyan. "Hmm… you know what, I like your profile. So, you tell. How much can you give?", hinted the husky voice. A smile did try to appear across Rhiyan's lips but he controlled it. "I was thinking if you can manage it with 14k including gas and electricity. I mean except for boiled eggs and Maggie; I hardly cook anything. Most of the days, lunch gets covered at office itself", requested Rhiyan. "Including electricity, huh?", he scratched his forehead. Mr. Pradeep got into deeper thoughts. He looked into Rhiyan's clothes and then into his eyes. "Fine. I agree. But only on one condition", continued his words, "No Smoking, No Drinking and No Loud Music. Agreed?" A huge smile took a curve along Rhiyan's lips. "Definitely. I have avoided those vices my entire life, Sir. You don't have to worry about it. But regarding music, I usually play the guitar and sing along. So…", hesitated Rhiyan. "Yeah, that's okay. As long as you don't bombard our sleep, we are good", shaked the duo's hands. After a few more chit chats, Rhiyan was back in the metro train. Taking a seat by the window, he kind of calculated and figured out that including the travel the total cost would come to 15k which is half of his current rent. That night Rhiyan had a really good sleep, completely unaware that a nightmare was waiting for him just across the next day.

Chapter 18 --- Lock-In Period

Only one more week left, thought Rhiyan preparing himself mentally again for a new place, a new life. From the day he had stepped in Mumbai, he never had the chance to unpack his suitcase properly. He had been constantly on the run, first at an AirBNB, then at a PG in Malad West, then a flat in Malad East and now at Kandivali East. Fortunately all were in Mumbai. But now he finally wanted to put an end to these 2 months sprints and settle in for good. Purchasing a house in Mumbai is nothing short of a challenge, since the 1 BHK flats just start off from 1 Crore Rupees. Real Estate prices had surged significantly in Mumbai over the past few years and Rhiyan could feel that pinch.

Tring! Tring! Rang his phone as the clock hit 10 am. It was from the broker of his current flat. "Good morning. Kindly come to my shop. We have small issue", hung up his words, even before Rhiyan could reply back. Finishing up the cup of honey-milk, he got ready and moved towards the shop, *Apna Estate.* It was a small grocery shop which dealt with chips, chocolates, ice-creams etc. But the main business laid in the brokerage deals. That's where home seekers arrived in case they needed a flat on rent. Rhiyan liked him. Yes, inspite of being a broker, he was a likable person, not because he was a 60 year old soft spoken person, but because he had an amazing capability of multi-tasking. He was handling around 30 flats around the Malad East region, across different societies. And inspite of being that high number, he handled the agreement making and maintainance issues of each quite seamlessly. When Rhiyan shifted with his parents, there were some hiccups with respect to lights, fans and wifi. Fortunately his broker uncle was just a phone call away. Be it morning, afternoon or evening, he picked up each and every call, noted the issues and send in the right person to fix them.

"Yes, uncle. Tell me. What happened?", asked Rhiyan as he took a seat. "You know that you are breaking the lock-in period of six months, right?", asked uncle's grumbling voice. "Yes, I know that", replied Rhiyan;s straight forward answer. "The owner is planning to fine you a penalty of 30k", fired his missile. "What?", Rhiyan was in a shock. "Are you serious? I mean, we had a deal, right? If I get you a replacement, wherein the owner doesn't incur any loss, no penalty will be charged", fumbled Rhiyan's words. "Yes, I know that. But the lady is just not happy with how people keep on leaving the flat in less than six months, whatever the reason be", came his counter. Rhiyan knew that the ball was completely in the owner's court as far as legalities were there. He in fact tried reaching out to her before making the replacement plan, but she only communicated through the broker. And now he was in a fix. "So, what now? I mean I have already lost the 30k brokerage that I had paid you. I can't afford to lose another", Rhiyan sounded tensed. "Trust me. I am on your side. Even I explained to her how hard you worked to get a replacement so that she doesn't incur any loss, but she is not ready to budge from the rent agreement terms", sighed his words. *I hope this is not a joint plan of the lady and the broker to squeez money from me,* thought Rhiyan. But even if it was true, he had nothing to defend it with. "Here is her number. Go, talk to her. See if you can convince her to return at least some more", the broker shared the owner's phone number.

Rhiyan returned back with a heavy heart. *Had I known this would happen, I wouldn't have executed the plan. But then I had to bear the 30k high rent for another few months,* Rhiyan's thoughts were constantly bouncing in and out. *But how do I convince her to return the entire deposit of 1 lakh rupees?,* pondered his thoughts again. His eyes kept on staring at the owner's number until an idea somehow struck him. *But would it work? Who knows?* After a few more minutes, Rhiyan hit the dial button.

"Hi, this is Rhiyan, your tenant. And I wanted to speak to you regarding the lock-in period penalty charges", began his effort. "Yes, tell me", came back a stern reply. "Ma'am, I know I am breaking the lock-in period but to make sure you don't incur any loss, I worked hard myself to find you a suitable replacement. Kindly consider my situation and refund my entire deposit, if possible", pleaded Rhiyan's voice. "I understand but if I let you go today, tomorrow someone else will come and give me the same logic. Then what's the use of making a contract? And moreover according to agreement, I am supposed to charge you 60k, two months' rent to be precise whereas I am charging its half, right?", came in the fierce counter. "Yes, I know. But please try and understand. It was my parents for whom I took this house. But unfortunately, the lack of Bengalis, difficulties in communications made my mother feel so lonely, that she couldn't bear it a day more. She just couldn't adjust to the fast paced life of this city", defended Rhiyan's counter. For a moment there was silence, because even the owner felt the pangs of his words. "Hmm… I understand. Fine, I can give you a 10k relief more. I am making an exception just for you. But you have to bear the 20k penalty. Can't help you with that", shot her words. Rhiyan was relieved a bit, but for him 20k was still left. And he wanted to try out one last shot before giving up. "Ma'am, thank you for understanding my situation. But I have a proposal if you may consider", requested Rhiyan. "Okay. I am listening", the call was still on. "You may not know this, but I am trained guitarist, a musician. If you want, I can give your daughter a three months complete training and help her become a musician, everything for free. In return you just have to forgive the entire penalty", Rhiyan was not ready to give up just yet. The owner smiled and replied, "You know I really like the fact you are still trying. And truly the proposal is great. But unfortunately my daughter is more into painting than music, so I don't think the proposal would work out." Rhiyan stood silent. His plan didn't work out. "See, in life all plans might not work out the way we think. But there is no harm trying them out. You know what they say, right? *Shoot for the moon. Even if you miss, who knows, you might fall among the stars*", consoled the owner. "You know I didn't want to penalise you but had to. Can't let the lock-in period clause get violeted every single time. Anyways, I hope you have a good time ahead. Goodbye", and with that hung up her phone. Rhiyan was still a bit sad that his plan didn't work out. But was happy, he was able to save 10k at least.

The next day he received a 80k cheque from the owner, which he deposited at the nearby bank. Coming back he looked at his phone with his dad's number in front. *Should I inform them about this?* Logically he should have but he knew how hurt his mother would feel, since the loss stemmed from her decision to shift to Mumbai in the first place. Locking the phone out, he decided to skip the call.

Chapter 19 --- A mini adventure awaits…

Date – 24th November, 2023

With a lazy Friday at hand, Rhiyan was busy scrolling through the mails on his screen, some of which had red flags on them signifying the importance level. "Hello buddy, what are you looking at?", surprised Pawan. "Nothing. Just a bunch of incidents that had hit our applications last month", answered a startled Rhiyan. "Hmm. That's one of the key reasons why tracking each application's risk components becomes so important for us. One miss from our end and the hackers have their day of a lifetime", cautioned Pawan's introspection. "By the way, do you know where we are going tomorrow?", asked Pawan. "Umm, no. In fact tomorrow being a Saturday, shouldn't we be chilling at our homes?", Rhiyan sounded doubtful. "What are the five principals of Qrian, that we follow from the heart?", asked Pawan's curiosity. "Never support the wrong, Listen to the Client, Innovate to the core, Support each other and…", Rhiyan got a bit stuck. "And what Rhiyan?", persisted Pawan. Rhiyan closed his eyes to search for the words and spoke out, "Always give back to the society" "Yes, and that's exactly what we will be up for tomorrow", winked Pawan leaving Rhiyan clueless.

The next day, Rhiyan found himself standing at the gate of Sanjay Gandhi National Park, Borivali, Mumbai. Around 20 others from the team had joined in as well. And leading the squad, Jay and Anirudh took the steps inside. "I hope everyone has downloaded a step counting app from the playstore. If not, do it fast. Because you need to attach the screenshot showing the number of steps and distance covered in the system and based on that proportion the firm would conduct the giveaway to the needy", Anirudh spoke out firmly. "And if you forget to keep the tracker on, you will have to redo the trekking again", added Jay with a smile. Everyone took out their phones and started off with the step counters activated. Rhiyan had never visited the place before. Naturally, he felt excited on seeing the greenery around and so did the others. With fresh air around, everyone felt energetic. *And that's how it starts, isn't it?* But what they were not aware of, was how long they had to walk for. Fortunately for them, the roads were smooth with mild hilly slopes taking the turns from here to there. Mahesh and Pawan had quite an athletic body with the duo already having trekking experience through rocky uneven paths. But Rhiyan had none. Neither was he athletic nor did he have any trekking experience. He could barely drag his skinny body beyond a point after walking for around 5 km. After a mile or so, the squad halted around a rocky area, that had a few old railway tracks covered with spriling plants on one side and some huge boulders on the other. Everyone sat down and drank water. A few started off clicking pictures along the old railway line and moments later others joined in. "So, enjoying the trek?", asked Jay, as he helped Rhiyan with a bottle of water. Gulping each and every drop like a thirsty bird, Rhiyan finally heaved a sigh of relief. " Absolutely. I just wish the route to the final destination would have been a bit shorter", smiled his heavy breaths. "By the way, what is the final destination here?", continued his question. "We are enroute to some 2000 year old Kanheri caves, carved out by Buddhist monks out of these rocky cliffs", smiled his answer. "Caves, huh?", Rhiyan didn't seem to make much out of it. *Must be similar to those at Elephanta,* thought his already tired thoughts. After a brief halt, the squad began their journey again.

On the other side of the spectrum, were Dhruv and Rajneet busy conducting a philanthropic event for the unsung heros of the firm. Yeah, when the opportunity to give back comes, employees' efforts come in from all sides. While one squad was busy logging more than 3 lakh steps through trekking, another was busy planting tree saplings and another was busy with beach cleaning activities. Some were even busy conducting learning sessions for underpriviledged kids.

Starting from the floor cleaners, security guards to kitchen staff, all were welcomed for the philanthropic event. Yes, in any institute or firm, these are the unsung heros, who contribute day in day out without any hopes of getting recognition. But Qrian, as a firm treated everyone equally. So just like the times, when these unsung heros made the employees' lives easy, this time it was a reverse turn. "I know this might feel a bit new for everyone. But trust me the only thing we want to say is THANK YOU. Thank you for being there for us 24*7. Thank you for making us feel secured even in the darkest of the nights. Thank you for the delicious meals you serve us effortlessly. Thank you for everything", began Rajneet, the chief organiser for the event. "But today its time for us to give back. And that's why we have arranged this small gala session for you all", continued Anisha, the host of the event, "*Humein pata hai ki app iss seher se kitna pyaar karte hai. Toh aaj ki quiz iss seher ke naam.* (We know how much you all love this city. So today's quiz begins with it)."

"We all know that Railways is the lifeline of Mumbai. So who can tell us the names of all stations starting from Churchgate to Borivali in a perfect sequence?", asked Dhruv in hindi. 3 hands went up in the air, one of them being the cleaning lady who always helps in keeping the desks clean inspite of some spilling over coffee in a hurry. "Yes Ma'am, kindly tell us", Dhruv handed over the mic to her. "Churchgate, Marine Lines, Mumbai Central…", she went on till Bandra and then messed up the sequence but somehow reached to Kandivali and finally Borivalli. On finishing she seemed a bit sad on messing up the order. "Ma'am, I being a senior manager myself make mistakes more often than you all. I see no reason for that sad face to come up on just a sequence mishap", cheered Dhruv with a smile as he passed on the chocolate to her. A few more questions related to Mumbai city were fired, but the unsung heros defended quite well. "Hmm… I loved the energy with which you guys participated", began Rajneet after the quiz, "But trust me I am in no mood to let it go down. So let me invite our chief security officer, Mr Mudit, who had served in the Indian Army to enlighten us with a few words."

With that Rajneet welcomed Mr. Mudit on the stage. "First of all thank you for arranging such a lovely event for all of us. And secondly coming to inspirational words, I have many with one being particularly special. The story of my first operation", began his enthusiatic words. "It was around 1995, when I joined the batallion. I knew that the training will be rigorous. Rigourous like hell but what I didn't know was there is a hell and heaven difference between firing shots on a fixed target at a training center and firing the same shots on a crooked mind of a terrorist. From sources we got to know about the whereabouts of 4 terrorists, hiding somewhere in a remote village, the journey of which could only be made on foot not in a luxury bus", smiled his memories. "Braving the rocks over the hilly region, when we finally reached the spot, there was nothing but darkness and yet we had to extract and terminate those notorious terrorists. Yes, shots were fired, lives were lost but what we had to make sure was the safety of the villagers more than our own. But the real test came in when I had to shoot a person down for the first time. My breath was heavy and fingers trembling because I was about to take a life. Seeing the look in my eyes, my commander put his hands on my shoulders and said just one thing, *This is not for a personal revenge, it's a shot for the safety of the country.* Those words were enough to fill in required gaps and without flinching my fingers pulled the trigger", ended his words, as he heaved a deep breath. "Did you take the terrorist down?", asked a moustached guy from the audience. "Oh yes I did. But with that I learnt a lesson. The first shot is the most difficult one. But when you do it for the right reason, the subsequent ones become easy", smiled Mr. Mudit as everyone applauded his courage.

The event went on with some song performances and finally ended with some delicious snacks. The crowd left the room with a heartful of motivation.

On the other side, Jay, Anirudh, Rhiyan and company finally reached the Kanheri Caves, which were quite similar to those at Elephanta but yet a bit different. There was even a small pond with fishes swimming around. Everyone finally settled down on the rocks to celebrate victory. Photos were captured and so were memories. Everyone took a screenshot of the step tracking app. *10.5 km, huh?* Rhiyan still couldn't believe he walked it out till the end. "Ready to retrace your steps back to the main gate?", asked Anirudh to Rhiyan. "What? We will have to walk back?", Rhiyan was almost on the verge of having a heart attack when everyone laughed off. "Don't mind that. We were just pulling your leg a bit", smiled Jay as his hands pointed towards a bus that was taking passengers back. Rhiyan heaved a deep sigh of relief. After having a glass of lemonade, everyone finally returned back via the bus. The return journey lightened out everyone's heart.

Date – 1ˢᵗ December, 2023

Rhiyan had shifted to the new place at Lokhandwala, Kandivali East. The owner had already made all the arrangements for him, starting from bed, study table, internet connection to a decked up kitchen. Although it was December, the winds of winter had hardly reached the city. Good for Rhiyan, the pleasant weather saved him from the shiverring cold winds afterall. But there was one problem. A problem that flew across Mumbai in numbers that are just not countable, Pigeons.

Although the local municipal corporation was trying their best to get rid of the pigeon problem, the success rate was pretty low. For Rhiyan particularly, it was their cooing sound that somehow always managed to wake him up at 7 am. *Damn! The days of waking up at 9 seemed to be gone for him.* One good thing that happened as a result was him going to sleep early. No more late night movies or web series. But Rhiyan was content with the fact that he got a personal place for himself, that too at half the price he was paying earlier.

Taking the metro, Rhiyan reached office where the squad was back on its feet with people busy coding, troubleshooting errors and having some serious discussions on how the next application release would take place. "So, finally a big day coming up for you Rhiyan. Have you been a part of production releases before?", asked Aarvi, the program manager of the GenAI Config squad over the zoom call. From the first day itself, Rhiyan had found her to be a very cheerful lady who could understand his hesitations, shortcomings in an instant and yet helped him move up the learning curve along with Pawan and Dhruv. "Umm… To speak the truth, no. Even in my previos role, I mainly dealt with external stakeholders, leaving lesser room to dive in with the developers and testing squad", answered Rhiyan honestly. "No problem. You will learn that too, soon", smiled her reply. "To give you a heads up, this is a very important application for the firm. And as you might know, be it any firm any application, first we deploy things on Non-Prod environment and only after successful testing do we go ahead with Prod. So yeah, welcome to tussle between Prod and Non-Prod. Pawan will explain you how to proceed with the non-prod activities. Hope you have good day ahead", concluded Aarvi. "You too have a good day", replied Rhiyan as the call ended.

"How did the call go?", asked Pawan who came in with a hot cup of tea and took a seat next to Rhiyan. "Oh it was good. I just wished I could have met her in person. You know she looked very focused on what she wanted. I hope to get the same level of clarity someday", smiled his reply. "You will", assured Pawan's confident words. An hour later Pawan explained him the tasks needed to be carried out on the Non-Prod environment with the help of network team. But given that the team operated in US hours, he had to wait for the evening to dawn in.

Taking a deep breath, Rhiyan locked his screen and went towards the coffee machine. His fingers by default always went towards the milk section. "Not a coffee person, I see", startled Mahesh's words from behind. "I am. But only when I make it myself. I like to keep the coffee proportion to the minimum but somehow this machine doesn't understand that", laughed off Rhiyan. "That's why it's a machine not a human being", laughed off Mahesh too, "So what are you adding? Honey?", Mahesh sounded curious as he could see a Dabur Honey Squeezy bottle in Rhiyan's hands. "Yeah. I carry it with me everyday. Milk and honey is best for throat you know. Keeps my voice intact", replied Rhiyan while squeezing out honey and stiring the milk. "Hmm… I see. By the way, let me know once the non-prod part is done. We need to go for prod soon", with that Mahesh left.

Taking the cup of honey milk, Rhiyan moved towards the transperant wall. On the other side stood a huge city decked up with tall skyscrappers. The sky looked a bit hazy, probably the pollution from the never ending traffic had managed to touch the sky. There were some patches of greenery around but again, the count was less. Looking at the car miniatures that moved smoothly on the road ahead, Rhiyan got reminded of the hot wheel toy cars he used to play with in his childhood.

Having had the experience of getting stuck in the Mumbai traffic for two hours, Rhiyan had already given up the idea of purchasing a car, but what had always bothered him was the high rental issue in the city. In fact, real estate in Mumbai had always been the costliest in the country, with very few being actually able to afford a buy in.

The phone rang up. Sushant's name blinked on the screen. "Hey buddy, how is life? Enjoying the view of codes?", began his sarcasm. "Not really. But I am indeed enjoying the view of a magnificient city from the 22nd floor of a tall skyscraper", answered Rhiyan taking another sip from the cup. "Is it? Well then we have something in common because I am doing just the same", smiled Sushant. "So, how is the new place at Kandivali treating you?", asked Sushant's casual words. "Quite well. Just that, I am having some tough time persuading the pigeons around on how disturbing an early morning sleep is not a good thing", replied Rhiyan as Sushant laughed off, "Told you, someday or the other you will have to become an early riser. Anyways, take care. Have to go back to desk." "You too", smiled Rhiyan as both hung up together.

Returning to the desk, Rhiyan found that he had already received two pings from the network team but it just said four words, Hi. Are you there? *Of course I am here, where is the next sentence?* Thought Rhiyan. Fortunately the person was online, must have started his day early. Rhiyan pinged back.

"Hi, I am here. Are we ready to deploy the code in non-prod environment?", asked Rhiyan.

"Yeah, we do. Are you ready for the testing?"

"Yes, I am", replied Rhiyan confidently.

"Fine then, I am pushing the code to non prod. Will take around an hour and then you can test."

The code was pushed, with the stakeholders receiving an email notification. Meanwhile Rhiyan was going through the steps for testing. Although he was not from QA, for this application he had offered to help as he didn't feel the steps to be cumbersome. As the hour passed by, a ping came in, *We are good for testing.* Changing the configuration from prod to uat, Rhiyan went for the kill. *And bingo!* The login was successful. A huge smile came across his face. *The test was successful,* went his mail across all stakeholders.

Since the non-prod was successful when are you planning for the prod deployment. Just to give you a heads up, prod deployments are done only over the weekends. And that's not just for this firm, it's a common practice across the globe, popped up another ping on Rhiyan's screen. Rhiyan looked at the calendar. Damn! That means we have just two weekends, in short two attempts before the due date. He went up to Dhruv for a suggestion who seemed to be on the same page as him. But still to keep Aarvi in loop, he pinged in the common group chat to inform about the prod deployment in the next two days.

Even two minutes had passed by when a call came up. It was Aarvi. "Hey Rhiyan, hope you are doing well. I just saw your ping on prod deployment", began her worried words. "Yes, we tested in non-prod and it worked perfectly fine", commented Rhiyan. "I am glad that it did. But that doesn't mean prod would be smooth as well!", exclaimed Aarvi. *Umm… if it worked in non-prod, why would it break in prod?* Rhiyan seemed a bit confused. "But why would it break in prod? It worked fine in non-prod", Rhiyan spoke his mind out. "Starting from Version control, update, storage issues to conflicts in software version, the reasons could be endless, Rhiyan. And if by chance it fails, do you have rollback pland in hand?", questioned Aarvi to which Rhiyan didn't have any answer. *Damn! Why didn't I think of this?* Rhiyan was stupefied. "I know this is your first application release. Relax. We need to get all approvals first from all stakeholders, make sure we are tracking all events in real time and most importantly have a rollback plan handy", explained Aarvi. "I understand. Sorry, I didn't think it out straight", apologised Rhiyan. "Actually you did. Its just that you forgot to take into account other variables that can break the prod like anything", added Aarvi. "Yeah, true. By the way, I have just informed the same to network team and have requested a halt till we have all variable on board", smiled Rhiyan. "Good", smiled Aarvi back as the call hung up.

Damn! Rhiyan was still in shock. He had always thought if it works in Non Prod, it would definitely work in prod. But had never thought about the external variables that can come in from anywhere. He thanked Aarvi in heart for helping him avert the possible mishap.

Paan, Chuna and Kattha

Date – 2ⁿᵈ December2023

Aarvi might have saved Rhiyan from one blunder. But unfortunately another one was just in queue, waiting for the right opportunity. "Hey Anirudh, we have 2 developers in hand, but falling short of one QA person", informed Umesh, the scrum master of the Dev Squad. "Okay…", Anirudh took a pause, as his eyes moved towards Rhiyan sitting just a seat away. Coincidentally Rhiyan looked at Anirudh, completely unaware of what was approaching him. "I think we can use him. What do you say?", suggested Anirudh as his eyes moved towards Rhiyan. *Damn! Really? Come on Anirudh, I don't know how to setup test cases for this app,* Rhiyan's heart was beating fast. "But he is a Business Analyst. Would he have any idea of how to set up test cases for multiple scenarios?", Umesh seemed a bit doubtful. "Of course he would. If not, he will learn. Isn't it Rhiyan?". teased Mahesh a bit from the other side as Anirudh's steps moved towards Rhiyan. "Yes…", Rhiyan's words were about to tremble when Anirudh cut him off, "But for this time, I was thinking of him", Anirudh's steps moved past Rhiyan and his hands fell on the chair next to him, "Our new QA Intern, Roni." Rhiyan heaved a sigh of relief and so did Umesh. Ha ha ha ha… Anirudh and Mahesh just couldn't hold their laughter back, "Sorry Rhiyan. Didn't mean to scare you, but the look in your eyes was just irresistible."

The day was pretty much quiet until three figures arrived with trolleys in their hand. "Welcome back Maddy, JK, Shiva", smiled Anirudh, as the trio took their seats. Rhiyan had heard these names before. These were code names for the trio who along with Anirudh had developed the most pristine GenAI application with respect to a few in-house translatory applications. "I tell you AV *(Code name for Anirudh)*, its time you give us the Tech Excellence award. Dealing with the UK folks, diving into 7 foreign languages and building an end to end translatory application is not easy", began JK. "I agree. Had Shiva not found and fix the errors, your app would have still been in staging. Forget about going pilot", added Maddy. "Not to forget the last minute changes we had to accommodate while the UAT was going on", shot out Shiva. "Yeah yeah, I know. And thanks to you guys, with all issues resolved our app is finally live", tried Anirudh in an attempt to cool down the environment. *"Toh iss baat pe ek party toh banti hai* (This definitely calls for a party)", added Pawan and Dhruv who had joined in too. "Of course. Let me speak to Jay. Only he can sponser the celebration", consoled Anirudh. "What? No. It should be you. We are not letting you go away this time", defended JK. "We will see", smiled Anirudh in return. "By the way, I see some old faces have returned back, huh?", Shiva's eye first moved towards Rhiyan and then towards Priyanshu, a developer who had converted the PPO just like Rhiyan. "Oh yeah, didn't notice that. Welcome back to the firm guys", congratulated

Maddy to both. "Thank you Sir", replied Priyanshu with full enthusiasm. "Sir? No way. Call me Maddy. We all have code names in here", shaked a few hands.

"Anirudh, not sure when your party would come. But to at least begin with, we brought these", JK opened a box to unveil a few *Banarasi Meetha Paan* (Betle leaves packed with chuna, kattha, gulkand, chopped dates, cherry and elaichi). "Wow. Now that's called a way to start", Mahesh sounded excited as he picked up one. The others picked up too. The paan was so delicious, it literally melted in the mouth. Anirudh was feeling a bit odd though. "What happened? Didn't like the taste?", asked JK. "No. Its delicious. Just that I like *sada paan* more. But yeah, this one is good too." "Really? What is there in a sada paan? You won't get so much of toppings", an argument was about to hit the court. "For the taste yes, but the betel leaf, chuna and kattha are the only ones that serves the benefit, right?", came along Anirudh. The converstation on benefits vs taste went on for the next 5 minutes when Maddy had just enough. "Hey hey, hold on to that. We have just returned back, in no mood for a logical vs illogical argument", Maddy poured the water even before the fire could take shape. "And you guys, get back to work. These things goes on day in day out. Get used to it", smiled Shiva, as he advised the newcomers and turned to return back to his desk.

"Guys, we have a small issue", spoke out Sam from the corner of the bay, another BA who had joined just a year ago and yet had managed to grab some significant eyeballs with his automation skills. "And what is that?", asked JK. "We are having some issues with the translatory app. Its not being able to translate Spanish to English", replied Sam. "But how is that possible? We tested it successfully with Spanish too", JK seemed a bit confused. "Where exactly is the issue, Sam?", Anirudh tried to dig deeper. "Its able to convert the printed

Spanish letters, yes. But not the hand-written ones", explained Sam. Things started making sense. "Of course, we tested all with printed documents not with hand written ones", clarified Maddy. "But translating hand written words was not even in the scope, right?", defended Shiva. "True. All docs are supposed to be printed only. But in Spanish ones, there seems to be a few Hand Written words as well", sighed Sam. Everyone seemed a bit worried since the app was already in pilot phase.

"What if we use OCR aka Optical Character Recognition Technology? Can't it help?", suggested Mahesh. "It could have, had all handwritings been uniform. OCR faces a lot of challeneges with inconsistent style of handwritings", Maddy sounded a bit worried. "Of course. Why didn't I think of it?", murmered Sam on his own. "What are you thinking?", Anirudh was curious. "Do you remember our last tech session, where the speaker was telling something about advanced OCR Tech. There he spoke about Google Vision that can help with human handwriting recognition and extraction. Can't we use its API? Integrate it with our App and who knows, maybe it will work", Sam sounded excited. "Maybe… yes, there is a huge MAYBE in there", JK sounded a bit skeptical. "But worth trying it. What do you say Shiva?", Maddy and AV looked at each other and then at Shiva. "Lets do it", smiled Shiva, as everyone got to work.

Umesh had to scramble among different squads to find the right resources for the dev and testing work. It took them around 10 days to get the integration done at a functional level. And yet there were mistakes. Not all words were getting converted accurately. "Thought so", sighed JK as the team sat for a mini discussion. "Its okay. At least we had a 60% success rate", tried Umesh's consoling words, when a knock tapped open the door. "But JK and AV would never settle with just

60, would they?", smiled Pawan as he entered. "What do you mean?", JK felt a bit offended. "I mean, cheer up guys, I went back to our stakeholder, understood their requirements and did some analysis", Pawan sounded excited, "We never needed the translation of the entire 20 pager doc. We just needed data from page number 4 and 5 of that Spanish doc. Its just 5 values that needs to be provided." "What?", Maddy and Shiva rose up from their chair. "Couldn't you have told this earlier?", JK sounded surprised. "No my friend. A few in-depth analysis do take time", smiled Pawan.

Without wasting any time, the team got back to work again. It took another 4 days. But yes, they did it. They were able to narrow down their search and extraction became easier. "So, 95% success rate it is, huh! Congratulations guys", congratulated Umesh to the whole team. "Couldn't have done it without you. Thanks for arranging the resources from the other teams. I think you are fit enough to help out a few more squads as Scrum Master, what do you say Anirudh?", Maddy was quite happy. "Of course, but only if his heart wants to", laughed off Anirudh and so did the others.

Chapter 20 --- The Final Convocation

Date – 5ᵗʰ December 2023

As the day passed by, next morning Rhiyan woke up to a reminder on his phone that showed up a date, 10ᵗʰ December 2023. A date which was important for the entire 2023 batch. Yeah, you guessed it right. *Convocation!* A day where all the passed out students would be presented with their degrees. Fortunately for Rhiyan, he had already made the to and fro bookings in time and so did the others. *I mean come on, what would a convocation be without friends teaming up for that one last party.* Just the thought of it brought a smile on Rhiyan's face. He looked at the clock on his phone. It showed as 9 am. *Really?* He was not surprised that it was late but was surprised on how he managed to brave the cooing sounds of the pegions just above his head. Maybe they decided to give him a piece of relief for a day at least. As otherwise 7 am was by default their calling alarm.

As he came back from the washroom, his phone rang up. The name did bring a smile on his face. It was Samrat. *The chap must have called to remind him of the convocation dates,* thought Rhiyan. "Hey Samrat, glad to hear you out again…", began Rhiyan but was interrupted inbetween. "Rhiyan, listen to me carefully. We are in a bit of trouble. Can you come over? I have asked others to join in as well", Samrat sounded serious. "Umm… okay. What happened?", fumbled Rhiyan. "You come over and we will have a discussion together", hung up Samrat.

Is someone sick? Did Aarav leave Feast on Wheels? Are they in some legal trouble? Multiple thoughts kind of struck Rhiyan from all sides. The only way to find out was to reach there first. Packing a few chocolates for the group, Rhiyan left for Churchgate.

The same evening everyone gathered in. Sushant and Antara being busy with some personal work couldn't make it there in person but had joined via conference call. But others including Emily, Samrat, Sameer, Aarav and Jaanvi had gathered on. "Most of us are aware but for you guys let me fill you in", began Samrat. "The thing is that we are about to expand. But for that we need money. Don't worry, I won't ask you to empty your wallets but we need a strategy for the expansion. I mean Rhiyan can't be everywhere playing on his guitar to attract foodies, isn't it?", smiled Samrat. "But the question arises where will you arrange the finances from? We all know how difficult it was to purchase just the first food truck?", pondered Sushant's thoughts. "I have found a solution for that. So recently a startup called Leaser has come in which kind of leases out food trucks on a 50-50 profit sharing arrangement. And these are all decked up with latest equipments including all safety features", Samrat sounded confident. "Interesting. But that means they have identified a possible food truck market here. Ready for competitions?", chuckled Rhiyan. "Yes correct, that also means there will be head hunting, poaching of the best chef around. By the way I hope Feast on Wheels is profitable and not burning cash?", chiped in Antara. "When did we have cash to burn? Come on Antara. Of course we are profitable and that's the reason we were able to negotiate with Leaser on a 50-50 profit sharing deal in the first place", defended Emily. Antara heaved a sigh of relief. "And for the chefs, we have already identified a few possible Aaravs, you know", smiled Aarav himself. "But the problem is competition. That's why we called you guys here", commented Sameer. "Which areas are you exactly targeting for expansion?", asked Rhiyan. "Andheri, Dadar, Goreaon and Malad", answered Jaanvi. "Dadar? Are you serious? That would have the highest number of competition in terms of affordable food stalls, forget food trucks", reacted Rhiyan vigourously. "I expected nothing less from you. From when did we start competing in price, we compete on quality Rhiyan", countered Samrat. "I agree. Its not the price it's the quality that we need to maintain", tried Sushant to support Samrat. "Fine. But how would we compete with the heavy workforce employed in each avenue? I mean we would have just two chefs in each food truck. Would they be enough?", Rhiyan was still skeptical about Dadar at least. *"Tezi goli mein nahi, chalane wale mein hoti hai",* commented Antara over the call. "What?", Rhiyan fumbled. "Come on Rhiyan. Did you forget what you told me over our last call, when we were talking over the upcoming grads at my firm. "Yes, I do now", smiled Rhiyan as he nodded out. It was one of Rhiyan's favourite dialouge from a movie called Dhoom. It said that, the speed is never in the bullet, but in the person who pulls the trigger. "So what do you suggest?", asked Rhiyan. "I suggest we implement the discount strategy but in a different way", suggested Antara. "But just now we agreed upon not competing on price, right?", Rhiyan countered. "Which part of *in a different way,* didn't you understand?", continued Antara. "Samrat, do you remember how we collected the primary data for our consulting club project from those shopekeepers? Nobody had time to share data and yet we managed to get it, right?", Antara tried to bring in some memories from the past. "Of course. Why didn't I think of that?", Samrat's eyes lit up. "Think of what?", asked Emily. "Umm… so we needed some primary real time data from the grocery shopkeepers in and around our college are for some projects. Now generally, those shopkeepers neither did have patience for that nor did they want to spend time. And we didn't want to spend any money too", elaborated Samrat, "So what we did was, sell them a few movie tickets at 50% discount that we got on various card offers for free. And that was enough to buy some of their time for the primary real time data." "Exactly. So wherever we are planning to expand, we will be using the local shopkeepers as our focal points", continued Antara, "We will place a few discount coupons with grocery shopkeepers nearby. In return purchase things in bulk that we would need. Based on regular intervals, the shopkeepers will offer our coupons as a freebie to whoever comes to their shop and does a heavy purchase." "In this way we might will not only be able to segregate the heavy spenders but also bring them straight to our food trucks", realised Rhiyan. "Exactly, who will spend more on our food and help generate more revenue", added Emily. "Hmm… Interesting. Any other strategies you applied back at college?", Aarav sounded curious. "Nothing more, I guess", reflected Antara. "May not be a strategy, but I think we should keep two spots handy for each and every location. If for any reason we are unable to park at one spot, we must have another one in mind", added Sushant. "Also we have to keep a track of all the upcoming local festivals wherein we can offer to serve. Foodtrucks being mobile could be driven anywhere, right?", added Sameer. "Hmm… Seems like we have a few strategies to begin with. Thank you so much for chipping in your thoughts, guys", smiled Samrat. "By the way, don't forget to wear the cream colour kurta for the convocation. You guys always mess up the dress codes, remember? For now goodbye", chuckled Antara as she hung up.

Date – 9ᵗʰ December 2023

Ideas can be copied, specially if it involves just printing some discount coupons and handing over to shopkeepers. It didn't take more than a week for other competitors to find out Samrat's tricks and try implementing the same. They even went a step ahead by giving out cash insentives to the shopkeepers. Fortunately Samrat and company had already anticipated this and had thought out of something different.

10th December being the convocation day, all students had been instructed to report by 9th December evening. And so have they did, but with one issue. Fooding by college was supposed to be provided from 10th, not 9th. And that's where Samrat and company kicked in. Taking permission from the required authorities, Feast on Wheels had set in a small food stall with an exact replica of the food truck and bugs bunny cardboard cut out. And the best part, whoever posts a selfie with it on social media, gets a 50% discount on whichever item they purchase. And since only college students were allowed on campus, the entire MBA BA and Core Batch came in for help.

As the sun set in, the evening came down like a fine wine. Almost 2000 students had set in their foot at their beloved college again. The streets and trees were lit up with beautiful lights and the way the heritage building was decorated, it was nothing short of Diwali. But pulling in the students as customers was not an easy task. Mere discounts couldn't lure them. "What to do now?", Antara sounded a bit worried and so did the others. "Hey guys, need some help?", startled an unexpected voice as everyone looked up. They couldn't believe their eyes. It was their juniors, Sudhanshu, Bharat, Souvik, Imran, Nayara and others. They were carrying two huge loudspeakers in their hands. "You forgot these while leaving the hostel a few months ago, remember? Thought you might use some extra hands", reminded their cheerful words. "Of course. We bought them for the concert", reflected Sushant, who had come in a few moments ago. "In that case, its time to reap the harvest", commented Samrat, as he took both of them and plugged in to the extension chord. Connecting to the bluetooth, they went on to play the latest bollywood music. "Hey guys, we hope you didn't forget the revolving lights", spoke out a voice from behind. A huge smile came across all faces. The 9 musketeers had set in their foot at the campus.

"Hey Piyush, how are you?", Samrat was excited to see the entire batch coming in. "We are good. And why wouldn't we be? Atleast one of us is living the startup dream", replied Piyush. "Yes, we keep following the Feast on Wheels social media page", winked Apurv from the side. "I hope we will get a bit more discount than the usual 50% for tonight", Megha tried to pull his leg. "Come on guys, tonight's party is on me. You just focus on sharing the selfies on social media tonight", smiled Samrat as the feast began.

Hearing the music and seeing the revolving headlights, a few folks from the B.Tech and M.Tech came in to see what's going on. And before they could turn back, the sweet smell of imli, paneer and aloo parathas atrracted their nostrils. Within an hour the ground filled in with students tapping on to the music beats, most having feasts and sharing selfies on social media tagging *Feast on Wheels* to get the 50% discount. By the end of the night almost all social media platforms were teeming with *Feast on Wheels* posts. "Hey guys, check this out. I just received 16 mails querying if Feast on Wheels would be available at others locations. Some of them even want to book us for parties", Samrat was excited. "That sounds perfect", everyone was overjoyed.

Date – 10th December 2023

The next day everyone got up early and dressed up for the mega event, the final convocation. Yes, there was a special dress code. Boys had to wear cream coloured kurtas whereas the girls had to wear sarees of the same colour. Shiny stoles was provided to each before the event. In fact the colour of the stoles bifurcated the bachelors from the masters. All B.tech students had a blue coloured stole around their neck, Masters students had red and the PhD students had green. But all had one thing in common, the emblem of IIT Dhanuj. As Rhiyan's hands passed over it, feelings of pride did surge from the bottom of his heart.

Rhiyan, Sushant along with the 9 musketeers reached the Grand Auditorium, the venue where the convocation ceremony was to be held. Jayesh Sir, being the current director of the college had already arrived. Seeing him, a lot of corporate finance memories surged through everyone. But the real surprise came in when a fleet of 12 Scorpio Cars moved in the campus. "I have seen this fleet only in Delhi before once, when the governor was travelling through the city. Are we having any governor as chief guest?", Rhiyan sounded curious. "Even better, we have the Vice President of India as our Chief Guest", commented Sushant. "What!", Rhiyan still couldn't believe his ears, "Bur how?" "That's because the IIT council fall directly under the purview of the President of India", replied Sushant. The car's door opened and it was indeed the Vice President of India who had stepped into the IIT Dhanuj campus for the Convocation. All eyes were wide open.

In the first batch all B.Tech Students were convocated. In the 2nd it was the Masters' turn. Within minutes everyone took their alloted seats. "Good morning everyone. First of congratulations. Yes you have made it to this day. All professors including me are really happy for you", began Professor Singh. "Knowledge is power and with great power we all know what comes in. Great responsibilities. And today we all shall take an oath to use our knowledge for the benefit of the society as a whole. With that I will hand over to Shashank, who will read it and you will repeat after him." Everyone had a pamphlet in their hands on which was written an oath both in English and Sanskrit. Although Rhiyan attempted to read the Sanskrit part, his words gave up after the first line. *Damn! Its difficult,* thought his mind. But fortunately

Shashank read it out with pauses in between, enabling everyone to repeat with ease. The English part was the smoother one.

Moments later, the entire convocation committee led by Jayesh Sir and the Chairperson moved in. As everyone took their seats, Jayesh Sir took the podium's mic, "Today is a great day. Not just for you but for us, the country and most importantly your parents who have made countless sacrifices to see where you stand today. Life is journey, as we know it. But what matters is how we use our knowledge to help people around us. And by now, I am sure you are all enroute to that destination. So without wasting any more time, let's make your memorable for life. With that I would like to invite the hounourable Vice President of India and honourable chairperson to do the honours", concluded his opening speech.

With perfect co-ordination in place, students moved in one after the other. As the turn for the MBA batch came in, Harigaran moved in first, with the Vice President honouring him with the Gold Medal from the Business Analytics Batch, followed by Shruti who won the Gold Medal from the MBA Core Batch. After that the rest followed. The Degree Certificate was presented by the Director himself. So when Rhiyan's turn came, he walked in with a huge smile on his face. "Many many congratulations, Rhiyan", congratulated Professor Jayesh. Although Rhiyan didn't win the gold medal, his heart was happy since he was receiving his MBA Business Analytics Degree from the God of Corporate Finance, himself. Touching his feet, Rhiyan took his blessings, posed for a photograph and finally returned back to his seat. Opening the degree, he checked if all details were correct and once verified, his heart was finally at peace. And this was not just for Rhiyan, each and student had same feeling pride and hapiness in their hearts. When all students returned back to their seats, the photographer took a 180 degree turn because even he knew what the tradition was. *Woh ho...* Flew up everyone's stole in the air, marking the final celebration of their academic life at IIT Dhanuj.

Coming out of the auditorium, students teamed up with their parents to click a few photographs with their respective degrees. Some even had tears in their eyes. But only tears of joy, nothing else.

"So, finally done and dusted, huh?", came in a voice, which Rhiyan recognised to be of Surbhi's, the Gold Medallist from M.Tech Data Analytics batch. "Yes, finally done. But I am really happy for you. Many many congratulations on winning the Gold Medal, Surbhi", replied Rhiyan as his eyes fell on the shining gold medal hanging down her neck. "I wish I had more time to talk but unfortunately I have a train to catch. Hope we meet soon", and with that Surbhi flew out with her parents to catch a train to Delhi.

With everyone busy clicking group photographs, Rhiyan's eyes moved across the campus one last time, trying to capture all memories for a lifetime. Later he joined in for the photographs too. The day ended with a delicious meal arranged by the college itself for all the students and parents.

"Time to say goodbye, I guess", spoke out Antara as everyone reached the main gate. "Seems so, but don't worry we will meet again... soon", replied Rhiyan. "In fact, we all would", joined in others with a huge laughter. With that everyone returned back to their respective home.

Epilogue

Date – 14ᵗʰ January 2024

After a roller coster ride through 2023, everyone finally entered into a whole new year 2024. With an off-campus attempt Shristi had managed to hit a jackpot, a role and package that surpassed her own expectations and best part her location was the same as Kabir. Joy knew no bounds for the duo. As for others, each one had already embarked on their new corporate journeys. Rhiyan was back at his new place, Lokhandwala, Mumbai. Sipping out a cup of coffee on a Sunday evening, Rhiyan was scrolling through a mail on his laptop screen It was from Jay, the executive director himself. *Congratulations, you have been promoted from an Analyst to Associate role,* read the subject line. A smile of happiness had already parked itself across his face. Just a few days ago, the firm celebrated the Promotion Day, wherein multiple people got promoted. Champagnes had popped up across the floor, with everyone joining in for a dance to music.

With Pawan and Dhruv's help, as Rhiyan was learning more about business risk and its management on one side, on the other he was revising his cooking lessons with the help of his landlord. Last time he actually cooked full-fledged dishes was something around 2020. Now after 4 years, his heart wanted to be back in the game. So yes, starting off with Daal, Rice and Matar Paneer did make some sense for him.

Reflecting on the thrilling journey he and his friends had over the past two years., something clicked. Back in 2016, during his B.Tech college days, he had written and published a few short stories as anthologies. As his thoughts started wandering in a similar direction, Rhiyan thought why not assimilate all the thrilling experiences in the form of a book. Without any second thought, he opened a word file and typed in a title that had come to his mind, *The Hidden Gemstone… An MBA Saga.*

~ 238 ~

Thank You